DRIFTED

DAVID WOLF BOOK 12

JEFF CARSON

CHAPTER 1

"TWENTY-ONE INCHES DROPPED at the base of Points."
Detective Tom Rachette stepped up next to Wolf and put
his hands on his hips. "Said thirty on the top. Did you ski
last week?"

Wolf said nothing as he stood at the rear of the luxury
SUV, squinting against the nuclear-blast reflections
coming off the snow. It felt like he was standing next to a
perpetual lightning strike.

"Where are your sunglasses?" Rachette asked. "And,
my God, it looks like you need them. You get into it
last night?"

They were sitting six miles down the valley on his
kitchen counter.

Rachette dangled his mirrored lenses in front of
Wolf's face. "Take 'em."

"No thanks."

"Suit yourself. I feel your pain. But, believe it or not, I
didn't touch a sip of alcohol last night."

Wolf narrowed his eyes to slits, a glancing blow of

pain hammering in his temples. He felt semi-dizzy, and his mind was slow to form sentences worth speaking, so he opted for silence.

"You didn't touch alcohol last night?" Detective Heather Patterson finished her trudge up from the vehicles to where Wolf and Rachette stood. "Then who ..." She crinkled her nose and looked up at Wolf. "Geez. Looking fit today."

Wolf closed his eyes and savored a breeze sprinkling his face with ice crystals. It was unseasonably warm, the sound of trickling water permeating through the never-ending blanket of snow. The sun had warmed his beard to an uncomfortable temperature from the second he'd stepped out of the SUV.

"There you guys are." Rachette nodded to Deputy Ryan Yates, who walked up behind Patterson.

"Yeah, sorry," Yates said. "Got here as soon as we could. The drive is brutal up that last stretch. I guess this guy's not a fan of plowing, or he pissed off somebody on the council. Holy cow, what happened here?"

Patterson whistled at the vehicle in front of them. "That's not going to be good for the upholstery."

A gold Lexus SUV sat half-buried in drifted snow with all four windows rolled down to the doors. The interior had collected an impressive amount of snow, piling high enough to cover half the steering wheel. It was as if a giant had opened the sunroof and poured a dozen shovel-loads inside, then left the wind to smooth it over.

A breeze whistled through the pines and pushed through the SUV's openings, kicking up more snow. Wolf unzipped his Carhartt jacket, letting the cool air wick the hot alcohol leaking from his pores.

"What's the story?" Patterson asked. "I heard from Wilson that Chris Alamy came in looking for his boss. I take it these are Chris's tracks." She gestured toward the twin vehicle ruts in the snow that led up to where they stood at the front of the house.

"Rachette." Wolf stepped away from their powwow and took in the scene as best he could without facing the sun. A single set of footprints led from the spot where Chris Alamy's car door would have been, then up a flight of sturdy wooden stairs to a sun-sheltered porch.

Rachette cleared his throat. "Chris Alamy came in this morning and filed a missing-person report with me. Said his boss, a man named Warren Preston—"

"The rock guy," said Patterson.

"Yeah."

"The place on the north edge of town."

Rachette blinked. "Yes. Can I finish my briefing? Or do you want to guess?"

"Sorry. I just didn't know where Chris Alamy worked."

"I didn't know you knew Chris Alamy," Yates said. "Me and Rachette know him from the bars, but where have you met him?"

"He did karate for a few months last year," she said.

"Hey. Tweedle-stupids, I'm talking here."

Wolf broke through thick, water-compressed snow toward the steps.

They moved after Wolf while Rachette continued.

"Anyway, Chris came in this morning. Apparently,

Warren Preston left work last Friday, so, what? Ten days ago?"

"Eleven," Patterson said.

"Whatever, the Friday before last. I guess Preston left and said he was taking a week down in Arizona to do some warm-weather camping, and said he'd be back the following Monday. Yesterday. When he didn't show up for work, Chris and the rest of his crew thought it odd. Called him, didn't get any answer, but thought he'd show up soon enough.

"When Preston didn't show up this morning, Chris decided to drive out here to check on him." Rachette stomped his feet on a dry spot of the front porch and gestured down to the buried Lexus. "And found that. Look, he even opened his sunroof."

Wolf turned away from the reflection lancing off the windshield to a window next to the front door. He peeked inside, feeling his pupils dilate for the first time in an hour.

"It snowed last weekend," Patterson said. "Started that Saturday afternoon, ended ... what? Monday morning? So, if the interior's filled with snow, looks like Preston didn't get to his Arizona destination. At least, not in that car. Could have taken a Winnebago or something. But then why leave your car like that, and leave the state when it's snowing balls?"

Rachette nodded toward the door. "Chris said he went inside the house to check on him."

Wolf reached over and pressed his thumb on a cast-iron handle. A thick glass and wood door pushed open.

Warmth billowed out from the interior.

Wolf paused, stomped his boots, and took them off. The action of bending over sent a pulse of pain into his skull. He stepped inside onto a stiff-hair welcome rug and continued onto a rough-finished dark-wood floor.

Patterson followed first, Rachette and Yates behind her, and soon an open and airy entrance to the house was filled with their sniffling and breathing.

A cat came around a corner and meowed.

"Oh, hey there." Patterson bent down and held out her hand.

The cat meowed over and over, keeping its distance a few feet away.

The noise felt like a violin bow sliding across Wolf's brain.

"Have you had any Advil yet today?" Patterson asked.

"Huh-uh."

She looked at Rachette and shook her head. "Why did you call him? It's his day off."

"I don't know. I thought he should know. I didn't think he'd drive up here and meet us."

Her gaze rested on him again.

The cat meowed again.

Wolf put on a pair of rubber gloves and walked toward the cat.

It screamed some more as it rounded the corner, then sat at a closed door and looked up.

"What the hell's that thing's problem?" Rachette asked.

Wolf pulled open the door and saw it was a food pantry.

"I never liked cats," Patterson said.

"You're telling me," Rachette said. "Give me a dog any day over those clawed little demons."

Wolf took a bag of cat food off the shelf, poured a pile on the floor, and put the bag back.

The cat pounced onto the food and purred as it ate.

"Ah." Rachette pulled on rubber gloves. "And there's the reason he's our boss, folks."

"His wallet's on the counter," Wolf said. "Along with his keys, sunglasses, lip balm. Doesn't look like he ever left the house."

Rachette walked over. "That's what Alamy said. Said he came in and saw his stuff sitting on the counter, the open windows in the car, and wondered what was going on."

Wolf walked to the sliding glass door looking out to the rear of the property. Waves of snow stretched out for a few treeless acres and ran into a wall of pines. There were no other houses in sight, and there had been no other properties for at least a mile down the road.

"Why would he roll down all his windows like that?" Rachette asked. "And then come in here? Drop all his stuff out of his pockets?"

"Maybe he's lying dead in a bathroom," Patterson said.

"Chris said he searched the house, thinking the same thing. Didn't find him."

"Rachette and Yates, take upstairs," Wolf said. "Me and Patterson will take downstairs."

"Let's do it." Rachette headed back down the hall toward the entrance and a stairway that led up.

Wolf stepped around the cat and walked through the kitchen to a laundry room. An older-model washer and dryer stood on a dusty linoleum floor opposite another door. He cracked it open and poked his head inside a two-car garage. One side was filled with equipment and a work bench. The other sat empty.

"Why not park in the garage when he got home?"

Wolf started at the sound of Patterson's voice next to him.

"Geez," she said. "You are not looking good."

"I think you said something about that outside already."

"Yeah, but now I can smell you. Jesus, I think I might vomit."

"That's what you get for coming into work during your first trimester."

Her jaw dropped. "How did you know?"

He shrugged. "I guessed. You have that easily disgusted demeanor lately."

"Well ... good guess. Please don't tell anyone."

"Don't vomit and your secret will be safe."

"What were you doing last night?" She softened her tone and tilted her head. It was the same tone he'd heard Margaret Hitchens use last time he'd seen her in town. The same tone his mother used on the phone.

"Nothing."

She nodded and looked past him. "Doesn't make any sense that he would have parked outside with all the windows open if he has an electric garage door-opener and this nice open space for his luxury SUV."

He shut the door and pushed past her back into the kitchen.

The cat was a few paces away from the pile of food, licking its paw.

Searching the rest of the lower floor of the house took little time. They walked a lap through a family room adorned with large leather couches that suggested a budget at odds with the old washer and dryer. The dining room was off the family room toward the front of the house, darkened by closed wooden slat shades.

Patterson twisted a hanging rod and let in some light, and Wolf silently cursed her for it.

The photons that didn't assault his eyeballs illuminated stacks of bills, organized by type, and other papers that looked like invoices. A single wooden chair sat against the table facing the window. The space seemed to be used as a home office by Warren Preston when he was not at the rock yard, which Wolf knew sat along the river outside the north end of town.

Plastic file holders stood along the walls, and the floor was coated with dust where it met the floorboards. Crumbs littered the corners.

Wolf knew the signs of a single man living alone when he saw it. His floors, too, held a coating of dust at the edges, specks of food tracked around the house, kicked into corners.

"There a basement?" Wolf asked.

"Doesn't look like it."

They left the dining room and headed toward the front entryway just as Rachette and Yates were coming down the stairs.

"Nothing," Rachette said.

Patterson ducked into a hallway bathroom and flicked on the light. "Nothing down here, either."

They convened back at the kitchen, where the cat had dug in for a second helping.

"I have an idea about what happened." Yates tilted his head down and narrowed his eyes, a movement that accentuated his hawk's beak of a nose.

Deputy Yates was thirty-nine years old, had short blond hair underneath his SBCSD cap, and a religiously fit figure beneath his winter clothing, which was apparent just by looking at his chiseled face. He had been a recent addition to Wolf's squad, hired at the beginning of the fiscal year after Sheriff MacLean had relayed the county council's wishes that they add another detective from within the existing force of the Sluice–Byron County SD.

Wolf had always liked Yates. The man had plenty of ideas and was unafraid to voice them. His thoughts might have been wrong on occasion, but Yates fought a smaller ego than most deputies in the department and was rarely self-conscious—a combination Wolf found refreshing. Plus, Yates seemed to temper the fire between Rachette and Patterson.

"Warren Preston's at the office," Yates said. "And he takes off, drives home. But on the way here, he's feeling flush. Gets some chest pains. Opens his windows to get some air."

"And drives all the way home?" Patterson frowned.

"Sure. There's no cell reception on the way up the

valley. He has to come all the way home to use his landline."

Rachette pulled out his cell. "I have reception."

Yates shrugged. "I'm just spit-balling here. Okay, fine, he's not in a life-or-death heart attack situation. He's just uncomfortable on the way home."

"Has the shits."

Patterson frowned at Rachette.

"What? He feels flush, starts to sweat. Rolls down the windows, gets home just in time, puts his stuff on the counter, runs into the bathroom, paintjobs the—"

"Stop speaking." Patterson took a deep breath. "If he came home Friday night, it was dumping snow. It would have been like he was in a washing machine."

Yates put his hands on his hips. "Well, my initial idea was, what if he had a heart attack? Maybe he felt bad on the way up, rolled down the windows. Comes in. Feels better for a second, or whatever, puts his stuff there on the counter. Then goes back outside for more fresh air. Keels over, dies. Gets buried by the snow."

They turned and looked outside the sliding door. The cat went to the glass and meowed.

Wolf stepped to the window and scanned the waves of wind-blown powder. "We need K9 units up here ASAP."

"I'm on it." Rachette went down the hallway toward the front door.

"It's not a bad theory," Wolf said. "But the car's open windows are concerning."

Yates shrugged. "He does it to get some fresh air."

"Or air out the car," Patterson said. Her blue eyes

stared into nothing. She was on the same track as Wolf. With his hungover mind flipping the switches, she'd probably got there before him.

"There's no better eraser of forensic evidence than sub-zero weather, twenty-five inches of snow, followed by a soggy melt," Wolf said.

Yates's mouth upturned in a disbelieving smile. "So Warren Preston left his car wide open so forensic evidence would get erased?"

Wolf's brain hurt, and his throat felt like it was coated with hundred-grit. "I don't know. It all doesn't make sense. And then there's those tracks down by our cars."

"What tracks?" Patterson asked.

Wolf looked at Yates.

Yates shook his head. "I didn't see tracks."

"Tyler's on his way up with Mittens." Rachette walked up with cell phone in hand. "What tracks?"

"Well, would you look at that." Rachette swiveled and looked around.

They stood back at their parked vehicles. Wolf felt energized after the fresh-air walk, just enough to get back down the valley and to the couch calling his name.

Now you're a drunk. The voice taunting him was an eight-year-old girl's.

"Sir?"

Wolf looked down at Patterson through his slit eyes. "What?"

"I said, that's why you parked down here? Because of these tracks?"

The twin ruts were distorted by melting and blowing snow. They cast a wide arc, stopped, backed up, and headed back down the unplowed road.

"They caught my attention. They were left sometime after the snowstorm."

Rachette folded his arms. "What am I missing? What does this mean?"

"I have no idea." Wolf walked toward his SUV.

"Where are you going?" Rachette asked.

"Home." He popped his door open and sat inside the warm SUV. Ignoring the three faces watching him, he fired up the engine, turned around, and headed down the valley, back to his dark living room, a dozen episodes of *The Rifleman*, and maybe some hair of the dog that had bitten him.

CHAPTER 2

YOU'RE ASLEEP. *This is a dream.*

Wolf's conscious mind had a knack for cracking the curtains of his unconscious, poking its head in, then ducking out again just as the good part came.

He stood among the tall, swaying grass, watching a line of people board a CH-47 Chinook helicopter atop a small rise set in a clearing of the jungle. The heat suffocated him. Sweat streamed at odd angles across his body, like a demon's tickling fingers.

He pushed up his helmet and studied the Sri Lankan boy standing at the edge of the jungle.

He was eight years old, Wolf knew that with certainty.

Same age as Ella.

The boy wore a dirty yellow backpack that hung low, as if it contained half his body weight in lead.

Wolf stepped forward, seeing more commotion in the trees.

Men. They saw Wolf, turned, and disappeared into the leaves.

Wolf's skin slipped and slid underneath his ACU as he stepped forward. His stomach sank as he realized what was happening.

The boy held a black detonation rod in his hand, thumb poised over the button. He locked his eyes on the line of people boarding the helicopter and snuck through the grass toward them.

Wolf's heart raced. He raised the M4 scope to his eye and gasped at the bouncing image.

It was not a bomb detonation device, but a paintbrush with a tip doused in red paint. It was not a yellow backpack, but a pink one. The vision flitting through the grass was not an eight-year-old boy, but a girl with a bobbing auburn ponytail.

Wolf's finger tensed on the trigger. His heart hammered as waves of panic pulsed through his body.

Why was the gun still raised to his shoulder? She was not a threat.

A grasshopper landed on his face. The weight of the overgrown insect pulled on his cheek, its claws pinching his skin as it struggled to find purchase.

He pulled the trigger.

"No!"

Wolf sat up, slapping his face.

Sweat streamed from his hair down over his temple and ran down his neck.

He tried to free himself from the blanket wrapped around his body, but the fabric pulled him into the couch like a drowning man's arms.

His breathing accelerated. The room was dark, the blinds drawn. A television playing a silent episode of *The Brady Bunch* provided the only light.

Finally, he got to his feet and freed himself from his captor, the Denver Broncos World Champions blanket he kept draped over the back of the couch.

"Jesus." He sat down.

The glow of sunlight behind the window coverings told him it was still daylight. He eyed the half-empty fifth of Dewar's on the coffee table, felt the pounding headache for a few heartbeats, and knew he was wrong.

He walked to the front door and opened it.

A blast of frozen air chilled his sweat-soaked body through his boxers and T-shirt.

His breathing normalized as he stared out at a landscape in stark contrast to a Sri Lankan jungle. Snow blanketed the flat acreage in front of his ranch house, framed by the pines of the Chautauqua Valley coated in the remnants of last week's snowstorm. Movement caught his eye, and a bull elk snorted in his direction, sending twin jets of steam out of its nostrils.

Pink light licked the tips of the western peaks.

"Shit."

He shut the door and read the wall clock—6:35.

Through the alcohol-haze, his voice of reason had to scream to convince him it was the morning and not the evening.

Twenty-five minutes to get into work. He would be late again.

He stood rubbing his eyes, trying to think. If he put his clothes on now, he could probably get to the office right on time, but given he hadn't showered yesterday, that was a bad idea.

He walked into his bedroom and slipped into the bathroom, ignoring the half-folded laundry on his unmade bed and dirty clothing strewn on the floor.

He managed to brush his teeth without looking at himself in the mirror, but then decided to take a glimpse, if only to see the state of his beard.

The face that stared back at him would have startled another version of Wolf. His beard was an inch, inch and a half long, full and messy, with a white fleck of something dangling near his bottom lip. His normally large, chocolate-colored eyes were half-exposed through swollen lids.

The right side of his face was red. He felt the oversized insect hanging off his skin and rubbed his cheek. His shoulder twitched as he felt the rifle's kick, and he flinched. The memory had woken from hibernation.

He blinked, trying to bring his thoughts out of the fog.

Fifteen minutes later he toweled himself off and stared in the mirror again. He'd decided to shave the homeless-beard, but that only served to expose the red skin of his chubby cheeks. An image of a pile of dog shit with a dollop of whipped cream on top came to mind. His eyes were worse than before.

He hurriedly dressed, pulled on his boots, grabbed his Glock, and shot out the door.

The landscape was waking up, brighter as the peaks above gathered more sun. But the air was frozen solid, scraping his nostrils as he breathed.

The interior of his SUV was an icebox, and he shivered as he fired up the engine.

He accelerated down the driveway, adjusting the heating vent to blow its deathly chill onto the windshield instead of his face. As he passed through the headgate and tipped down the hill, he realized he was going a little fast, so he pumped the brakes. The tires locked and squealed on the packed snow. The world swirled in the windshield as he fishtailed sideways. The cab shuddered, and change rattled in his center console as his momentum carried him toward the river. He held his breath and let out an unintelligible shout as he slid out onto the road below. And then he came to a stop, pointed back up the hill.

"Shit." He checked the side-view mirror and saw the Chautauqua River flowing by behind him, indifferent to whether he decided to take a dip in her this morning.

He turned and headed along the river toward town, taking it slow in four-wheel-drive. The department-issue snow tires were top quality, and his last year's model Ford Explorer handled the elements like a snow mobile, but it had been warm yesterday and now the dash thermometer read five degrees. The road shone like a freshly Zambonied ice rink.

And he was still drunk.

He pulled a box of Altoids out of the center console and threw three in his mouth. If he'd had eye drops he would have poured half a bottle in each eye, but who was he kidding? He worked with three capable detectives. It was going to take them less than a second to see he was hungover again.

February had been a blur. And now he was working on his fifth or sixth hangover this March. That was a conservative estimate.

What was the date?

A small voice in his head said something about dangerous amounts of alcohol and job security, but he failed to make out the words behind the bluegrass floating out of his speakers.

Fifteen minutes later, he was stuck in an inexplicable traffic jam at the edge of town. What the hell caused a traffic jam on a Tuesday morning this early?

He sat watching the dash clock change from 7:20 to 7:21, then decided to hang a right on First and take the back roads. A minute later he was in the parking lot of the county building and jogging through the cold to the rear automatic sliding glass doors.

"Howdy, Chief." Deputy Tyler stepped out of the doorway as Wolf entered.

"Hey."

"Didn't find anything."

Wolf stopped in front of the second set of doors, puzzled. "What?"

"Yesterday. With Mittens."

"Oh. Yeah ... and she didn't find anything?"

Tyler shook his head. "Nothing. Covered the entire property and then some. Checked the trees on the west and south. Went up and down the driveway. We're headed back up now to continue."

Wolf could sense Tyler studying his appearance.

"Right," Wolf said. "Okay, thanks."

"Yep." Tyler turned and left.

Wolf headed for the elevator bank and pressed the up button.

"There he is!" Tammy Granger's voice echoed through the reception area at the front of the building. Then her footsteps came closer.

"Hi, Tammy."

He pulled out his phone and pretended he had something to check, then surprised himself with a stone-dead screen staring back at him.

"You going to the Equinox Festival Thursday?" Tammy asked.

The Equinox Festival. The traffic jam now made sense.

He turned toward her and tried to paste on a smile.

Her face dropped. "Oh, honey. Not again."

"Hi, Tammy."

She stared at him, and then at his profile as he turned toward the opening doors. "Have a good one," he said, stepping inside.

Tammy said something under her breath as she walked away, but Wolf was already out of earshot and pressing the third-floor button.

He took the ride up, pressing his knuckles into his eyes to relieve the pain, then removed them when an eight-year-old girl's face enclosed in a rifle sight flashed across his mind.

The doors slid open and Patterson stood a few inches outside, almost colliding with him as she barged inside.

"There you are." She backed up and out into the hallway.

He sidestepped her, but she followed him.

"What's up?" he asked, disappointed she hadn't continued on a trajectory away from him.

"I was headed down to talk to Tammy."

Wolf's office was down the terrazzo hallway, third door on the right. At the far end of the hallway, the squad room opened up, and this morning it was filled with bustling movement and noise. Beyond that stood MacLean's office, an aquarium that butted up against the exterior windows.

MacLean had stated that he liked to keep his blinds open at all times, that he valued transparency in leadership. This morning the blinds were closed, which meant he was having a meeting with someone that required opacity.

Wolf sighed as he reached his office door and pushed it open. Opaque-mode usually meant MacLean was meeting with DA White, or some other person Wolf had little desire to talk to this morning.

"MacLean sent me to come looking for you," Patterson said. "I called you. And yesterday. Both times your phone went straight to voicemail."

"Yeah." Wolf unzipped his coat and hung it on the tree next to the window.

He twisted open the blinds and took in the sight below. Two front-end loaders, probably operated by the Nanteekut brothers, pushed snow into evenly spaced piles for the skijoring race that would take place in two days.

Patterson stepped next to him and looked down. "You going to do it?"

"What?"

"The race."

The skijoring race consisted of strapping on your skis, grabbing a knotted rope, and being towed by one of the fastest horses in town while slaloming back and forth through gates and bounding off five evenly spaced six-foot-high jumps.

"Nope."

She looked up at him, an obvious hint of sadness in her big blue eyes. "I heard you won it one year."

He sat at his desk and shook his computer mouse.

The monitor crackled to life, revealing a screen-saver of him and Jack standing on Mount Harvard two summers ago. Wolf avoided staring at the thin, clear-eyed version of himself atop the fourteener, and pushed the email icon.

"To recap: MacLean's looking for you."

"What's he want?"

"He's with White. They want to talk Warren Preston, I guess. And I spoke to Lorber this morning. He's cracked into Preston's phone."

He nodded, knowing this was basic information for a sober person to comprehend, but it was like she was flinging topics of conversation at him like rocks.

She sucked in a breath as if preparing a long speech, then said, "Take some Advil."

He waved a dismissive hand.

The door shut and he sat back in his chair, thinking nothing as he felt the pain eddying inside his body.

His CSU Rams football clock ticked on the wall like a construction worker's hammer. The hum and rev of the front-end loaders' diesel engines seeped through the triple-pane glass behind him, sounding like a drag race had ensued outside. He needed a handful of Advil, but his mouth was dry and he had no water. He'd have to walk down to the squad room, grab a bottle from the refrigerator, and come back without being seen by MacLean. That, or suck it up and get it all done at once.

"Shit." He put his elbows on the desk and massaged his temples with his fingers.

A strange sensation rippled through his chest, like a fluttering of his heart. It caused him to suck in a breath and straighten.

A moment later the sensation passed.

That was new.

He pulled out the Advil bottle from his top desk drawer, shook out three brown pills, then another, and put them in the breast pocket of his flannel.

Before he could stand, two knocks hit the door and it swung open.

MacLean poked his head inside. "You're here." He ducked his head back outside. "He's here!"

The sheriff walked in uninvited, letting the door swing open and bang against the inside wall.

"Sheriff." Wolf nodded, not letting the pain inside his skull outwardly express itself.

"Look shittier than ever today," MacLean said, meaning every word of it. He scraped back one of the two chairs from the desk and sat down, keeping his eyes on Wolf's as he did so. Like a magician, MacLean produced a bottle of water from thin air and slapped it on the desk. "Here."

Wolf tried not to look too eager as he gripped the cold

plastic and scraped it across the desk toward him. He fished three of the four pills out of his pocket, tossed them into his mouth, and cracked open the dew-covered bottle. The water massaged his throat as he drank. And then it caught, and he coughed, spraying liquid across the desktop.

"Jesus, boy." MacLean remained motionless, watching Wolf mop the liquid with a sleeve.

DA White appeared at the doorway, shut the door, and sat next to MacLean. "My God, what happened to you?"

"Hi there, Sawyer," Wolf said.

"Seriously." White leaned forward and sniffed. "Smells like a distillery in here." His eyes never left Wolf's as he sat back.

MacLean was dressed in his formal khakis today, and the Sluice County district attorney in his customary pinstriped suit and earth-colored tie.

"What brings you down to our offices today?" Wolf asked, directing the question to White, who had an office almost directly above Wolf's head.

"What brings me down ..." White repeated under his breath as he got comfortable in the chair. "Well, Chief Detective, we have a man well-known in the business environment of Rocky Points who's vanished, leaving behind a vehicle filled with snow. Come noon, we're going to have a gaggle of reporters down in the press-room lambasting the sheriff, looking for answers. I'm here wondering what answers you and your team have, so we can avoid looking like buffoons today."

Wolf cleared his throat. "Right. Well, we've searched

his house and the surrounding area, and we've still not found him."

White pinched his brows and leaned forward. "Listen, Detective, this is the Sluice–Byron County Sheriff's Office that you're sitting in right now. This is your office, where you work."

MacLean turned toward White. "Sawyer."

"I'm just making sure our highest-paid employee knows where he is right now, Sheriff. Because from where I'm sitting, he's seven sheets to the wind. And from what I'm gathering, I'm already seven steps ahead of him in this investigation!"

"You are?" Wolf asked. "Let me in on the news."

White straightened in his chair and sucked in a breath. He stood up and walked to the windows.

Wolf knew the man was thinking about how to bolster his conviction rate, and anything less than black and white, eight months before elections, was like a triple shot of anxiety to his system.

MacLean would have been petting his silver walrus-style mustache if he'd been concerned about anything. But the sheriff sat preening his nails. He would be running unopposed.

Wolf turned and saw White's gaze leveled on him. Menace and calculation sizzled behind his eyes.

"I assure you, we're on it," Wolf said. "I would have my team in here right now, discussing our plan of action, if we weren't having this conversation."

White flicked a knowing glance at MacLean. "Just keep me posted." He exited the room in a hurry and left the door swinging open.

"What was that about?" Wolf asked.

"You know damn well what that was about. He's on the way out. He's hyper-sensitive to anything that might make him look bad."

Wolf sipped the water and watched MacLean's gray eyes never waver from his.

"And no offense, but if he was standing next to you right now, he'd look pretty bad."

"I'd think he would look good in comparison."

MacLean blew a puff of air from his lips. "A man in his position is very dangerous. You're not careful, he'll pull you under to save his own breath."

"Excellent metaphor, sir."

MacLean stood and went to the window. "You think I'm kidding? Listen, Wolf—"

There was a knock at the door.

Patterson poked her head inside. "Oh, sorry. I'll come back in a few."

"What's up?" Wolf asked, ignoring MacLean's staring at the side of his face.

"I have the cell activity from Lorber." She held up a stack of papers.

"Good. Wait, sir?" He looked at MacLean. "You wanted to speak about something else?"

MacLean sighed. "Get in here. Show us what you got."

Rachette and Yates appeared behind Patterson and they streamed into the office. Patterson walked up to the desk and set down the sheets next to each other, one by one in a matrix. Some were lists of text, others were color print-outs of ping maps and GPS location lines.

"According to Chris Alamy's statement, Warren Preston left work that day like any other normal Friday. Then Warren called him Saturday morning, wanting to speak to him Saturday night in the office. According to Chris, he went into work to speak to his boss at 6 p.m."

"We're talking about this last weekend?" Wolf asked.

His detectives looked at one another.

"No," Patterson said, flicking a quick glance to MacLean. "The Saturday they met was the weekend before last. According to Alamy, Preston's been missing for ... eleven days now."

Wolf nodded as if he remembered the detail. "Right."

She continued. "During the meeting that Saturday, eleven days ago, Mr. Preston revealed to Chris that he was going on vacation, apparently down to Arizona for some camping in the Superstition Mountains." Patterson flipped a page. "Alamy said he and his boss discussed upcoming work issues for that next week, and that was that. Chris left to go home. Then he told us he went to the Pony later that night and shut it down."

Wolf leaned forward and looked at the sheets of paper Patterson had organized on his desk to evade the stares beaming into him.

"I've written up the warrant for Chris Alamy's cell logs and GPS locations," she said. "I turned it into White's office and I'm just waiting to hear back. But, in the meantime, you can see we have a list of calls Mr. Preston made for the last few weeks, taken off his phone. Most of the numbers were listed with contact names, and those that weren't we tracked down via the number-lookup system."

Rachette scoffed. "Meaning we called half the numbers and saw who answered."

"Right," Patterson said. "Anyway, it looks like, on that final day of work on Friday the seventh, Warren Preston made a series of calls. One to a company called Hood Rock Supply up in Brushing. One to another supply company called Herald Flagstone and Rock Supply in Fort Collins. Two calls to a woman named Betsy Collworth. Goes on and on ... as you'd expect from a busy business owner during a day's work. I have a list of employees of his right here. Betsy is an employee. This call is an employee ... this one ... all of these."

She picked up a GPS map. "On Saturday the eighth, I have Preston's location coming from his house up the canyon, down to his work that evening. He stayed at the rock yard from 6:17 p.m. to 9:28 p.m. He made no calls during that time."

"And Chris Alamy says he met with Preston at work during that time," Wolf said.

"Correct."

MacLean scoffed. "Looks like we have an official person of interest."

Patterson shrugged. "I'd say so."

"What about Preston's vehicle?" Wolf asked. "Any clues found in there yet?"

"Lorber's still drying it out," Patterson said.

"Keep me posted." MacLean left the room, but not before shooting Wolf a look that said he was disgusted, or concerned, or both.

"Let's get Chris Alamy back in here," Wolf said.

"Right." Patterson collected her papers. "We'll get on it."

Wolf stood and put on his coat.

"Where are you going?" Rachette asked.

Wolf's stomach churned, demanding food. "Out."

CHAPTER 3

WOLF CONSIDERED TAKING the back exit, but even with a hangover he was not one to run from a good scolding, especially one he deserved, so he took the front entrance out to Main Street.

Surprisingly, as he walked through the glass-enclosed front waiting area to the county building, Tammy ignored him as if he were an apparition.

She was good.

He went out onto the sidewalk and into a stiff breeze. He put the wind to his back and headed down the sidewalk of Main.

Rocky Points's main thoroughfare had been covered by a few inches of packed powder by the plows. Dozens of people milled about, making preparations for the festival—erecting tents, hanging flags, setting cones for the skijoring course. It was a feat the town was, and should have been, proud of, but it left little impression on Wolf.

The sun had risen fully, and the glare off the thick

coat of snow on the western valley wall of mountains stung his eyes. He cursed himself for forgetting his sunglasses yet again.

When his eyes had fully adjusted, he snuck a glance at the resort. Skiers meandered down the slopes like slow-motion ants. Season-pass-holders were getting their money's worth this year, or so he'd heard.

He walked past the store fronts, keeping his head down to minimize the damage to his retinas, and skidded to a stop, almost passing the coffee shop.

If Wolf had had his pick, he'd have been sitting down for a full plate of breakfast at the Sunnyside Café, a few blocks in the opposite direction, but a quick stop at Dead Ground would do for a dose of grease and caffeine to battle the hangover.

He walked inside, happy that today's employees had picked a sane volume for their music. He joined a line of six people and stood with half-closed eyes. The scent of freshly ground coffee beans did little to perk him up, but the promise of ingesting the caffeine lifted his mood.

"David!"

He recognized the woman's voice and turned around to see Margaret Hitchens sitting at a table along the wall. Across from her sat James Pritchard, an ex DA from Denver turned Rocky Points local, turned current county-council member with more than a little clout, if MacLean's ramblings had any truth to them.

Wolf nodded and faced forward in the line.

A minute later, he grabbed his large dark roast and a sausage breakfast burrito and stopped at their table on the way out.

"How are you, David? You remember Mr. Pritchard?" Margaret blew on a steaming cup, her eyes on the rippling liquid.

Wolf nodded at the man and sipped his own coffee through the sliver in his to-go lid, scalding his lip.

Pritchard nodded and averted eye contact. He made no move to shake Wolf's hand, and Wolf felt the better for it.

Margaret looked uncomfortable.

"Well, you two have a good day." He nodded and went out the door.

The breeze blowing through the old buildings felt good now as it cut through his hair to the scalp. With the sun at his back and his vision restored, the Margaret Hitchens for Mayor posters appeared as if out of nowhere. Every lamppost had one, every store window.

"Hey!"

Margaret marched around him and stopped, blocking his path.

"What the hell is your problem?" Her eyes bugged. The curly silver locks poking out beneath her knit cap blew away from her face on the breeze, adding a touch of wrath to her expression.

He wanted to make a smart quip but his hungover brain came up with a single syllable response instead. "Huh?"

"Jesus. You're drunk. Last time I saw you, you were drunk. The time before that you were drunk. You sit up there in that office of yours, or in that house of yours, and drink."

"I don't drink at work." Wolf sipped his coffee.

She put her hands on her hips, narrowed and widened her eyelids, and turned away. "Shit."

He took that as permission to go, so he did.

She gripped his arm and spun him around. "Don't you walk away from me."

"Okay."

"Don't okay me."

He blinked. "What would you like me to say, Margaret?"

"How about something of substance? Like, I don't know, I'm devastated about Lauren and Ella leaving me, and I'm getting drunk every day to cope with the pain, but it's really, really not helping, so I ..." She stopped and studied his face with glistening eyes. "So I need to stop."

He turned and studied the ski slopes again.

"Shit, I'm sorry," she said.

He smiled. "About what?"

She shook her head. "You're impossible."

"Listen." He put on a concerned face. "There's a case, okay? I'm just a little preoccupied."

She stared at him, clearly unconvinced, then nodded. "Okay. A case, huh? What's going on?"

"You know Warren Preston?"

"Yeah. Preston Rock and Supply."

"What do you know about him?" he asked.

She shrugged. "Sells rock. A lot of rock. He supplied those boulders in the center of Ski Base Village. Took special trucks and a crane to place them. Other than that ... I've sold a dozen or so of those condos next to his rock yard."

Most real-estate agents saying they'd sold a dozen or so of something was an over-estimation, but Wolf knew Margaret often undersold herself when it came to already impressive sales statistics. Wolf suspected this was so that when the person inevitably found out the truth at some later time, from an online search or word of mouth, said person would be doubly impressed by her actual numbers. She was good.

"What'd he do?" she asked.

"Why would you think he did something?"

"I don't know. Didn't he? You brought him up."

"Can't really talk about it."

She rolled her eyes. "Bastard."

"Had to shut you up somehow."

She stared blankly at him, then shuffled close and wrapped her arm around his bicep.

They turned down the sidewalk and walked toward the county building.

"How's the campaign going?" he asked.

"Very well."

"Of course it is."

"But it's no done deal," she said.

But it was. She was running against Trip Wellmont, a former cattle rancher with his finger on the rear-end of the county, trying to find a pulse. He guessed it was good she was working so hard to ensure victory, though. To have Wellmont in power would have been a major disruption to the standard operations of the department. The man wanted cuts across the board, in a town seeing record growth. Of course, Wolf had no doubt that to have Margaret Hitchens in power would be no less earth-moving. He had yet to sit down with her and discuss her agenda. He'd been busy with other things.

They walked in silence until they reached the county building.

He pulled away from her near the sliding doors.

"Listen," she said. "My sister's coming into town tonight." Her sister, meaning Detective Patterson's mother. "We're getting a whole crew together tomorrow night and going to dinner at Black Diamond Pizza, then we're coming down here for the race." Meaning Margaret Hitchens was standing on the music stage behind him, yelling into the microphone about *responsible progress*, and other hot-button topics.

"No thanks. But thanks."

She opened her mouth to say something, then nodded and walked back up the street.

He watched her go. The rapidity of his answer had surprised him, but the quickness of her giving up was something else.

He headed back inside.

Tammy was on the phone, ignoring him as he strolled in on a gust of wind.

He made his way to the third floor without further social distraction. Once in his office, he locked his door and ate, letting the caffeine, protein, and ibuprofen battle against the alcohol in peace.

CHAPTER 4

WOLF WOKE WITH A START, wiping a stream of drool from his chin and the desk.

The doorknob rattled, and someone knocked.

"Come in!"

The knob rattled again.

"Just a second!"

The light streaming through the blind slats was brighter and coming in at different angles from the last time he remembered.

Had he slept here last night?

Details came to him, but it was like trying to recall the memories from the prior year.

More knocking.

"Yeah!"

He stood up and walked around his desk, planting a hand on the wood to keep his balance. My God, his throat. He picked up an almost-empty water bottle from the desk, sucked down the warm liquid, and threw it toward the trash, missing the bin.

He unlocked the door and cracked it open.

Patterson stood with a concerned face. "Sir?"

He turned around and made his way back to the desk, picking up the water bottle and trashing it on the way past.

There was silence for a few more moments, then she shuffled inside after him.

He sat. "Yeah?"

"We have Chris Alamy down in Interrogation B." She walked inside and placed a large, twenty-ouncer bottle of water on his desk and dropped a pile of pills next to it.

"Thanks."

"You have a bunch of lines on your face where you've been sleeping."

"I do?" He sucked down half the bottle and the pills. The liquid was sent from God. "Oh, thanks. I needed that."

She stared at him through half-mast lids.

"Interrogation B?"

"Yes."

"Okay. I'll be right down."

"You want me or Rachette in there with you?"

"Yes."

She stood still. "Which one? Me or Rachette?"

"You. I'll see you there in a second, okay?"

She left, leaving the door open. A pair of deputies walked past, staring at him intently, like he was a zoo animal on display.

He rolled his neck to straighten a kink, ignoring the

kick of pain in his skull. He sucked in a deep breath and almost gagged on the vapor as he exhaled. He rifled through his drawers and found a single piece of gum in the back corner. He unwrapped it, removed flecks of dirt from the green rectangle, and shoved it in his mouth.

Willing the spearmint to wash away the stench, he chomped away and walked down to the squad room.

The vaulted ceilings echoed with hushed conversation. Patterson, Yates, and Rachette stopped talking and turned to him.

"He have a lawyer?" Wolf asked.

"No, sir." Rachette sipped some coffee and lifted it. "You want a cup?"

"No, thanks. Let's go over what we have."

Patterson picked up a stack of papers and read from the top. "Chris Alamy's initial report from the other morning states that he was aware that Warren Preston was planning on taking a camping vacation in Arizona. Chris Alamy said that when Mr. Preston never came into work the following Monday he was suspicious, but not overly concerned. When he never showed up Tuesday, however, he became anxious. Drove up to his boss's house. Found the vehicle wide open and filled with snow. Found the keys, wallet, cell phone inside, but no sign of his boss. Came down the valley and gave his report to Rachette."

Wolf looked at Rachette with a raised eyebrow.

"That's about it," Rachette said.

"Okay. Patterson, you're in there with me."

"Yes, sir."

Wolf forked his fingers and pointed at Rachette and Yates. "You two watch carefully, please."

"Yes, sir." Rachette smothered a jealous expression behind his Styrofoam cup.

Chris Alamy wore a purple-and-white checked flannel buttoned to the mid-chest, untucked and draping over well-worn jeans. His brown hair was long, hanging in shampooed waves that splashed on his shoulders. A beard trimmed to perfection framed an oval face. The mustache had been grown longer than the rest of the hair and curled up at the edges, like an old-timey barber-shop quartet singer. He stood up from the plastic chair upon their arrival and nodded.

"Mr. Alamy," Wolf said, shaking his hand.

"Yes, sir."

Wolf studied Chris's eyes and saw a hint of fear peeking out. "I'm Chief Detective David Wolf. Please, take a seat."

Patterson pressed a button on the audio recorder mounted in the center of the table. "This is Detective Sergeant Heather Patterson, here with Chief Detective David Wolf, speaking with Chris Alamy ..."

Wolf watched Alamy as Patterson spoke. The man sat down and nodded, looking little fazed by the audio recorder and two video cameras mounted in the corners of the room.

"So, for the record, Mr. Alamy, do you agree to have

our conversation audio and video recorded today?" Patterson asked.

"Yes."

Wolf and Patterson sat.

"I don't think we've ever met," Wolf said, not recognizing the man's face, which was rare. Wolf had been born in County Hospital and, other than his years in the army, had lived every year of his life in Rocky Points.

"I grew up north in Brushing."

"How long have you lived down here in Points?"

"Three years."

Wolf nodded. A long time to not see the guy around. But people could go years keeping a strict routine, and clearly their routines had failed to cross paths.

"So, you went up to Mr. Preston's house," Chris said.

"Yes, we did." Wolf nodded.

Patterson pulled a legal pad onto her lap, crossed her legs, and scribbled to get the pen flowing.

"Nobody's told me what happened," Chris said. "Did you find him?"

Wolf took his time answering, noting how Chris's skin flushed red.

"No, we didn't find him."

Chris leaned back hard in his chair, as if he'd been waiting on the outcome of that question for days. His thumb and forefinger came up beneath his mustache and he petted his beard.

Patterson gestured to a piece of paper. "It says here in the report you gave Detective Rachette that you went into work Saturday, March 8th to meet Mr. Preston."

Chris nodded. "That's right."

"And what happened at that meeting?"

Chris frowned. "We talked."

"About what?"

"Just work. I was taking over for him while he was out of town. He wanted to discuss some orders. Some specific things I had to take care of while he was gone." Chris held frozen eye contact with Patterson.

"And where, exactly, did Mr. Preston say he was going?" she asked.

"Arizona."

"Where in Arizona?"

"He said the Superstition Mountains."

She nodded. "Nothing more specific than that?"

Chris shook his head. "No." He shrugged. "He never told me the exact spot. It's some family gold-mining claim."

Silence took over for a beat.

Wolf raised a finger and looked toward the one-way mirror. "Hey, Rachette!"

After a brief pause, the door knob rattled and Rachette poked his head inside. "Yes, sir?"

"Can you please get Mr. Alamy a bottled water?"

"Yes, sir."

The door shut.

Wolf turned a kind smile to Chris. "Sorry. Bad manners on our part."

Chris crossed his legs and bounced his leather work boot on his knee.

Wolf said nothing as he waited for Rachette's return. The lull in conversation seemed to ramp up Chris's anxiety. He scratched the side of his nose, petted his beard some more.

Rachette returned in short order and plunked a sweating bottle of water in front of Chris.

"Thanks," Chris said. He picked up the bottle, cracked open the lid, and took a sip.

"What time did you meet with Mr. Preston at work that Saturday night?" Wolf asked.

Alamy looked at the ceiling. "I was there at like six-ish?"

"That was your agreed-upon meeting time?" Wolf asked. "Sometime around six?"

Alamy nodded. "Yeah. Six."

"And how did that meeting go?"

Alamy shrugged.

"Could you please use words for the audio recording?"

"It went fine. We just had a discussion about the upcoming workload for that week. Last week's workload."

Wolf nodded. "And what time did you leave the meeting?"

Alamy looked up again. "Let's see. It was about seven, seven fifteen. We met for an hour. I remember we met for an hour."

Alamy's face had gone beet red, and the man seemed to know it, which only ramped up his anxiety. A bead of sweat glistened on his forehead.

Wolf sat patiently, watching the physical reaction sweep through the man's body.

"He was still at work when I left," Alamy said.

"Where did you go after the meeting?" Patterson asked.

"I went home."

"And where is that?" she asked.

Alamy gave his address.

Patterson wrote it down.

"And then I went to the Pony Tavern at around ten thirty."

Patterson wrote that down.

"Who were you with at the Pony?" Wolf asked.

He shrugged. "The usual Saturday-night crew. There's a bunch of them. Vic Brooks, Cameron Tate ..." He ticked off some more names on his fingers and Patterson wrote them down, too.

"So, from seven to ten thirty, what were you doing?" Wolf asked.

Alamy looked at Wolf with narrowed eyes. "I probably got home from the meeting at like seven thirty."

"Okay, yeah. You had to drive home."

"Right."

"Okay, from seven thirty to ten thirty, what were you doing?"

"I just sat around. You know, watched some television, had a beer or two."

"Were you with anyone?"

"No. I live alone."

"And then you went to the Pony."

He nodded. "Yes."

"At ten thirty."

Alamy nodded. "Yes."

"What did you watch?"

"What?"

"On the television? What did you watch?"

Alamy's eyes glazed over for a second. "I was watching a movie. The new *Iron Man*."

"Which one?"

Alamy glared at Wolf. "The new *Iron Man* one. What is this?"

Wolf put up his hands and pulled at a stray thread coming off his jeans. "And how long did you stay at the Pony?"

Alamy took his time answering. "Until it closed down. I took an Uber back home. Left my car there. I was too drunk to drive."

"That's good," Wolf said.

"Can you tell us more about what happened the day you went to Mr. Preston's house to check on him?" Patterson asked.

"Yeah, sure. Like I said, I was concerned that he never came back to work this Monday, but I figured ... I don't know ... you know, he's the boss. He doesn't really have to answer to anyone at work."

"Did you call him that day? On Monday?" Wolf asked.

"Yes. I've already told Detective Rachette. I called Mr. Preston Monday."

Wolf nodded. "My mistake. Go on."

"Then, when he never showed up on Tuesday morning, I got concerned. That's when I decided to just drive up to his house. When I got there, I saw his car. And then I kind of freaked out, you know? The vehicle was completely covered inside and out with snow. It hadn't snowed for over a week. Then I remembered the last time it had snowed was that Saturday we met.

"I kind of freaked out. Wondered what was going on. I ... think I called him again. And then I went to his front door. Knocked. Rang the bell. But nobody answered. I went inside. And I saw that his stuff was lying out on the counter.

"None of it made any sense. I started wondering if something, you know, bad had happened. Like, if he'd had a heart attack or something and ... shit, I don't know. I wondered if he was dead in there. So I searched the house, went room to room, but I never found him. That's when I came here and reported him missing."

"Why didn't you feed the cat?" Patterson poised her pen over the paper, waiting for the answer.

"Feed the cat?"

"Yes. The cat was starving when we got there later that morning. Meowed at us until we fed it."

Alamy blinked rapidly. "Yeah. I don't know. I must have not noticed."

Wolf resisted looking at Patterson.

She scribbled something in her notes.

Chris's breathing accelerated. He volleyed glances between them.

"What do you do at Preston Rock and Supply, Chris?" Wolf asked.

He hesitated, looking as if he'd been caught off-guard by the change of subject. "I'm VP of operations."

"And the president is?" Wolf asked.

"Mr. Preston is president and owner." Alamy opened his mouth to say something else but closed it.

"Were you going to say something?" Patterson asked.

"No, well, I'm part owner, too. Twenty-five percent."

Wolf nodded. "And if something were to happen to Mr. Preston? Would that make you a hundred-percent owner?"

Alamy straightened, an affronted look twisting his face. "I can leave, right? I'm not under arrest, am I?"

"No, you're not," Wolf said. "We're just talking about the—"

"Yeah, but I don't have to talk anymore. I'm not liking the direction this is going. I'm gonna get a lawyer." He stood up. "Can I leave?"

Patterson and Wolf looked at one another.

"I asked you if I can leave."

"You can leave," Wolf said.

Chris walked to the door and twisted the handle. "It's locked."

The doorknob rattled, and the door pushed open.

Chris backed away and squared off with Rachette.

Rachette took his time stepping aside, but as soon as the opening was big enough Chris darted through.

Rachette watched him go. "Geez. Guy looks like Yates after eating a pound of cheese."

Yates came up behind him and they stepped into the room.

Rachette looked at Wolf. "You wanted us to watch, and I just saw a guilty man get up and dart out of here."

"Guilty of what?" Patterson asked.

"Guilty."

Yates stepped to the table and pushed in the chair,

then reached over to grab the bottle of water from the table top.

"Bag that bottle and get it down to Lorber."

Yates pulled back his hand. "You brought that in to get his fingerprints?"

"Are his prints on file?"

Yates looked at Patterson and Rachette.

"I don't know," Rachette said.

"They are now." Wolf left the interrogation room, went through the cramped observation space, and out another door to an office manned by Deputy John Tyler.

"You get all that?" he asked Tyler.

Tyler clicked his computer mouse and sat back. "Yep."

"Upload the footage," Patterson told him, referring to some place on or in some cloud unknown to Wolf.

"You got it."

They left for the hallway and walked toward the squad room, passing MacLean's office. The blinds were closed again, and a bark-like laugh vibrated the windows.

"How are we doing on Alamy's cell records? A man's life could be hanging in the balance."

"I'm on it." Patterson veered into the squad room.

Wolf stopped and turned around. Yates came up behind him with a plastic bag containing the empty bottle of water.

"I'll take that."

Yates handed it over.

"Rachette, you two look into Alamy's internet presence. Social media, all that."

"You going down to see how the Yeti's doing?" Rachette asked.

"Yep."

Rachette and Yates walked to their desks.

Wolf sighed, thinking about the couch inside his office.

CHAPTER 5

WOLF RODE the elevator to the first floor and walked down the hallway to the hanging sign that read *Forensics Department*.

"Hello?" Wolf said into the empty room.

Electronic scopes, other devices, and accompanying electronic screens hummed under blinding white lights.

A black knit sweater and a pair of gray slacks were laid out on a metal gurney. Water streamed off them. Wolf deduced the objects had once been inside Warren Preston's drifted-over vehicle. Unless there were other current cases he was unaware of. He caught a whiff of his breath, still strong enough to kill a deer, and decided that could have been a possibility.

He walked through a pair of double doors. The next room was small and rectangular with white-tiled floors. Boxes and unused equipment spilled off metal carts.

A heavy steel door waited on the far side of the wall, opening out into the garage. Wolf pushed through into exhaust-tinged cool air.

The garage inside had been created for forensic analysis of vehicles and was large enough to house four fire trucks parked side-by-side. It had been dubbed The Bomb Shelter for obvious reasons. In the center stood Warren Preston's Lexus SUV. The doors were wide open and powerful lights mounted on metal stands illuminated the interior. Water streamed away from the vehicle in dark swaths, burbling as it flowed out of sight into drains in the floor.

"Hey." Dr. Lorber stood studying the vehicle with folded arms.

The Sluice–Byron County medical examiner stood six foot seven, a few inches lower when he stood in round-shouldered contemplation, like now. When he let his arms hang down, they were long as a gorilla's, like the mythical Yeti, as Rachette had referred to him earlier. The man was skin and bones though. More of an anemic gorilla or Sasquatch.

"What's happening?" Wolf asked.

Lorber pushed a pair of John Lennon-style glasses up his nose and double-took the plastic bag in Wolf's hand. "What's that?"

"We just interviewed Chris Alamy—Warren Preston's employee. As far as we know, he was the last person to see Warren Preston Saturday night. I have his prints on this bottle in case we need them."

Lorber raised an eyebrow. "Funny. I was just going to come up and talk to you about prints."

Wolf held up the bag.

"It's wet."

"Yeah."

"Damn it. If I see another drop of condensation I'm going to piss myself."

"Seems counterproductive."

Lorber donned a pair of latex gloves and took the bag. He extracted the bottle, brought it to the lights, and set it on the concrete.

"Prints?" Wolf asked, referring to Lorber's earlier comment.

"I found a single partial. Nothing else."

"Whose?"

Lorber shrugged. "No match in the databases. And we should have found way more than just a single, partial print. Doesn't matter if the vehicle was left out in the snow or a torrential rain storm. Unless Warren Preston drives with gloves on all the time, never touching the interior of the vehicle."

"It was wiped."

Lorber nodded. "Come here." He loped to the open vehicle.

Wolf followed into the hot lights. The leather of the SUV interior was covered in patterns where condensation had evaporated.

"See this?" Lorber clicked on a black light and pointed it at the bottom of the door. "Turn off those lights."

Wolf turned around.

"Flip the main switch on the side of that stand."

Wolf did as he was told and the room went pitch-black.

He stood blinking, feeling like he'd been transported

to the deck of a swaying ship socked in with fog at midnight.

"Over here." Lorber waved the black light.

Wolf shuffled nearer and studied the passenger seat headrest as Lorber swept the light across it.

"See this? Up here where the snow didn't reach." Lorber's light revealed swipe marks on the leather where someone had wiped it with a rag and cleaner.

"Yeah."

"It's the same all over. No fingerprints. Just this thorough wipe-job."

"Where'd you get the partial?"

Lorber shut the door. "Outer driver's-side handle. Underneath."

"Want to bet that partial belongs to Chris Alamy?" Wolf asked into the darkness.

"He was with Preston Saturday night?"

"That's what he says."

"That's when that storm hit, right?" Lorber asked.

"Yep."

"Turn on that light again."

Wolf fumbled around for a few moments and found the switch. The light blasted his eyes, and when his eyesight returned to normal he noticed Lorber staring at him.

"You look like shit today. Again."

"How about you get to lifting Alamy's prints off that bottle, and we can check it against the partial."

Lorber failed to hide a faint, amused grin as he picked up the bottle with a thumb and middle finger.

Wolf followed him back to the interior lab doors and back inside.

The ME wasted no movements as he gathered the necessary equipment and supplies to process the prints.

"You want me to come back?"

"It'll take me a minute or two."

Wolf fantasized about a minute or two on the office couch. He decided that after this he'd sit while the rest of his team accomplished their other tasks.

"There." Lorber flicked a switch, displaying a full set of prints on a monitor. "Glad I didn't bet. Partial's not Alamy's."

Wolf studied the screen.

"Alamy's loops are all ulnar," Lorber said, pointing.

Which meant the fingerprints spiraled away from the pinkie side of the hand. Or was it the thumb side?

"The print on the handle is less than half a complete pattern, but you can see it's looping the opposite direction. And it's all wrong, anyway."

Wolf nodded. "Okay. And you're certain that partial's not Warren Preston's?"

"Yep." Lorber clicked on the keyboard, fingers like an Irish stepdance. A second later another set of prints came up onscreen, replacing the prints from the bottle. "These are Preston's prints from his phone and all over the house. See?"

Wolf did. The partial clearly didn't match any of Preston's.

"So we're looking for a third person," Wolf said.

"And our third person wiped the car," Lorber said. The ME folded his arms and looked Wolf up and down, judgment pinching his forehead. He opened his mouth to say something but Wolf cut him off.

"What about any other forensic evidence? Hair? Clothing fibers? Blood?"

"That's another matter. I'm starting on it now. Daphne's coming in to give me a hand. I'm not that optimistic, considering the amount of snow swirling around inside that vehicle. But we'll see."

Daphne Pinnifield was Lorber's new intern. She lived over the pass to the south, where she was pre-med at a branch of Colorado Mountain College in Ashland.

Wolf let a yawn stretch his face.

"Looks like you need to go back to sleep," Lorber said.

Wolf wished. "Keep me posted."

He headed out the doors and down the hall. A group of uniforms were chatting, waiting for the elevator, so he stepped into the stairwell and began the climb.

His lungs heaved by the second landing, but he pressed on without stopping. By the third floor, an itchy sweat had broken out under his shirt. It beaded his forehead and prickled his scalp.

He exited the stairs and saw Patterson standing with Rachette and Yates outside his office door.

Patterson spoke first. "My guy's not there at Summit Wireless, but they know we're in a hurry for Alamy's records. Should be a few hours."

Wolf walked inside his office with his squad in tow. He pointedly avoided eye contact with the couch and went to the window. Cool air radiated off the glass. A bank of clouds had rolled in from the north, looking like they might spit a few flakes by the afternoon. He recalled vaguely that the forecast was calling for trace amounts. But when? For the second time of the day he questioned what day it was. Wednesday?

He pulled his cell phone from his pocket and looked at the screen.

Wednesday, March 19th. 10:45 a.m. Nailed it.

More people scrambled on Main Street below. Two men with snow shovels were slapping one of the jumps, while a woman sprinkled chunks of green pine boughs over the landing zones.

"Sir?" Patterson cleared her throat.

Wolf turned and saw his squad looking at him. "Yes?"

"So? What now?"

Wolf rolled his neck and eyed the couch for the first time. The cloth looked warm and soft.

"Time to go to Preston Rock and Supply."

CHAPTER 6

WOLF SAT in Patterson's passenger seat, feeling heat from her glances hitting the side of his face. Or was it the heater, which was cranked on high? He had a vague memory of Patterson being hot her last pregnancy. Now, she apparently liked to sit in a pool of her own sweat for this baby.

"Seems like you're drinking a lot lately," she said, breaking the tension with a grenade.

Wolf studied the Chautauqua Valley sliding past his window.

"Even more than the last couple of months. Which was a lot then."

"I know," he said. Because not saying anything would have pissed her off.

She huffed, then seemed to give up.

They drove the short distance along 734 North, then turned onto Wildflower Road. A quick right and they were driving along the river. The water ran high, carving into the snow piled alongside it. It had been a heavy winter, and now that spring was here, there would only be more precipitation.

New condominium complexes had sprouted up along the river over the past few years. They were overpriced, and every one of them was either occupied or owned by a Denverite weekend warrior. The properties were appealing to the eye, if one was into tall metal-and-wood structures blocking mountain views.

And then there was Preston Rock and Supply. The business consisted of a large, vaulted metal building situated in the center of five or so acres of land on a bluff raised above the river—a scarred piece of land surrounded by metal fencing, and the stark opposite of the manicured condo properties upstream.

The road turned to packed powder-covered dirt and circled around the space, giving them a good look inside. Concrete retaining walls cordoned off different colored and textured rocks piled in varying quantities.

A large dirt-mover revved, spewing thick diesel exhaust as it rolled on huge tires through the lanes between the retaining walls. A truck billowed dust as it finished dumping a load of gravel into a slot.

Patterson pulled through an open gate, then parked in front of what looked like an office on the end of the metal building.

They stepped out into chilly, damp air. Even after the blast-furnace interior of Patterson's SUV, the wind cut through Wolf's clothing and made him zip his jacket to his chin.

Rachette's SUV barreled into the entrance and parked behind Patterson's.

While the other two detectives climbed out of their vehicles, Wolf edged to the front bumper and eyed the Chautauqua below. The sound of the river burbled faintly behind the noise of diesel engines. Flakes floated down from the now leaden sky.

"Hello, ma'am." Patterson said.

"Is this about Warren?" A heavy-set woman had come outside. She wore a red-and-black flannel that hung open, revealing a gray T-shirt that read *Sexy* over ample breasts. The puffy flesh of her face framed a worried expression.

"Are you Betsy?" Patterson asked.

"Yes."

"I just spoke with you on the phone. I'm Detective Heather Patterson. And these are Detectives Wolf, Rachette, and Yates."

Rachette made a show of pacing and observing the premises while Yates stepped up and shook Betsy's hand.

Wolf had seen Betsy around town. Besides a cordial hello here and there, he doubted they'd exchanged words. He opted to stand mutely and nod, knowing that sometimes the four of them barreling in on somebody could be overwhelming.

"We'd like to ask you a few questions, ma'am," Patterson said.

Betsy nodded. "Sure. Come on in."

Rachette walked to Wolf, pointing a discreet thumb at a window. Wolf had seen it: Chris Alamy inside, looking out through open blinds with an exasperated expression. The man had probably just driven here, maybe gotten a single call in to a lawyer, and now here they were again.

They streamed into an office filled with all the blue-collar furniture one would expect to find inside a rock-supply business—metal desks, file cabinets, a countertop with a drip coffee-maker, faux-wood folding tables surrounded by folding chairs.

Wolf noticed the table top was strewn with papers in much the same fashion as they'd been in Warren Preston's dining room.

"What's going on?" Chris Alamy stood in the doorway of his office.

"These are detectives from the Sheriff's Department," Betsy said. "They want to ask us some questions."

"Not you." Patterson held up a hand, stopping the protest about to make its way through Chris's mustache. "We're here to talk to Betsy and the other employees. You don't have to speak to us any further."

Alamy shuffled for a few seconds, then backed into his office. He shut the door, revealing a gold name tag that read *Chrissy* affixed to the wood.

Betsy frowned. "What's this all about? Where's Warren?"

Wolf folded his arms and moved to look out a window to the rock yard. Rachette and Yates gave Patterson the floor.

"Betsy, as you probably know by now, we're looking for Warren," Patterson said. "When's the last time you spoke to him?"

Betsy looked shaken, then stared hard out of intelligent blue eyes. "Last I spoke to him was Friday. Friday night before I left work. Twelve days ago." She closed her eyes and exhaled. It sounded like air being let slowly out of a tractor tire. "Twelve days. My goodness."

"What did you talk about before he left that night?" Patterson asked.

"Nothing much. The usual, I guess." She blinked as if recalling memories. "I was just telling him how the grandkids were coming over from Grand Junction. You know ... 'Have a good weekend,' small talk." She shrugged. "He didn't talk to me about no vacation."

Patterson straightened. "He didn't speak about his vacation?"

"No. Not at all. I had no clue he was even going."

Wolf studied Betsy's face. She was telling the truth.

"He never said anything about going to Arizona for camping to me."

"And that's strange?" Patterson asked. "Out of character for him to not tell you before he left for vacation?"

"Hell, yeah, that's strange. He doesn't do anything without telling me."

"Chris told us that Mr. Preston told him he was going on vacation. Is that strange to you that he told him but not you?"

She stared at Patterson, then flicked her eyes to Chris's closed office door. "That's what he says."

Patterson lowered her voice. "Are you saying you don't believe him?"

"Warren never told me he was going to Arizona." She lifted her chin, using a loud enough voice for Chris to hear in the next room. "Which is ludicrous. I run the day-to-day here. So he goes telling Chris and not me? We have shipments coming in and out of here every day. Pickups and drop-offs change all the time. I run the reschedules."

Chris's office door cracked open. The man stood like he wanted to say something.

"Yes?" Patterson asked him.

"He told me," Chris said in a low voice. "Mr. Preston told me he was leaving for Arizona. I don't know why he didn't tell you, Betsy."

They volleyed their gazes back to Betsy.

She reddened from the attention, defiance in her lowered eyelids, and looked down at her desk.

Chris stepped out from his office door, through the room, and went outside. His feet crunched on the packed powder as he walked to a beat-up Ford Ranger and got in. The engine fired up and he drove away at speed through the gate and out of sight.

They exchanged glances while Betsy ran a fingernail over a spot on her desk.

The dump truck outside killed its engine, dropping the office into complete silence.

"What about Saturday?" Wolf asked. "Did you know that Chris and Warren were going to have a meeting here on Saturday night?"

Betsy's eyes narrowed. "No. They had a meeting? Saturday night?"

"That's what Chris told us," Patterson said.

"That's the first I've heard of that."

"He never told you anything about Saturday?" Rachette said.

"Who, Chris? No! He didn't tell me anything about

Saturday. And Warren didn't tell me he was going on vacation. He didn't tell me shit. And now he's gone." She opened her mouth and shut it.

"What aren't you telling us, Betsy?" Wolf asked.

Betsy glared hard at him. "He told me to bring him some brisket on Monday. I mean, it was a joke, but he knew I would if he mentioned it, so I did. I packed up a Tupperware and brought him a couple of pounds of meat that Monday. The way he lives up there in that big old house of his alone? He never cooks for himself, and he knew I would bring it. I made two extra pounds. He would have known I'd go out of my way and make extra. If he didn't want it, he would have kept his mouth shut." She shook her head. "Something doesn't make sense. Something happened to him." She looked out the windows.

They said nothing.

Her hardened expression melted, and she shook her head. "I don't know. Maybe he decided to go after he talked to me. Honestly, he had been talking about camping down there. He goes down to Arizona every year. Looks for gold in the Superstitions on some family claim of his. But ... I still think he would have told me. I run the day-to-day."

"How's business going, Betsy?" Wolf asked.

Betsy looked up, first startled and defensive-looking, but then her expression softened and she sighed. "I tell you, we're not doing as hot as other years."

"And is there pressure on Mr. Preston due to the strain on the business?" Wolf asked.

"Well, of course there is. He's responsible for feeding

a number of families with the income generated here." She sat back and nodded with narrowed eyes. "But he's a determined man. His father started this business forty-five years ago. Warren took it over fifteen years ago, and that was after he'd worked for his father for, geez, twenty years? So he's seen tough times before. He could have sold out to the developers years ago, but he's determined to continue the business."

Wolf nodded.

She cocked her head. "Wait. Why are you asking that?"

"I'm just ... trying to get a full picture of what we're looking at here."

"If you think he ran away, you can get that out of your brain."

Wolf nodded. He'd seen people lie, cheat, steal, and kill others or themselves over money before. "Was he in any major debt?"

She leaned on her elbows. "Detective Wolf, isn't it? Warren Preston doesn't run from debt collectors. He pays them. Mr. Preston did not run away."

"Okay." He smiled. "I understand."

Betsy's eyes lingered on him.

He leaned and looked into another open door. "Is that Mr. Preston's office?"

Betsy blinked out of a zone. "What's that?"

"Is that Mr. Preston's office?"

"Sorry. Yes, it is."

Rachette and Yates moved toward it. Wolf kept still, opting to lessen the appearance of a pack of sniffing dogs moving in on a bag of chow.

Wolf cleared his throat. "Do you mind if we take a look, Betsy?"

Rachette and Yates stopped in their tracks.

"No. Go ahead."

Rachette and Yates disappeared inside.

Wolf followed them in, leaving Patterson and Betsy to converse some more.

The floor creaked under their boots as they paced around a decent-sized office. It looked bigger than Chrissy's office next door, as the owner's office should have been, he supposed. He noted the sign on the door. *Warry*. A lot less clever than *Chrissy*, and with less backhand.

Rachette went behind the desk and bent close to the desktop.

Yates joined him. "Guy liked to doodle."

A big paper calendar sat on the desktop, covered in blue, black, and red ink. Cubes, mountains, palm trees, faces, and a hundred other streams of consciousness were etched onto the page between phone numbers, names, and other notes for Warren Preston's reference.

Wolf read some.

Flagstone—6 yards ...

Granite slab—Tony, Wednesday, 12th ...

Zack Hood. 20% off first five shipments ...

PG 1308, 1309, 1310 ...

He pointed. "Granite slab, Wednesday, 12th."

"Yeah." Rachette nodded. "That was last week. So what?"

Wolf stood straight, rubbing a kink in his neck, and walked to a bookshelf. Dark-blue binders stacked every inch of the shelving from floor to ceiling. Black writing was scrawled along the bindings of each.

A picture of Warren Preston hung on the wall. He was holding a fat rainbow trout in two hands, a smile plastered on his face. He was dressed in waders and a black Harley-Davidson shirt. According to their research, he was sixty-one years old, and given three chances Wolf would have guessed his age by looking at him. The man's hair was flecked white, gray, and black, like granite. His eyes were hidden behind fishing glasses. He was clean-shaven with skin like worn, tanned leather. Judging by the belly bulging against his waders, he was thirty or forty pounds overweight.

"Sir?" Patterson stood at the doorway.

"Yeah?"

"Betsy was going to take us outside and introduce us to one of the other employees."

Betsy stood behind Patterson, leaning to the side and watching Rachette like an old shopkeeper watches a teenager.

Wolf pointed at the pad of paper on the desktop. "Betsy, could you come in here?"

"Yes, sir."

"Who's Tony with the granite slab?"

She edged past Patterson into the office and came to Wolf's side. "What's that?"

"This here. It shows he set up an appointment for the twelfth."

Betsy planted both her palms on the paper and leaned close. "My eyesight's crap. Oh, yeah. Tony, granite slab. Delivered on the twelfth." She straightened. "What about it?"

"Did he tell you about it?" Wolf asked.

She shook her head and poked the paper. "No. See? It's stuff like this I'm talking about. He never told me about Tony coming. He does this all the time—just writes his little appointments on this paper. Or he'll shove a Post-it into his top drawer. Every few days I'll come in and make him tell me what he's got in the works."

She stormed around the backside of the desk, pushing Rachette aside. She pulled open the top drawer and looked inside, seemingly surprised by what she saw. "Oh, well, I cleared it out. Well, if you would have been here last Monday, you would have seen a desk drawer filled with a pile of notes. All sorts of delivery orders from the week before. You gotta understand. This business isn't repeat. Just about every customer's repeat but the orders are as varied as they come."

"Okay," Wolf said.

Betsy's eyes bulged. "So, if he would have been going out of town, he would have brought me in here and debriefed me. He knows that's how we work."

She turned and looked at Rachette.

Rachette backed up a step.

"I heard something about you guys finding his car. Chris said it was wide open and parked in front of his house, filled with snow. Now what's that all about?"

"That's why we're here, ma'am," Patterson said.

Betsy sagged like a deflating balloon.

"Ma'am." Wolf cleared his throat. "Are there any

people you can think of that would want to hurt Mr. Preston?"

She went pale. "No, not that I can think of."

"Is there anything else he spoke about two weeks ago? Anything at all that you're thinking might be out of the ordinary?"

She shook her head, then jerked it to the side as if a thought had hit her. "Well ..."

"What?"

"Our equipment was breaking down lately. I guess that's something. Well, maybe that's not something—stuff breaks down all the time. But his reaction this time was something else. He was paranoid. First, he thought the mechanic was slacking, so he fired him. Then it kept happening, so he thought somebody else was doing it. Somebody, like, breaking in overnight and sabotaging the machines or something." She shrugged.

"And then what?" Patterson asked.

She gestured outside. "I tell you what, Dennis is your guy if you want to talk about that."

"Who's Dennis?" Rachette asked.

"The guy I was just going to introduce you to outside."

━━

Dennis Lamont was a beefy middle-aged man. Despite the cold rushing in from the north, he wore a thin long-sleeved shirt rolled up to reveal tattooed logs for forearms.

Wolf knew him. The man had volunteered to help set up various festivals and town events. He looked different today, Wolf thought, and realized it was because he was used to seeing the man laugh. Today Dennis's brown beard seemed to hang lower from his sullen face.

"Hello." Dennis nodded.

"Dennis," Wolf said. "Listen, we heard something about equipment breaking down lately."

Dennis pinched his brows. "What does that have to do with anything?"

"You know Warren was all paranoid about it," Betsy said. "Tell him what he was telling you."

"I don't know." Dennis shook his head. "There were a few times in the last couple of months the loaders were acting up. One day, one of them had a flat tire, and what looked like a cut hydraulic line. Could have been wear—it was a close toss-up. Basic stuff that could have been caused by sitting over the weekend in cold, varying temperatures, like we have here in the Colorado Rockies."

Betsy scoffed. "But it was more than just that one time. There were more breakdowns."

"Yeah, fired our best mechanic over it. And the breakdowns kept happening, what do you know?"

"Who was this mechanic?" Wolf asked.

"Rick Welch. Bartends down at the Diamond now. But, like I said, it wasn't his fault. Just shitty old equipment if you ask me. Stuff breaks. Components need to be replaced."

"Oh, Dennis." Betsy turned to Wolf. "He was sure it was somebody coming in and deliberately causing the damage. He brought in that razor wire." She pointed to a shiny pile of coiled wire sitting in the distance. "He was fixin' to put that up on the fence. It's not shitty old equipment."

Dennis upturned his hands.

"Did Mr. Preston mention anyone by name?" Wolf asked. "You know, who he thought might have been causing the damage?"

"No."

"Did you hear anything about Mr. Preston going on vacation last week?" Wolf asked Dennis.

"Nope."

"And do you think it's strange that he went on vacation without you knowing about it beforehand?"

"Nope."

Wolf sucked in a breath and let it out. "Care to elaborate?"

"Guy doesn't tell me much." Dennis chuckled. "I show up, run the rigs, load the rock, move the rock, push it where he tells me, dump it where he says."

"Do you two not get along?" Patterson asked.

"What? No, we're okay. We're tight. You know, he's my boss though." Dennis scratched his arm. "I don't know, when I heard he'd left for Arizona, I guess I found it a little strange. But, then again, he's left for days on end without me knowing before."

Wolf stared at Dennis.

Dennis straightened and looked at Wolf. "What?"

"Did you know we're looking for Mr. Preston?" Wolf asked.

"Yeah, I heard."

The snow falling out of the sky thickened, sticking to the back of Wolf's neck.

Dennis stood unmoved, letting it pile onto his face and exposed arms. "So, what's the status?"

"How many employees work here?" Wolf asked.

"Five," Betsy said.

"Six." Dennis ticked his fingers. "It's me, Chris, Betsy, and we have two drivers. And then Mr. P. So, six."

"Oh, right. I didn't count myself." Betsy scoffed.

"Where are the two drivers?" Rachette asked. A winter cap had appeared on his head.

"One of them, Jack Murphy, is up making a delivery in Brushing. The other, Brad Wells, isn't working today."

"Wells drives here?" Rachette asked.

"Yep."

"I didn't know that."

The conversation fizzled to silence.

"Do you remember what you were doing two Saturday nights ago?" Wolf asked Dennis.

Dennis popped his eyebrows, looking like he'd understood the significance of the question. "I have two kids—six and two years old. Me and the wifey don't get out much anymore. So, sitting at home."

"And do you happen to remember anything about what Mr. Preston was doing that night?"

"How would I know? I don't hang with him on the weekends."

"Thanks, Dennis."

"Yep."

"Well," Wolf said, "if you guys think of anything else, please let us know. And if you two wouldn't mind keeping available, we'd appreciate it."

Dennis jogged to the loader parked in the distance.

He climbed up, shook himself free of snow, sat inside, and fired up the engine.

They walked briskly back to the office through a thickening curtain of snow and said their goodbyes to Betsy.

"And one last thing," Wolf said over the din of the diesel engine.

"Yes?" Betsy stopped inside the doorway, brushing snow from her nest of curly hair.

"If something were to happen to Warren Preston, what happens to the business?"

"Geez, I don't even know. I guess Chris would take over. He owns a portion of the business as it is. And as far as I know, Mr. Preston's been grooming Chris to take over once he retires, which was set to be in the next few years."

"And what about you?" Wolf asked.

"What about me?"

"None of it would go to you, huh?"

"What am I going to do with a rock business?"

"Thanks, Betsy."

The door shut, and they convened next to Patterson's SUV.

"What now?" Patterson brushed snow from her eyebrows. "Dang, it's coming down."

The flakes were thick and wet, hissing as they accumulated on the hood next to them.

"We need to check the Pony," Rachette said. "See if Alamy's telling the truth about that or not."

"We'll know for sure once we get the phone GPS readout for his phone from Summit," Patterson said.

Wolf's phone vibrated in his pocket. He pulled it out and read MacLean's name through the flakes.

He would have screened it, but the other three detectives had seen it.

"Hello?"

"Where are you?"

"Preston Rock and Supply."

"Come back."

"Okay. We were headed to the Pony Tavern to check out Chris Alamy's story."

MacLean said nothing.

"You there?"

"Yeah. All right. Go to the Pony and then back in my office first thing."

The phone went dead.

"What did he want?" Rachette asked.

Wolf shrugged. "He wants us to brief him when we're done at the Pony. Let's roll."

"You think MacLean would mind if we got a pitcher or two before the briefing?" Rachette asked, bouncing his eyebrows at Yates and Wolf. "I'm getting thirsty."

Patterson shook her head and walked to her door. "Let's go."

Wolf followed her, thinking of how a beer would have done the trick. Damn, he needed this day to end.

CHAPTER 7

"I'm staying here," Wolf said.

Patterson slid off the driver's seat and looked at Wolf. He was even paler now. She'd scarcely seen him looking worse, and she'd seen him pretty bad. It could have been the sun poking through the clouds, but she thought his skin had taken on a yellow hue.

"What?" he asked.

"Nothing. Sure. Stay here. We have this."

Wolf closed his eyes and leaned his seat back.

She shut the door, wondering who she'd left in the vehicle. How far had the Wolf she knew been pushed behind the hangover?

She met Yates and Rachette at the rear bumper and walked past them through the Pony Tavern parking lot.

"Aren't you waiting for Wolf?"

"He's staying in the car."

They walked in silence, her boots squeaking underneath the thin blanket of snow the only sound. It was 2 p.m. and the parking lot had six cars in it.

The Pony Tavern was a day-drinkers' bar, more so than Beer Goggles, or Black Diamond, or any of the other establishments in town. At least, that's the impression she'd always had. She hadn't spent much time in any of the drinking holes in Rocky Points, but she made it a point to stay far from the Pony.

Rachette pushed through the door first, followed by Yates.

She took up the rear and immediately wished she'd stayed with Wolf. The sour stench of beer soaking the floors mixed with bar food hit her hard. Her mouth watered, and she had to blank her mind to calm her gag reflex.

Rachette walked in like he owned the place, threaded between two cowhide barstools, and slapped the counter. "Hey, Crystal."

A bleached-blonde bartender turned around and smiled. "Hey, there they are! Hi, Deputies. What can I get you? Shots? Beers?"

Rachette smiled. "Funny. We're here to ask you a few questions."

Crystal stacked some receipts near the register and walked toward them. She placed both hands on the counter. Yates and Rachette leaned forward, like they were basking in the heat billowing out of her low-cut tank top.

"Doin' all right there, Heather?" Crystal asked.

Patterson pasted on a smile and nodded.

"Still doing ka-ra-te or kung fui, or whatever that's called?" Crystal karate-chopped the air, sandwiching her fake breasts together.

"She's pregnant," Rachette said. "She's gotta take a few months off."

"Oh my gosh, is that true?"

Patterson felt the blood drain from her face.

Yates looked back at her and lowered his eyes to her belly. "Is that true?"

"Ha. Thanks. Tom. I wasn't telling anyone yet. But, yes, I am pregnant with my second child."

"Well, congratulations."

"Hey, congrats!" A guy sitting at the bar raised his beer.

She failed to recognize him but nodded anyway. "Thanks, Crystal." She may as well have posted the ultrasound on the internet. The news would travel like a tropical mosquito-borne disease, infecting the town by the week's end. Or maybe she was a little too full of herself.

Crystal cocked her head. "What's up?"

"You know a guy named Chris Alamy?" Rachette asked.

"Yeah, I know him. Why?"

Rachette struck a pose on his elbow. "What's his story?"

Patterson rolled her eyes.

Pool balls clacked together. One man rounded the table, stalking another shot while his opponent sat hunched, staring with bloodhound eyes at Patterson.

"He's just a regular, I guess," Crystal said. "Comes in most weekends."

"How about last Saturday night?"

Crystal stared at the ceiling.

"It would have been the night of the snow storm," Rachette said.

"Ah, yes. The snowstorm." She shrugged. "Probably."

"Can you check the receipts?" Patterson asked. The flexing of her abdomen as she spoke set her mouth watering anew.

"Oh, I guess I could. I'd have to go into the back office and check."

"Chris Alamy?" one of the pool players asked.

She turned around. "Yeah, you know him?"

"Yeah. The rock dude."

She nodded. "That's him."

"He's in here every weekend."

She nodded again. "Thanks."

The guy bent over to line up a shot.

She moved out of the way but caught the scent of the man and wished she hadn't.

Rachette clicked his tongue. "If you could check those receipts, Crystal, that would help us a lot."

"Why? What's going on? Tell me the inside dirt." She leaned further forward, giving them all a spelunker's view into her cleavage.

Patterson tried to swallow, but her throat worked backward, and she made a pre-hurl noise.

The room stopped dead and all faces turned to her.

She ran outside, rounded the side of the building, and vomited.

Her mind went blank as she emptied the contents of her stomach. After the past couple of months, this was old hat to her. She knew this was just a temporary discomfort and then she'd feel a hundred times better.

She wiped her mouth and straightened, surprised at the cramp in her lower back from flexing interior muscles.

Gotta love pregnancy.

"You okay?"

She turned around. Wolf was standing behind her.

"Yeah."

His eyes were glued to the discoloration in the snow.

"I'm fine." She put a hand on his shoulder and tried to turn him away from the scene.

He pushed her aside and bent over.

"Jesus." She walked away, leaving the sounds of Wolf emptying his own stomach as she rounded the building.

"Hey, there you are." Yates walked toward her. "You all right?"

"Yeah."

Wolf coughed, and the sound echoed around the corner.

"Is that Wolf?"

Wolf appeared, wiping his mouth and sniffing. "What did you guys find out?"

"We ... Rachette's in there getting Alamy's receipt right now. Patterson ran out here, looking like she was going to be sick. Are you okay?"

"I'm all right. Thanks."

Rachette strode out and skidded to a halt. "What's happening? You puke?"

"What did you find out?" Wolf asked.

"Alamy paid a tab at one thirty-seven in the morning that Saturday night, or Sunday morning.

"Does she remember when he got here?" Wolf spat into the snow.

"No, she doesn't. But it's a pretty hefty tab—eight beers. That's a few hours' worth of drinking for me." Rachette shrugged. "Okay, two hours of drinking for me." He narrowed his eyes and studied Wolf. "You okay?"

Patterson walked toward the parking lot. "Let's go."

CHAPTER 8

WOLF KNOCKED on MacLean's door and twisted the knob.

"Come in." MacLean sat with bridged fingers behind his desk. The afternoon sun streamed through the windows, silhouetting the sheriff in his big leather chair.

Patterson, Rachette, and Yates followed Wolf inside.

They lined up at the desk, Wolf squinting against the glare. After the Pony parking lot, he found himself yearning for a little hair of the dog. More alcohol was his only hope of breaking up the chunks of concrete rattling in his skull.

MacLean looked at him expectantly, then looked out the windows. "You know what? Save it until he's in here."

DA Sawyer White's Italian loafers clicked on the terrazzo outside. A few paces behind him, Deputy DA Hanson walked fast, a cell phone pressed to his ear.

Quick knocks rapped against the door and the two DAs strode in on a cloud of cologne.

Wolf nodded, ready to offer a hand, but White

ignored his team's presence and took a seat while everyone else stood.

Hanson walked in pocketing his phone and gave a round of nods. Patrick Hanson dressed the part of a city deputy district attorney, but Wolf knew the man to be an avid outdoorsman. Wolf and he had fished before and Wolf had enjoyed his company. The invitation to the river had come from Hanson, clearly a gesture of good will to get to know the chief detective better on a non-professional basis. It had worked.

"Looking good, Detectives," Hanson said.

"Hi, Patrick," Patterson said.

"Hanson," Rachette said.

White crossed his legs and stared at his phone. He made a face, shoved the phone into his breast pocket, and bridged his fingers. "What do we have?"

"Looks like Preston's employee-slash-partner, Chris Alamy, could be up to something," Wolf said. "Or not. We can't tell for sure. We're waiting on his cell records. They'll tell us more."

Patterson raised her chin. "I have another call into Summit. I don't know what their problem is."

White kept his eyes on Wolf. "What did the co-workers at the rock yard say?"

"Everyone but Chris Alamy was unaware of Warren Preston going on vacation. Chris says that's why he was with Preston Saturday night—to discuss the next week of work while he was gone. But Betsy Collworth, the woman who runs operations there, says there's no way he would have gone out of town without telling her."

"So she's saying Alamy's lying," MacLean said.

"She never said that. But she implied it, yes."

"Where in Arizona was he supposed to be going?" MacLean asked.

"Superstition Mountains," Wolf said.

"We talked to anyone down there yet?"

"Preston doesn't have any other vehicles," Wolf said. "How's he going to get down there? And then there's his car, clearly wiped, with an unidentified partial on the exterior handle."

MacLean sat back.

"What else happened at the rock yard?" White asked.

Wolf recapped their visit, touching on Dennis Lamont, the outside employee they'd spoken to, and the story of Rick Welch and his firing.

"Sounds like we have a few more candidates to check against that partial," White said.

"Agreed," Wolf said.

"What else?" White flicked a glance toward Rachette and Yates.

Rachette hitched up his belt and folded his arms across his chest. "We talked to the bartender at the Pony. She confirmed that he left when he said he did, but we don't know when he arrived."

"Was he with anyone else?"

"It's not clear if he showed up with somebody else. But he got an Uber ride by himself at closing time."

"And still nothing up at Preston's house?" White asked, turning to MacLean.

MacLean shook his head. "K9s are still coming up empty."

White folded his arms and exhaled. "It looks to me like we have a missing person. Other than that, we don't have shit." White leaned forward and got up.

"The car was wiped," Wolf said.

"And we haven't matched the partial." White eyed his watch. "I gotta go. I don't see any potential charges. I'll tell the press as much." He glanced at Wolf. "Mac-Lean, I hope you'll take care of your side of things right now. Hanson, let's go."

The DA and his deputy left.

"You three can go," MacLean said.

Wolf saw that MacLean was speaking to everyone but him.

Patterson, Rachette, and Yates walked out of the office.

"Take a seat." MacLean stood and closed the door with a soft click.

Wolf sat and waited while the sheriff moved behind him and twisted the blinds shut.

MacLean returned to his desk, petting his silver mustache, and sat down.

If they'd been playing poker, Wolf would have doubled his bet. "What's up?"

"We went for over a year running this department with a squad of three people," MacLean said.

"Yep."

"And now we have four," MacLean said.

"I'm not looking to cut anyone from my squad, if that's what you're saying." He remembered the glance from White and the order for MacLean to take care of his side of things, whatever that meant.

"Why do you think we hired internally for that fourth detective?" MacLean asked.

Wolf blinked.

MacLean let the silence take hold. It magnified his next words. "I'm all for standing by my people while they go through tough times, but there's only so much I can do. There are a lot of people out there wondering if you aren't becoming a major detriment to this department. They say it's only a matter of time before you crash your car on the job. Hurt someone."

Wolf said nothing.

"You went through a tough time last year, I get it. Those two girls left you high and dry."

Wolf stared ahead at the desk. "White. That's what you were talking about in my office before. He's pulling me under so he can stay afloat."

MacLean smiled with cold eyes. "You've spent more time unconscious than conscious on the job over the last few months. Are you seriously going to put the blame on White?"

Wolf put his elbows on his knees.

"And it's not just him," MacLean said.

Wolf remembered councilman Pritchard averting eye contact earlier that morning, Wolf's hasty exit.

"We were doing just fine with three detectives." MacLean's voice softened. "That's why we hired another detective, to make sure we could transition as smoothly as possible."

"I'm fired."

MacLean slapped the desk. "No! You're not!" The

sheriff's face quivered and turned red. "I'm not firing you, dumbass. You're the best detective I've ever met."

Wolf sat back heavily and crossed a leg. The knee of his jeans were scuffed with black soot. The stain looked old.

"Are you listening to me?"

Wolf lifted his eyes. MacLean stood with his hands on the desk.

"What."

MacLean turned to the back window. "Jesus. I just said you're suspended for a week and you don't even hear me." He turned back and stepped away from the sun, revealing a hard glint in his gray eyes. "Are you listening to me now?"

Wolf folded his arms and raised his eyebrows.

"I said you're suspended for seven days. If you don't clean up by next week, just save us both some pain and don't bother coming back in."

MacLean walked to the door, twisted it open, then sat back behind his desk.

"We're at the beginning of an investigation," Wolf said. "A man's life could be hanging in the balance."

"We'll take care of that."

Heat rose in Wolf's cheeks.

I told you, the voice said.

He needed to get the hell out. He stood and walked out the door.

"Badge. Gun."

Wolf stopped, turned around, and put his paddle holster and badge on the desk. Then he left, ignoring the squad-room glances as he strode out.

CHAPTER 9

WOLF PULLED THROUGH THE HEADGATE, bouncing on his seat as his house came into view.

The snowstorm skirted south just as fast as it had moved in. The sun hid behind the western peaks, but the eastern mountains ahead were half-ablaze in sunlight reflecting off the fresh blanket of snow. Through the searing brightness, Wolf saw twin tracks in the powder leading to a black Toyota Tacoma parked out front.

Jack.

He looked over at the box of Scotch poking out of a brown bag in the passenger seat and thought about the couch and a bottomless glass. This would put a wrench in his plan.

His breathing accelerated as he neared. Damn it. Why was he here? What did he want? He was probably up from Boulder to ski, but it was Wednesday afternoon. Spring break? That had to be it.

Wolf slalomed around Jack's truck and parked in the car port next to the kitchen.

The frigid air burrowed under his collar as he stepped out. Bag in hand, he stood for a moment, looking at the freshly shoveled wall of snow, and realized the carport was free of the drift that had been building for months. Instead of his SUV-sized groove, now there were vertical walls set wide apart, like Inuit architecture.

"Thanks, Jack," he said under his breath, more annoyed than grateful.

He hurried around the back bumper and up the steps to the kitchen door. Inside, he stopped dead. His boot soles squeaked on the tile as he looked down at a wriggling animal nipping at his feet.

"What the—"

A puppy, a tiny German shepherd with squint-eyes and no larger than his foot, licked his boots.

"Drifter!"

Wolf started at a woman's voice and looked up. "Oh. Hi, Cassidy. Hey, who's this?"

"That's Drifter," she said.

He bent and ran a hand over the dog.

He stood up and froze. Cassidy wore jeans and a sweater underneath an unzipped fleece. Her blonde hair was in a ponytail pulled back from a smooth, tanned face. She smiled and Wolf thought if he squinted she'd have been Sarah reincarnated.

"Hey, Dad." Jack appeared in the kitchen entrance to the living room, pulling on a jacket. "What's happening?" The question was literal, not small talk.

Wolf followed Jack's eyes down to the bag in his hand. The silvery box poking out of the paper reflected the light from the windows. He couldn't remember the last time he'd opened all the blinds.

"More booze, huh?" Jack zipped the jacket to his chin.

Cassidy lowered her gaze. "Oh, no! Drifter! Sorry, Mr. Wolf. He keeps peeing everywhere."

"No worries." He stepped over a tiny puddle and set the bag down on the counter.

The surface smelled of cleaner and shone like new. At least a dozen empty or near-empty bottles were clustered. All Dewar's, the contents long passed through Wolf's system.

Correction: two of them were still half-full. He wondered how that had happened.

The tiny puppy sniffed and panted, its tongue slopping as Cassidy tried to wrangle him into her arms.

"What are you guys doing here?" He turned and straightened.

Jack squared off with him a foot away.

The last time he'd seen his son wear that expression, Jack had just finished blaming him for Sarah's death.

"We talked last week. It's our spring break, and I told you we were coming up to pick up a puppy from the Watts farm. I told you we'd stop by, and you said you'd make us dinner. Said we'd have some steaks and some baked potatoes. We said we'd bring the salad." Jack gestured toward a Tupperware container on the counter.

Wolf nodded, his face slacking. "Oh yeah, right."

"You obviously don't remember shit about our conversation, otherwise you'd have cleaned this shithole up before we came." He swiped a hand behind him.

Wolf looked into the living room.

"Hey!" Jack snapped his fingers.

Wolf stared at his son, his insides turning to ice. "Don't do that."

Jack stepped forward until his face was inches away.

Cassidy shuffled to the door, opened it, and went outside.

"What the fuck are you doing?"

"About what?"

"About your life?"

Wolf put a hand on his son's chest and pushed.

Jack slapped his arm away and stepped close again. "You gonna sit here and drink yourself to death? Because of a bitch who left you?"

"She's not a bitch."

"Hey, whatever you gotta say to pull yourself out of the gutter. She's a bitch. Fuck her and that daughter of—"

Wolf slapped him across the face. The sound seemed to last a full five seconds.

Jack stepped back and stared at him with lowered eyelids.

"Don't ..." Wolf raised a finger.

The space between them seemed to crackle.

"Don't worry." Jack turned away and walked to the door. With one hand on the knob, he turned back. "Your happiness matters, too, you know."

The door slammed shut.

Wolf watched through the window as Jack and Cassidy climbed into the truck. The engine revved and the tires spat snow as the pickup disappeared down the drive and through the headgate.

He stood rooted on the kitchen tile. The sting on his palm turned to a burn. His whole body shook.

He eyed the living room and his gaze was pulled down to carpet striped with vacuum marks. The coffee table was bare, devoid of dirty glasses and used paper plates. The dryer hummed in the laundry room.

He stepped onto the carpet. The space looked like it had been visited by a fairy godmother and her bag of magic dust.

He walked to his bedroom. The bed had been made with new sheets. More vacuum marks striped the floor and a calm flame licked off a scented candle perched on the nightstand.

The bathroom was spotless, including the toilet. Another candle flickered, the rising tendrils of smoke exuding a more feminine scent. He remembered the shopping trip into town when Lauren had picked the candle. He stepped up and pinched the flame with his thumb and middle finger.

The pain burned to the bone, but he ignored it.

A tear rolled down his cheek, licked his neck and fell onto the collar of his jacket. He stared at the smoke through blurry eyes, and when he blinked more tears cascaded down his cheeks.

"Damn it." He roughly wiped his face with his jacket sleeve, then turned and stormed to the living room, through the kitchen, and outside. As he marched to the barn, his feet squealed on the snow. His face lay slack. The cold burned his eyes but he didn't blink as he walked to the barn and opened the workshop door.

The fluorescent lights flickered and sizzled overhead

in the freezing-cold space. He crossed the dirt floor and flicked on the second bank of lights.

He searched and found the wheelbarrow leaning against the wall behind the John Deere. He grabbed the cold wooden handles, worn smooth by his father.

The front wheel was completely flat, but the rubber rolled well enough, staying on the rim as he pushed it through the workshop and out the door.

For an instant his resolve dimmed. As he stopped and zipped up his jacket, his breath clouded in the fading light, evaporating on an icy breeze.

He remembered the sound of his hand bouncing off Jack's face. His son's frozen gaze.

And the last time he'd seen Ella. She'd been so excited to toss flower petals in front of him and her mother. He imagined equal doses of her disappointment.

His mouth watered, and he envisioned a cool, ice-filled glass touching his lips.

Slowly, he bent over and clasped the wheelbarrow handles again. He grabbed too high with one hand and a splinter dug into his thumb. He ignored it, turned back and heaved the rusty metal and decaying wood up the stairs into the kitchen.

Inside, he placed the bottles into the wheelbarrow's bed, and topped the heap with the heavy bag he'd just purchased. The glass clanked as he grabbed the handles and wheeled the barrow into the living room to the front door.

He pulled the Browning twelve gauge out of the hall closet. The cover's zipper sang as he pulled it open, revealing an oiled over–under model his father left him when he died.

He took a box of shells and placed it in the barrow. Followed with the gun. Then he opened the front door and pushed it outside.

The snow chilled his feet through his boots as he pushed the heavy payload through the powder to the side of his house. A deer stared at him, then shot twin jets of steam out of its nostrils and ran into the woods.

With cold hands, he broke open the shotgun and draped it over his shoulder, picked up the box of shells, and upturned the wheelbarrow.

The bottles clanked as they splayed out into the snow.

He second-guessed his location—no more than a dozen paces from his bedroom window. Then he cursed under his breath and dragged away the wheelbarrow.

He pushed two shells into the barrel, closed it, and walked back to the pile of bottles.

His mouth watered again, and he stared at the undamaged box spilling out of the paper bag atop the pile. He stutter-stepped forward, shifting the gun to his left hand to grab the box.

One final swill would be a fitting goodbye. That felt right. He'd never been an alcoholic, never had trouble holding his liquor or controlling his desire for drink. Never had the shakes like he did every morning now or felt a wave of pleasure as liquid passed down his throat. This was all new to him.

He pinched one end of the bag and let the box slip out.

What the fuck are you doing? Jack's voice replayed in his mind.

Wolf dropped the bag and stood upright.

"Good question."

He pointed the barrel down and fired.

CHAPTER 10

JUNE 18th. 8:47 a.m

Three months later ...

Wolf bared his teeth and leaned on both knees. His lungs pumped hard, his heart double-timing to keep the oxygen flowing through his body at the high altitude.

Without looking, he stopped the timer on the new digital watch he'd purchased for this occasion. He didn't have to look to know he'd beaten his best time by at least a few seconds, but he checked anyway—00:36:41.

His eyebrows popped with surprise. He'd never broken the thirty-seven-minute mark, and he'd just shattered the record without feeling especially exerted the entire hike.

A shadow was peeling back across the Chautauqua Valley below, revealing a green carpet and shining river hemmed in by forest.

As the sound of his breathing subsided, the roar of rushing water filled the air. He spotted a deluge racing down a crag in the mountain off to his left. It had rained hard last night on his roof and judging by the saturated ground under his feet and lack of fresh snow, it had rained hard up here, too.

He turned around, looked up, and saw new streams of water webbing the mountainside.

His eyes were drawn back to the valley floor and the shining Chautauqua. It had been a large run-off year already, and today river conditions would be especially dangerous.

But it was his day off.

He unzipped his fleece and welcomed the cool air licking the sweat off his body.

He sucked from his CamelBak water pack, then took it off and placed it on the granite slab rock in front of him. He opened the top zipper and pulled out two bananas.

Breathing calmly through his nose, he stood and ate the two pieces of fruit and raised his eyes to the jagged horizon. June in the Rockies. The bottom of the valleys were carpeted in never-ending green, while the mountain tops were still covered with white frosting left behind by a late May storm. He loved the juxtaposition.

He finished the two bananas, and with more than a little ceremony, added the skins to a pile under the overhanging lip of granite. There had to be at least fifty now, in varying shades of black and degrees of decay.

His phone chimed in his pack and he pulled it out.

Two text messages and three missed calls. The first message was from Patterson, the second from Rachette.

Call me ASAP!

Call the station as soon as you get this!

He pressed the first message and tapped the call button.

"Hey, there you are," Patterson said.

Wolf checked the time on his wrist. It was still before 9 a.m. "I'm here. What's going on? Flooding?"

"What?"

"It rained hard on the snow above my house. Is the river flooding?"

"No, it's not. I know it's your day off but you have to get in here immediately."

"And why's that?"

She told him.

He grabbed the pack and took off down the hill at full speed.

"You coming in?"

"Yeah, yeah," Wolf said into his phone. "I'm on Main, almost there."

"Okay. We'll be in MacLean's office." Patterson sounded like she was in the squad room. Somebody hooted with laughter in the background.

He hung up and slapped the wheel. He should have taken First and cut one street over. Now he crept along in a train of cars passing through the heart of downtown.

The Rocky Points Mountain Bike Festival banner spanning the road bounced on the breeze, reminding him why traffic on this June Friday morning was more like a Sunday ski season rush hour.

A woman stood at the edge of the road, holding a coffee cup and the hand of a little girl.

A small jolt rippled through his body. The sight of any woman with a young daughter did that now. The passing cars were preventing them from stepping alongside the driver's side of their vehicle, so he slowed to a stop and waved them out.

She peaked her eyebrows and mouthed *Thank you*.

A car sucked up against his bumper and honked. The train behind came to a halt.

The girl, unprepared and yanked by her mother, twirled and landed on her backside. Her eyes clamped shut and she screamed.

Whoops.

The car behind him honked again, this time a full whole note. Obviously, the guy had failed to recognize the significance of the folded spotlight mounted to Wolf's side-view mirror, or the government plates, or the dark paint job and tinted rear windows.

He flicked the dash switch on and off, which set his spoiler alight with red and blue strobes.

The man behind him put up his hands and sat back in his seat.

Girl now kicking and screaming under her arm, the woman stepped off the sidewalk and went to the rear driver's-side door. Red-faced, she moved fast while she set her coffee on the roof, shoved the kid in, strapped her into the car seat, shut the door, and jumped behind the wheel. It was like a new rodeo event and she'd broken the record time.

Wolf honked, but it was too late.

The woman waved out her window and took off. The car lurched forward, sending her coffee tumbling off the roof and onto the pavement.

She pulled over and jammed to a stop. A moment later, her hand came out again, this time waving him on.

He rolled down his window and eased up next to her. "Geez, I'm sorry. I tried to—"

"Just"—she was barely audible over the screaming in the back seat—"go."

"Right."

He let off the brake and accelerated up the two blocks of now open road, took a right turn, and parked at the rear of the Sluice–Byron County building.

He jogged through the lot and into the double automatic doors. Two uniforms were getting into the elevators, but he passed them and took the stairwell instead. His legs were tight from the morning's exercise, but as he summited the third flight of steps his lungs barely strained.

Down the hallway, MacLean's office window blinds were open, revealing a swarm of people inside.

Wolf's leather boots thumped down the terrazzo hall, out under the vaulted ceilings of the squad room, and into MacLean's aquarium office.

"There you are!" MacLean waved him inside. "Dr. Sheffield, this is Chief Detective David Wolf."

A man Wolf recognized well held out a hand. "Hello, I'm Dr. Steve Sheffield."

"Detective Wolf."

Dr. Sheffield wore a pair of nylon hiking pants, hiking boots, and a red North Face fleece. Frameless glasses perched on a triangle nose, magnifying intelligent brown eyes. He seemed wired, and from what Wolf had heard so far, he could understand why.

"You know him, right?" Rachette thumbed toward the doctor. "Has all those radio and TV ads right now. Has the clinic in town."

Sheffield flashed a self-deprecating smile. "That's right."

Patterson nodded to Wolf and stepped aside.

Yates stood behind the doctor, looking over his shoulder, and Undersheriff Wilson took up post near the sheriff on the other side of the desk.

Wolf turned back to the object of focus lying on MacLean's desk: a cell phone.

"Take a look," MacLean said.

Wolf stepped forward and looked down at the illuminated phone screen. The naked upper torso of a human corpse had emerged from shiny, glass-looking snow. The skin was jet black, sucked against the bone. The mouth was wide open in morbid hilarity, its lips shriveled, revealing white teeth. Patchy gray hair streamed from a misshapen skull.

"Where is this?" Wolf asked.

"Huerfano Pass."

"Huerfano Pass? That's ..." Wolf had been going to say *so far from Preston's house*, but he left the sentence unspoken. They'd have plenty of time to discuss the nuances of the case when the civilian was gone. "Why don't you tell me what happened."

"I was up hiking on the pass, just off the north side, by the gate, where they close the road for the winter."

Wolf nodded him on.

"Anyway, I saw a flock of crows ... a murder, I guess the correct term is." The irony was obliviously lost on Sheffield. "And I was curious. I wanted to see what kind of animal the birds were eating." The doctor exhaled hard. "And I was surprised to see this."

Wolf took off his SBCSD cap and scratched his freshly buzzed scalp.

"I'm an orthopedic surgeon. The last time I saw a corpse was back in med school." Sheffield looked mesmerized by his phone. "Anyway, it freaked me out. I considered covering the body because of the birds, but I had nothing to cover it with. I was going to put snow over it but thought that might be frowned upon by ... well, by you guys. That, and the snow is really dense and icy right now."

"It rained last night," Wolf said.

"It looks like the storm uncovered the body," Patterson said.

Wolf looked at MacLean. "Lorber?"

MacLean nodded. "Lorber and his team are on their way up there now."

"Again, I'm just in orthopedics, so I can't tell. How old do you think this body is?"

The room met his question with silence.

"Dr. Sheffield, how are you?" White appeared from nowhere and strode into the office. "I just got word you were here," he said, shooting MacLean a glare.

"How are you, Sawyer?" Sheffield and the district attorney gave each other double handshakes and fake-looking smiles.

"What in the name of heck is going on here?" White asked, looking down at the cell phone.

Sheffield gestured. "I was up on Huerfano Pass and found ... something interesting."

White stepped next to Wolf and looked at the phone. He straightened abruptly.

"I was going to thank Dr. Sheffield for his discovery and quick action," MacLean said.

"Of course," Sheffield said. "Anyone would have done the same. You can't exactly ignore something like this."

"Detective Rachette, could you please escort Dr. Sheffield to the squad room and take his statement? After that, you're free to go about your business, sir. Thank you again."

"And what about my phone?"

MacLean nodded. "Yes, good point. We'll get that to you while you're filling out your statement."

The doctor looked apprehensive. "I could send the pictures to you."

MacLean deliberated, then nodded.

Patterson cleared her throat. "Why don't you send them to my phone?"

MacLean and Wolf exchanged a glance while Patterson gave her number. Wolf knew that depending on the personal settings of one's cell, pictures could be stored in many places. Who knew how many servers the images had already been uploaded to?

"Have you told anyone else about your discovery, sir?" Wolf asked.

"No. Not at all. I came straight here."

"No texts to anyone else? No phone calls?"

He shook his head. "No."

"Got them, thanks." Patterson held up her phone.

"Uh, Doctor." MacLean held out his hand. "If you don't mind."

"Yes?"

"We're going to need to erase those pictures from your phone."

Sheffield looked unfazed. "Of course. You don't want me selling these off to the news channels, eh? Darn it. I was hoping to get a bonus payday." He smiled.

The room looked at him.

"Sorry. Bad joke."

MacLean gestured to Patterson again, and she took the device from Sheffield.

White raised a finger. "Uh, when Detective Patterson is done, why don't you let me escort Dr. Sheffield, Sheriff? Detective Rachette, if you wouldn't mind going out and brewing a fresh pot of coffee, we'd much appreciate it."

Rachette nodded curtly and left the office.

They watched Patterson. Judging by the number of flicks and taps, she'd had the same thoughts as Wolf and was checking the nooks and crannies of the phone thoroughly.

"There. Thank you, sir," she said, handing back the phone.

The doctor nodded, and Wolf thought the man looked slightly violated.

"Come with me, Doctor."

Wolf watched White and Sheffield leave out the door.

"So, how's your county-council campaign going?" White's question echoed around the corner.

Sheffield's signs were as numerous around town as Margaret's, and the recent ads Rachette had mentioned were associated with the doctor's bid for council and not his orthopedic clinic.

According to Margaret, the DA was looking bad in the polls against Blair Hanquist. White's nose planted firmly in the doctor's ass suggested Sheffield's political prospects were looking good. Wolf had seen less angles played by billiards champions.

"Well?" MacLean asked. "What are you thinking?"

Wolf blinked out of a stare, realizing the sheriff was talking to him. "I think we have to get up to Huerfano Pass."

CHAPTER 11

WOLF TWISTED and looked back down the road snaking up the east side of the valley. The late-morning sun was high overhead, and spotty shadows slid across the green landscape below. He zeroed in on a cut into the mountains over Rocky Points and on the other side of the valley.

Rachette stepped up next to him and followed his gaze. "That's Wildflower Canyon, right?"

Wolf nodded.

"We're pretty far from Preston's house."

"Yeah." Preston's house was up the canyon. They were miles up the other side of the valley. The distance between the two points was exactly that: pretty far.

Wolf's boots crunched on wet, rocky earth as he turned and looked up the slope again. Just like behind his house, this mountain was shedding a lot of water to the valley below.

Lorber was crouched on a snow bank with his CSI team. The ME stood to his full height and waved to Wolf.

"It's him?"

Lorber nodded. "You wanna see?"

Wolf did. He stepped up onto the snow and followed a line of footsteps. The snow was pitted and crusted with jagged daggers of ice, eroded artistically by the overnight rain.

Daphne Pinnifield turned her mirrored glacier glasses toward Wolf and smiled. "Hi, Detective Wolf. How you doing today? I mean, besides the dead body."

"Not bad, thanks."

Wolf eyed the exposed hole beyond her. The snow surrounding the opening was stained reddish black. He caught his first in-person glimpse of the body. The birds had been feasting, and it was in worse shape than in the cell-phone pictures from earlier.

Crows circled overhead and sat in the stunted trees a short distance away.

Hungry beaks had torn and shredded the upper part of the body. The lower limbs—black, shriveled, and whole—had been dug out by the two other members of Lorber's team.

"Warren Preston." Lorber waved a hand. "The myth. The legend."

"The body," Daphne said.

"The body," Lorber repeated.

"How do you know?" Wolf asked.

"Dental." The ME held a cell phone in one hand and pointed with the other. "See?"

The corpse's teeth and shiny dental-work were on display, lit by the overhead sun.

"It's a perfect match." Lorber held his phone out for Wolf.

He waved it away. "I'll take your word for it."

Lorber pointed. "See his skull?"

Wolf took a closer look at Preston's head. At first, he assumed he was looking at part of the decomposition process or damage from the birds, but then he saw that the man's skull was caved in.

"I see it."

"That's a major blow to the head," Lorber said. "Looks like last night's rain washed enough snow off for him to emerge. Lucky for the crows. And lucky for us, he didn't wash off the mountain. His lower body anchored him down."

"I'd say he was dumped," Daphne said. "The angle of his body? The way he looks like he's in the middle of a sit-up, with his arm over his head? It looks like he was killed elsewhere to me. Rigor set in, and then he was dumped here."

Lorber shook his head behind her.

She snapped her head around. "What? Did you just shake your head?"

"You tend to jump to conclusions early, my pupil."

Wolf had seen some doozy-arguments between the student and teacher, and another one ensued as Daphne raised her voice and pointed out some more nuances of the body position. The two forensic technicians thought opinions needed to be vocalized at all costs, and usually theirs differed greatly. And Wolf suspected they were sexually attracted to one another and had probably acted on their attraction, but that was none of his business. He left them to argue and walked away from the hole.

He stretched his neck and surveyed the crested horizon to the west. His eyes latched onto the top of Aspen Mountain. Out of sight, below the undulating sea, sat the town of Aspen. And Lauren and Ella.

"Hey, Wolf."

He blinked, pulling his thoughts back thirty miles in an instant. "What?"

Lorber was bending over, pointing at the wispy gray hair surrounding the hole in Preston's skull. "See this?"

Wolf walked back and bent down.

Daphne ducked in next to them and Wolf caught the scent of patchouli oil from her white suit.

"Look at that. See that little piece of red rock embedded in the skull?"

Wolf nodded.

A noise floated to them on the breeze.

"What is that?" Lorber stood up and looked at the sky. "Oh, no."

The crows flapped their wings and took flight to the south.

A helicopter's rotors flitted in and out of earshot, then Wolf spotted something coming straight for them from the north.

"News copter," Lorber said. "They must have heard something on the scanner. Who mentioned Warren Preston on the radio? I'll murder them!"

Wolf thought of Sheffield.

"You did," Daphne said.

Lorber's mouth dropped open. "No, I didn't."

"You said his name on the way up. Right into the radio. 'Get the DNA bag, Johnson. I want to know if this is Preston by lunch.' That's exactly what you said. I remember thinking, I hope nobody's combing our scanners right now and figures out what we're doing."

Another technician nodded.

"Bullshit."

Wolf slid down the snow and stomped his feet on the dry ground. He eyed Yates. "Get on the horn to MacLean and see what you can do about that."

Yates broke off and moved fast down the hill.

"Geez, boy can move." Rachette watched him leave and turned to the approaching helicopter.

As it neared, the rotors biting the air echoed off the mountains. It sounded like there was more than one.

"Blunt-force trauma to the head," Patterson said. "Is that what I heard?"

"Yep. Lorber says there's rock embedded in his skull."

Wolf started walking down the muddy path back to the road.

The helicopter was on them now, straight overhead.

"—coincidence!" Patterson said.

"What?"

"I said, rocks—that's quite a coincidence!"

Wolf nodded, not bothering to answer over the noise.

They stepped fast down the slope toward the road.

Wolf felt a vibration in his pocket and pulled out his phone.

The name on the screen made his heart leap. He felt like he'd stepped off a cliff.

"What is it?" Patterson shuffled around him. "What?"

Only then did he realize he'd come to a stop. He sucked a breath and put the phone back in his pocket. "Nothing."

"What?" Rachette asked.

His heart raced. He felt a shortness of breath. He'd experienced it once before but couldn't put a finger on when exactly. When he was a kid? No. It had been a few months ago. Right after *they* had left, and the drinking began.

"Sir?"

"Yeah. Hey, head down and help out Yates if he needs it. I have to ..." He pulled out the phone and held it up. "I have to take a call. I'll be right down."

He walked off the trail, out into a field of boulders and wind-warped trees.

When he was certain he was alone he pulled the phone out again and tapped the message to open it.

He read, and as he did it felt like a giant's hand was squeezing him tighter with each breath.

The screen spun, like he was drunk. The tightness in his chest amplified, turned to dagger-like pain.

The phone dropped from his hands into slush. He hadn't even realized he was standing shin-deep in wet snow.

He ripped off his cap and sucked in deep breaths, but the air was thin. Too thin.

Were his lungs even working?

His chest.

He felt like he'd been buried alive. Like the mountains surrounding him had risen up and crashed onto his back, smothering him, pressing him into the earth.

He clutched a hand over his chest.

"Sir!"

Somebody grabbed him.

He felt flecks of ice hit his face.

He opened his eyes and saw feet scurrying around him, crunching in the snow. He felt his body being lifted. Saw Rachette's face, then Patterson's, then Charlotte's. They carried him.

"You're okay!" they told him between yelling at one another.

The pain intensified. His jaw hurt from clenching his teeth, his eyes from clamping them shut.

Then there was wind and dust stinging his skin, and the sky above him, and he was set on his back and strapped into a leather cushioned chair. A gruff man wearing earphones yelled something back at him, and then Rachette was there, right in his face.

"You're okay!" he said. "You're gonna be okay!"

The cushion pushed up into Wolf's back and he felt himself being lifted again.

"It's okay!" Rachette's eyes told him he was anything but okay. "We're flying you to the hospital! Hang on!"

Wolf passed out.

CHAPTER 12

HEATHER PATTERSON's hands were numb from gripping the wheel.

An hour and twenty minutes had passed since she'd begun the frantic drive from the top of Huerfano Pass. With flashers and siren still blaring, she sped along I-70 into the eastern side of Vail Valley.

This place always felt claustrophobic. The valley was too narrow, threaded with the interstate highway. She preferred Avon and Eagle only a few miles back. There one could breathe.

"Take a right here," Yates said. "West Vail exit. Then hang a left at the traffic circle. Then right on the frontage road. It'll be on the left."

She logged the directions in her mind and slowed the vehicle at the West Vail exit. That's why she liked Yates —the guy knew how to think ahead. And knew when to shut up. Those had been the first words out of his mouth in thirty minutes.

"Thanks," she said.

She flicked off the siren.

Never in her life had she seen David Wolf with that look twisting his face. It was so strange. He'd been eating healthily, exercising daily.

But, then again, maybe it wasn't so strange.

"Right here!"

She cranked the wheel, almost missing the exit. Geez, how had she done that? She felt her face redden as she jammed the brakes and pushed into the seatbelt.

"Left at the traffic circle."

"Yeah. And then right on the frontage road, then it's on the left. Sorry. Just ... a little freaked out, I guess."

"Rachette said he's fine." Yates said. "We're just lucky that chopper was overhead."

Patterson nodded.

They swung onto the frontage road and turned into a parking lot behind a modern wooden building that was all boxes and right angles.

Whereas County Hospital, down over Williams Pass to the south of Rocky Points, sat in the middle of a wide valley surrounded by sage and air, Vail Health Hospital was socked in by evergreen trees on all sides. A red sage-covered mountain rose on the horizon to the south. The mountain to the north was a carpet of pines. Ski runs gouged the forest, dipping down into Vail Village.

The dash clock read 12:15 p.m. as she parked and shut off the engine. Was it only lunch time? It felt like she'd been awake for days already.

She lowered the window and drove up to a gate arm leading to an underground garage. The air was saturated with the scent of pine and some sort of baked goods wafting from somewhere beyond the trees.

They made their way to the rear sliding glass doors, and into a quiet reception area.

Yates took the initiative, asking the receptionist for Wolf's room, and they were directed to the third floor.

The glass elevator rose above the trees, giving them a view of the Vail Valley, and the cars sliding down the pass on the interstate into town. Just like Rocky Points, snow clung to the uppermost peaks.

"Patterson."

The elevator had stopped and Yates waited outside.

She was in mild shock.

Their feet pattered silently on a low-pile carpet as they made their way down a long hallway toward a waiting room.

Rachette sat in a chair, looking half-asleep. He stood. "There you guys are."

They were alone in the room. A pair of closed double doors stood at the far end.

"What's the news?" she asked.

"The news is there's no news. I'm about to shove my foot up the nurse's ass, I'll tell you that. She's a wench." His voice rose and he looked over his shoulder toward a window in the wall.

Patterson put a hand on his shoulder. "Can we not start a fight? Why don't you sit down and I'll figure out what's going on?"

"Please do." He sat and Yates perched next to him.

She walked to the window and saw an empty cloth

chair inside some sort of records room on the other side of the counter. "Hello?"

No answer.

A moment later, a woman in pink scrubs walked past with a folder in her hand.

"Excuse me."

The woman continued on. "You here for Detective Wolf?"

"Yes."

The nurse studied a shelf, found a spot, and shoved the folder in. Avoiding Patterson's eyes, she moved to her seat and sat.

"Can you tell me his status, please? We haven't heard any news."

"You haven't?" She wiggled a computer mouse and clicked on her keyboard. "I told Detective Rachette out there that he's stable. He's visiting with the doctor now. When the doctor comes out and talks to you, you'll have more information."

"But ... has he had a heart attack?"

The nurse looked at her without expression. "He's stable."

"Stable."

"Yes."

"So, no emergency surgery?"

The nurse blinked.

"Thanks. You've been a pleasure to speak to."

The woman slid her gaze to the computer screen and began typing.

Patterson walked back to Rachette and Yates. "Yeah,

good thing she's got a big ass, cause it's going to have to fit my foot, too."

"Told you."

The double doors swung open and Wolf strode out. He cinched his belt and fixed his flannel shirt, then threaded his arm through his jacket. "Hey." Without slowing, he passed them and walked down the hallway.

"Hey, what are you doing?" She strode after him. "Hey."

"What?" Wolf kept walking.

"What are you doing?"

"Going home." He slowed. "Who drove?"

"I did," Rachette said, hurrying down the hallway to them. "Patterson did. What's going on?"

"I've been discharged." Wolf held out a hand between them. "I'll take your vehicle."

They stood mute and motionless. Wolf's hand was steady, his gaze relaxed, matching his demeanor.

Patterson looked down the hall toward the waiting room, then back at him. "You have to explain yourself, sir. You were just airlifted off Huerfano Pass, and now you're walking out of the hospital? That doesn't make any sense. They have to keep you for observation for more than ..." She looked at her watch, remembered she'd stopped wearing one, and dug for her cell phone. "You've been here for like an hour and a half. Where's the doctor?"

Wolf snatched a set of keys from Rachette's hand and walked away.

"I have to get my bag out of the back," Rachette said, following Wolf. "And here, take your cell phone. You dropped it on the pass."

"Thanks."

Her mouth dropped open as she watched Yates follow silently behind them to the elevator.

"You coming?" Rachette poked his head out of the open door.

She turned and walked back to the waiting-room window, where Nurse Human-Interaction was still typing on her computer.

"Excuse me."

She raised an eyebrow, continuing at two-hundred words per minute.

"Did you discharge David Wolf?"

"No."

"You didn't?"

"Did you see me leave my station in the three minutes you've been here?"

Patterson reached in and slapped the top of the computer monitor. The sound reverberated like a bomb. Immediately, Patterson regretted her action. The nurse outstretched both her arms and pushed back in her roll-chair, her face a mask of horror.

"Listen to me. David Wolf just walked out of here. It was my impression he's had a freaking heart attack. Why is he leaving right now?"

The nurse volleyed her gaze from Patterson to the still-wobbling monitor.

"Hey." Patterson calmed her voice. "I'm sorry. Okay? Now can you please page David Wolf's doctor for me?"

"I should call the cops, that's what I should do."

"I am the cops." Patterson was short, so her beltline was out of sight and had been since she'd shown up.

Had Rachette not informed this woman who they were? Patterson picked her badge off her belt and showed it.

The nurse blinked rapidly, her eyes searching the room for an escape route.

Damn it. She was surrounded by idiots. "Never mind."

"No. Sorry." The nurse scooted back to her computer. "I just don't do very well with confrontations. Apparently ... you do."

Patterson felt heat rising in her cheeks. "No. I'm sorry." She closed her mouth and breathed, letting her impatience dissipate with each exhale.

The nurse clicked the keys, then leaned in, studying the screen. "He's not on the discharge list. Which means he hasn't been discharged. This list shows recently discharged as well as scheduled estimations. He's not even on here yet."

"Is he in the system?"

She nodded. "I entered him when he arrived."

"Thank you."

Patterson went down the hallway and rode the elevator down to the garage. When the doors opened, Rachette and Yates stood like a couple of abandoned dogs outside the door. She caught the side of an SBCSD vehicle climbing out of the ramp and disappearing into the daylight outside.

Rachette turned to Patterson. "I think he just ditched out on the doctor."

"No shit, Sherlock."

Her phone vibrated in her pocket and she read the

screen. "Ah. It's MacLean." She pressed the button. "Hello, sir."

"What's going on?" MacLean was yelling over a lot of background vehicle noise. "Damn cell reception's been shot for the last thirty minutes. How's he doing?"

"He's ... stable."

"Stable."

"Yes, sir."

"So what's that mean? He had a heart attack?"

"I don't know."

"What happened? What are the doctors saying?"

She looked at Rachette and Yates, who stared sympathetically. "We haven't talked to the doctor yet."

"Okay. I'm just driving past Eagle now. I'll be in there in a few minutes."

The line went dead.

"Great," she said.

CHAPTER 13

THE DRIVE HOME to the ranch took all of an hour and forty-five minutes, but it felt like a full day had passed.

It was dark by the time he parked in his carport. His hands ached from clutching the wheel. He stepped out into the calm night and stood, staring into the cloudless sky and the spray of stars sparkling above.

He walked back to the vehicle, opened the rear driver's-side door, and searched for his phone. After ignoring the fourth call from MacLean, he'd thrown it in back. The first mile he'd listened to the radio chatter. It was all about him so he'd shut it off.

There were three new missed calls from the sheriff, two from Patterson, two from Rachette. He stopped reading and shoved the phone in his pocket.

Now he knew what a criminal felt like fleeing the scene of a crime. And he, too, felt no remorse.

He could stretch his hands but not his chest—it still felt like a large man was sitting on him.

His boots swished through the grass as he stepped to his front porch and took a seat on a metal chair.

Visions of a girl playing with a dog danced across the moonlit lawn, so he stood and went inside.

The living-room electronics hummed. Strips of moonlight streamed through the open blinds. He sat on the couch and got comfortable for the night ahead. His eyelids grew heavier, but his willpower was stronger.

Nobody came to visit him. Which meant they knew. Meaning it was going to be a long day tomorrow. But he'd never been one to shy away from a challenge, so why was he ignoring his phone as it chimed like a Cripple Creek slot machine?

Because this was different.

⸺

Six and a half hours later, as the valley outside started to glow, he stood up from the couch.

He shaved and showered, and made a vegetable smoothie and a bowl of steaming oatmeal with bananas. By 6 a.m. he was out the door and back in Rachette's vehicle.

At 6:24 he pulled into the rear parking lot of the County building and parked. People were streaming in for the early day shift and flowing out from the night shift. Wolf and his team worked on their own schedule and Wolf was a full thirty-five minutes early, but he noticed Patterson's unmarked at the far end of the lot.

As he climbed out, Patterson's car jostled and lit up as she opened her door.

She bee-lined him, flicking her eyes between him and the ground.

"What's up?"

She looked around. "I wanted to catch you before you went in."

"Okay."

"MacLean knows you left without being discharged. Everyone was worried about you and wanted to come out to your place last night, but he stopped them."

Wolf walked.

"I think I know why."

"Why what?"

"Why you left the hospital. Why he stopped everyone from going to your house."

He slipped to the left, putting a car between them.

"Sir."

He said nothing.

"Remember when I quit?" Her voice bounced as she walked next to him. "I'd just been drugged and shoved in a trunk with Charlotte. I'd been flown on a helicopter to County. When the memories came back, they haunted me."

She grabbed his arm and stopped him.

He looked down at her hand.

"I know what it's like. Because it happened to me." She let go.

He opened his mouth to say something, but nothing came out so he walked inside the automatic doors.

A group of deputies sipping gourmet coffee waited at the elevators.

"Hey, there he is." Deputy Nelson turned toward

him. "Geez, what are you doing here? I heard you had a heart attack on ..." He looked at Patterson and his voice trailed off.

Wolf felt heat blossom in his face. He stepped over to the stairwell and pushed through. No one followed.

He climbed the stairs with ease, propelled by strength in his legs that he'd built over the past three months. At the third floor he pushed through the doors, his breathing relaxed as he walked down the hallway toward his office.

As he unlocked the door the elevator opened, and he slipped inside before he had to face Patterson and the elevator-goers a second time.

He leaned against the wall and took some deep breaths. The same heaviness clenched his chest, but this time it dissipated with each exhale. There was no clamp of a giant's palm, no swirling vision, no searing poker pain in his sternum.

The deputies' footsteps passed.

For thirty minutes, he sifted through his messages and missed calls. They were all from MacLean, Rachette, and Patterson. Clearly word hadn't gotten out to the civilian population, otherwise his mother, Jack, Margaret, Nate, and a few others would have been kicking down his door—digitally or literally.

Somebody knocked.

"Come in!"

Rachette poked his head inside. "Situation meeting in five. Lorber just got in with his report."

"Thanks."

Rachette eyed him. "How are you doing?"

"I'm doing fine. Thanks, Tom."

Rachette gave him an unreadable look and ducked out.

The door clicked shut.

Wolf waited ten minutes and made his way down to the situation room. The squad room was still bustling, the sound echoing off the ceilings. Conversations turned hushed or were muted altogether when he strode in.

"Hello, sir," somebody said. "Glad to see you're feeling better."

Wolf nodded at a few other well-intentioned comments and slalomed his way into the situation room.

He took the side route, descending into the auditorium along the exterior windows. Patterson, Rachette, Yates, Undersheriff Wilson, DA White, ADA Hanson, and MacLean populated the central seats in the first two rows.

Lorber stood hunched over a laptop at the front table next to Daphne Pinnifield. The screen behind them had been pulled down and showed a blackened body entrenched in a snow grave.

The memory of Warren Preston's body was like a confused dream. He thought about the text message and his chest seized up. He felt the cold of the snow on his face, saw the shuffling feet.

"Wolf!"

He snapped back to the present and saw everyone was staring.

His eyes went to his hand clutching the back of a

chair. He was about to look up, but the afterimage of them looking at him wide-eyed was already seared in his brain.

Chairs squeaked and flapped shut as people stood and rushed toward him.

"You okay?" The question came simultaneously from a half-dozen mouths.

"I'm okay!" He raised a palm. "Sit."

He went to the front row and sat next to Patterson. Everyone else's chairs groaned as they sat back down, a low murmur sweeping through the room.

Lorber raised a long arm to the screen. "Okay, everyone's here. Let's get started."

Daphne walked to the front row and sat next to Patterson.

The door clicked shut, snuffing out the noise from the squad room above. Motors whirred as blinds automatically lowered over the windows, darkening the auditorium.

A closeup of Warren Preston's head glowed on screen.

"I've confirmed this is Warren Preston. Dental records match. DNA match. It's him." Lorber raised a laser-clicker and pressed the button, switching the photo to a closer angle.

Wolf pushed his inauspicious entrance to the back of his mind as he stared at Preston's black, misshapen skull —just as he'd remembered it from yesterday. Thick gray hair twisted in different directions from the caved-in portion of his head. The two eye sockets were empty, leaving dark holes, and the mouth was agape.

"Holy shit," somebody mumbled.

"You can see that, for three months out in the elements, he's decomposed relatively little."

With such a decrepit version of a man who'd been alive only three months earlier, Wolf's mind begged to differ, but he'd seen more decay happen in much less time.

"Clear sign of blunt-force trauma." Lorber swirled the laser. "We found evidence of four different blows to the head. Fragments of rock that do not match the surrounding strata on Huerfano Pass were found lodged in his remaining brain matter and skull: Sandstone composed of feldspar and quartz, arenaceous in nature, bound with iron oxide."

"English," MacLean said.

"Flagstone. Red flagstone, commonly quarried on the front range of Colorado or north of here near Brushing." The medical examiner cocked an eyebrow, as if he'd just revealed a vital clue.

Wolf tilted his head toward Patterson. "Does Preston Rock and Supply have red flagstone in their inventory?" he asked under his breath.

"Good question," she said, scribbling in her notebook.

MacLean pointedly cleared his throat. "Have you guys—"

"We'll check," Patterson said.

Lorber turned back to the screen and pressed the button. The next picture showed Preston's left arm raised above his head.

"The position of the arm suggests he was either trying to reach up and out of his snowy grave to free himself, or he was deposited there after death and after the onset of rigor mortis. Daphne and I posit he was killed and laid on his side, like this, with his arm outstretched, something close to the fetal position, but with straight legs." Lorber struck a pose to illustrate.

Wolf eyed Daphne and saw a satisfied twinkle in her eye as she watched her boss regurgitate her arguments from the pass.

Click. A picture of Warren Preston's body on a gurney in Lorber's County Hospital lab glowed on screen. The clothing had been cut away, exposing darkened flesh looking like wispy, opaque Saran Wrap over misshapen features.

"We don't see any other wounds on the body so I'm declaring cause of death the head trauma. You don't survive a hole like that in your skull."

Click. The screen shifted to a white place-holder.

The motors hummed and sunlight blazed into the room.

"That's it?" MacLean asked.

"For now." Lorber walked to Patterson and handed her the laser pointer.

She closed her notebook and got up, sliding her slightly bulging belly around the fold-out table.

"You feeling all right?" Lorber asked quietly as he sat down on Wolf's other side.

Wolf ignored him, keeping his eyes forward.

Patterson walked to the table at the front of the room, twisted the laptop toward her, and clicked on a file. A PowerPoint presentation lit up the screen—boxes containing names and places, interconnected with lines.

"Overachieve much?" Rachette asked.

Patterson ignored the laughter and pointed at the first name.

"Chris Alamy. Alamy came to the station on the morning of Tuesday, March 18th, telling us that his boss, Warren Preston, was missing. When we pressed him on that, he told us he'd known that Preston had supposedly been on vacation in Arizona the week before. When he hadn't returned on Monday, Alamy was concerned. When he hadn't returned on Tuesday, he decided to go visit his home."

Patterson clicked. Warren Preston's snow-buried vehicle came up onscreen.

She pointed the laser at the car's open windows. "Alamy told us he'd found the car this way and was worried. He went inside the house, found Preston's personal effects, but no Preston."

Patterson flicked through pictures of Preston's keys on the counter next to his cell phone and wallet. She left a picture up and paced side to side as she spoke.

"Dr. Lorber found a single print on the driver's-side door handle of Preston's vehicle. We've yet to find a match. Doesn't match Alamy. Doesn't match any of the five employees at Preston Rock and Supply." She stopped and raised a finger. "Doesn't match the disgruntled former employee named Rick Welch."

Wolf knew all about Welch, though he hadn't spoken to him during the initial investigation. Wolf had been on his forced vacation. He thought of evenings laced with nightmares, slick skin, hours on the toilet, and the shakes, and felt a sweat bead on his forehead.

"I want to touch on Welch." A man came up onscreen, pulling Wolf out of his memories.

The picture had been taken from Facebook and showed him smiling with a raised beer. He was slim, with long brown hair, a short beard of the same color, and wore glasses over brown eyes.

"When we visited Preston Rock and Supply, we were told that Warren Preston had fired Welch. Welch had worked as a mechanic at the rock yard and there were a lot of breakdowns of the large equipment and earth-movers over a short period of time. Welch said somebody was tampering with the equipment, but Preston thought he was a poor mechanic. They got into a fist fight, and Welch went home for good."

Patterson clicked back to her PowerPoint diagram and circled Welch's name. "Rick Welch, our disgruntled mechanic, looks to be a good suspect, but his alibi is rock-solid." She stopped pacing. "Sorry. Pardon the pun. Welch went to work as a bartender at Black Diamond Pizza after he was fired, and we've confirmed he was working all night on the Saturday in question."

A picture of Chris Alamy came onscreen. "We're back to Chris Alamy. During the interview, he told us he met with Warren Preston Saturday night. Why? He says they needed to discuss the upcoming operations for the business, because Preston was going down to Arizona on a camping trip." She clicked back to Preston's car. "Obviously he never went. His car is filled with the snow that fell that Saturday night into Sunday.

"When we went to Preston Rock and Supply and

spoke to one Betsy Collworth, she swore she'd never heard about Warren Preston's vacation plans. She contended that was very much out of the ordinary, and she flat-out told us she thought Chris Alamy was lying."

"What about the Chris Alamy interview?" MacLean said. "What exactly did he say again about what happened that night? He said he went to the Pony, late night. But his cell records show him going home earlier, right?"

Patterson nodded. "Chris Alamy told us he met with Preston at the rock yard from around 6 to 7 p.m." She picked up a sheet of paper from the table and read. "The records indicate he's telling the truth there. His phone GPS has him traveling from home to the rock yard, arriving at the rock yard at 6:03 p.m., staying at there until 6:45, and arriving back home at 7:05 p.m. He stayed home until 10:36 p.m. when he drove to the Pony Tavern. He stayed at the Pony until 1:30 a.m., grabbing an Uber ride from one Matt Jenkins. Alamy left his car at the Pony that night. The next day he went back and got his car just before noon—took another Uber to get there. Comes back home. Stays there for the remainder of the day."

They sat in silence, digesting the information.

"What about Alamy's calls?" DA White asked. "Any leads there?"

"Potentially."

"Meaning?"

Patterson sucked in a breath. "The guy spends a lot of time on his phone. According to Chris himself, he helps run the day-to-day business of the rock yard. He's on the phone all week to a hundred different people."

"What about Saturday?" MacLean asked.

"Saturday not so much. He speaks to Warren Preston in the morning and makes no other calls all day."

Wolf narrowed his eyes. That piece of information had been bothering him for the past month and he'd voiced it before. "That seems oddly quiet," he said.

Patterson nodded and flipped to a page in her packet. "The previous weekend, Alamy makes six different calls to various local friends. Our investigation shows he's a social man."

"But not the Saturday his boss goes missing," MacLean said.

"Right."

"How about the weekend before that?" Wolf already knew the answer, but he was following a thread of thought.

Patterson flipped back several pages. "February ... here. He makes nine calls."

"So what?" MacLean asked. "Where we going with this?"

"So, he makes numerous calls before he goes out drinking for two weekends. Why not the Saturday night Preston goes missing? He went to the Pony to meet his pals and tie one on. But he makes no calls."

The room fell silent.

Wolf stood. "Lorber, can you pull up Google Maps?"

Lorber drew his phone like a gun. "Got it."

Wolf paced. "We know Alamy met with Preston at work on Saturday night, then left and went back home.

How long does it take to drive from Preston Rock and Supply back to his house.?"

Lorber looked at Patterson. "What's Alamy's address?"

Patterson clicked some keys and read it off.

Lorber nodded. "Twenty-four minutes, according to the app."

"Okay, write that down," Wolf said to the room.

"Got it," Wilson said.

"But it's a sunny June morning right now," Lorber said. "Alamy would have been driving at night, with a biblical snowstorm rolling in."

Wolf pointed toward Patterson. "But the phone GPS data said he left work at 6:45 and got home at what time?"

Patterson flipped her pages. "He left at 6:45 and got home at 7:05."

"That matches what the app is telling us," Wolf said.

Lorber nodded. "The storm must not have hit yet."

"What time did it snow that night?" Wolf asked.

"Pffft." MacLean flailed his arms in the air. "What color outfit was Patterson wearing? How strong was the coffee in the squad room that day? Jesus, there's no way to know."

"There're numerous websites that document weather history and observations," Lorber said.

MacLean's face turned red. "Pull it up."

Lorber stood, walked to the laptop and crouched over.

They watched on the screen as he conducted his Google search. He clicked on a webpage run by the state of Colorado, then on Chautauqua Valley, Rocky Points, March, and scrolled down to the eighteenth.

Rachette cleared his throat. "There's another website that actually documents what Patterson was wearing—"

"Shut up."

"Yes sir."

"Here," Lorber scrolled down, showing the hourly weather observations. "It's all here. Looks like the snow hit at around 11:05 p.m." He looked up sharply.

"Okay," Wolf said. "We have Chris Alamy at home at 7:05. Write that down."

"Got it."

"Time to get back to Preston Rock and Supply again?"

"Twenty-four minutes," Lorber said.

"Time from Preston Rock and Supply to Warren Preston's house?"

Lorber typed on the laptop. They were all watching on the screen now. "Twenty-nine minutes."

"Now let's do Warren Preston's to the Huerfano Pass road gate."

"Shit. How do we do that?"

Patterson pointed. "Do the intersection with County 707 and Huerfano Pass road. That's no more than one mile from the gate."

Lorber typed it in and a line shone on the map. "That's forty-two minutes."

"And now, from there back to Chris Alamy's house?"

"Twenty-three minutes."

They looked at Wilson.

Wilson scribbled. "Twenty-five plus twenty-nine plus forty-two plus twenty-three minutes ..."

"One hundred and nineteen minutes," Lorber said. "Two hours' driving time." His forehead crinkled. "So what?"

They looked at Wolf.

"That's how they did it," he said. "Alamy and our partial-fingerprint unknown. They killed Warren Preston, bashing his head in with a rock from the rock yard. From that point on, they started thinking ahead. They knew we'd be able to read Alamy's cell-phone data, so they drove to Alamy's and left the phone at his house.

"The first leg was Alamy's car. The other guy followed. They had to drop off Chris's car and his phone, make it look like he went home. So they did that and returned to Preston Rock and Supply. They loaded Preston's body into the back of second guy's car. Probably a pickup. One of them drove Preston's car up to Preston's house. The other followed. They dumped Preston's car, wiped it down, and opened all the windows to make sure the coming snow would wipe out any remaining forensic trace evidence. But Alamy's friend left a partial on the handle.

"Then they were in the truck with the body in back. They drove from Preston's, up to Huerfano Pass to the gate. They hiked up the hill, put down the body, then drove back to Chris's house."

Lorber folded his arms and put a long finger over his lips. "Chris left work and got home at 7:05. His phone was next on the move at what time?"

"10:36," Patterson said.

"That's one hour thirty-one minutes total time. One hundred and nineteen minutes gives them only twelve minutes to do their business, like loading Preston's body into the back of the truck, wiping down Preston's car when they drop it off at Preston's, and burying the body up at the pass. That seems too tight."

"The body was dumped," Daphne said. "There were feet of snow beneath him. They tossed him into a drift, probably kicked some snow on top of him, and then the storm buried him further. Otherwise, he would have been deeper."

Lorber looked at Daphne and nodded. "She's right. That takes few minutes to carry him up the hill, a few seconds to drop him. It fits."

The intern looked out the window ignoring Lorber's appraising gaze.

"Plus, the storm hadn't hit yet, not until around 11 p.m.," Wolf continued, "and you're using an app that calculates drive times by using the exact speed limit. I'd say they probably used the speed limit in town since they had a body in back, but once out on the roads they were hopped up on adrenaline and driving fast. I'd say they had at least twenty-five, thirty minutes to do their dirty work between driving."

Wolf looked at White and MacLean. "Chris Alamy. It was always him. It fits too perfectly."

White smoothed his tie, staring into nothing. "He's lawyered up. This is all circumstantial. We need to match the rock buried in Preston's skull with one sitting in Preston Rock and Supply, three months ago mind you." He shook his head.

"So, we search Preston Rock and Supply for the rock in question," Wolf said. "We also search Alamy's house for solid evidence."

"Specifically, what are we searching for at his house?"

Wolf shrugged. "A red flagstone with blood on it. Clothing with blood. Something."

The DA exhaled. "Write it up."

CHAPTER 14

WOLF LOOKED TO PATTERSON.

She nodded and walked up the center stairs. "I'm on it."

The room burst into movement as people stood up.

Wolf nodded to Rachette. "We'll roll once those warrants are ready."

"Got it."

It felt good to be in motion, on the hunt again. The memory of his situation-room entrance was shrinking into the past.

"Wolf!"

MacLean craned a finger.

"See you in a few." Rachette went up the steps.

"What's up?"

"I need to see you in my office." MacLean strode out the doors to the squad room.

Wolf followed, feeling like a kid being called to the principal's office.

They walked inside and MacLean shut the door.

"Sit."

Wolf did as he was told and waited.

MacLean walked the perimeter of the office, twisting shut the blinds, then exhaled hard as he sat. His eyes wandered the room for a few moments and landed on Wolf. "Panic attack."

The words hit Wolf like a punch in the stomach, but he didn't move.

MacLean bridged his fingers and studied him. "I was shocked to hear that. But I'm sure not as shocked as you were, Dave."

Wolf said nothing.

MacLean stood and turned to the exterior window. "Well, at least it makes sense why you left the hospital, stole a deputy's vehicle, and drove away without explanation after having a heart attack."

MacLean turned back to him. "You know, Bonnie had these episodes for a while. A few years ago, she got stressed out by the crash in the real-estate market and went cra ... shit, sorry. She had a few of the episodes that you had yesterday. It wasn't fun to watch my wife go through that."

Wolf looked past him to dark clouds building in the southern sky.

"Then she got scared that the attacks were going to keep happening, which led to more attacks. That only exacerbated her problems. But in the end, it was a pretty simple fix. You want to know what helped her?"

Wolf studied a bird circling over the forest.

"Talking about it."

Wolf nodded.

"Not with me. With a professional." MacLean sat back down in his chair. "So I've set up your first session, which starts in"—he checked his watch—"forty-five minutes."

Wolf shot him a glare. "We have a case cracking wide open."

"Yeah, and a detective doing the same."

They stared hard at one another.

"I haven't slept lately. I hadn't eaten enough yesterday. I had hiked up the mountain behind my house when Patterson called me into the office. The doctor said it could have been physical stress."

"You haven't slept in how long?"

"I don't know. A couple days? A week?"

MacLean's eyelids slid down.

"A few months."

"A few months? Jesus."

"My point is, it's physical. I know what I have to do—get more sleep. Eat better."

"Bullshit. I've seen your Buddhist monk diet lately, and the way you've been exercising, you should be sleeping twelve hours a day, not having panic attacks."

Wolf sucked in a breath. "Are we done here?"

"Nope." MacLean stood, rounded the desk and sat on the edge in front of him. "If word were to get out that a detective suffering panic attacks was walking around town with a gun on his hip, the community would want my head. Both of our heads. You know White's already jumpy with the election. Do you think he'd willingly back an investigation where you search Alamy's house one day after your episode?"

Wolf said nothing.

MacLean sighed. "Nobody knows about what happened yesterday. They think you had an unspecified heart 'event' and went home on doctor's orders. Although, I think the more people talk about it, the less believable that explanation becomes."

MacLean tilted his head. "There are two ways this can go. One: You go to the therapy session in thirty minutes down the street at the Old Bank Building. You kick this thing and that's that."

"And the second way?"

MacLean raised his eyebrows and let silence hang.

Wolf sat back in resignation.

"Thirty minutes," MacLean said. "Ten a.m. The Old Bank Building. His name is Dr. Hawkwood. Some new kid in town."

Wolf blinked. "Kid?"

"Younger man. A certified psychologist."

"Certified. Impressive."

"Comes highly recommended."

"By whom?"

MacLean shrugged. "The receptionist at the Old Bank Building."

CHAPTER 15

PATTERSON STEPPED out of the elevator and walked fast down the hall, the signed warrants in hand. She slowed at Wolf's closed office door, then spotted him leaving MacLean's aquarium at the end of the hall.

Her boss's expression made her halt. He was stretching his face, trying to relax the tension in it, and with little success.

He saw her and wiped his nose. "What's up? You get the warrants?"

"Yes, sir."

"Good. You guys go ahead without me. Take Wilson for extra muscle, just in case. Keep me posted."

He walked past her and went into his office.

"Yes, sir."

Down in the squad room, Rachette was standing next to

Charlotte's desk at the head of the room, which meant they'd seen the interaction.

"Got 'em. Wilson, you're coming with us!"

Wilson was the undersheriff, ranking a full few levels above her, but he stood from his desk and nodded without a second's hesitation.

Yates finished typing something on his desktop computer and stood up. "Coming."

"What was with that?" Rachette crowded close to her, sipping coffee and looking down the hall toward Wolf's office.

"He's staying here."

"Why?"

"Probably something to do with the heart attack yesterday."

Rachette nodded. "Good. He needs to rest. He shouldn't even be here today."

She eyed him. There was no hint of irony in his voice. He was speaking sincerely.

Both he and Yates seemed oblivious to the truth, but she could spot a panic attack clear as day, having watched two occur in the mirror. Just recalling of those moments in her life sent a ripple of fear up her spine.

"So what's gonna happen next week?" he asked.

"Next week? What?"

"The party."

"Oh, shit. Yeah. I don't know."

Rachette scoffed. "Really? I'd say a surprise birthday party for a man who just had a heart attack is definitely a bad idea. Let me save you some deliberation there. Cancel it."

Rachette was right, though she hated to say it. So she said nothing.

She hoped MacLean had slapped some sense into Wolf just now, and he was going home. He needed to rest. He needed to speak to a professional. What was that look on his face she'd just seen?

"Patty!"

"What?"

"Wake up. We going or what?" Rachette was walking down the hall with Yates in tow.

"You okay?" Wilson stood next to her and put a beefy hand on her shoulder.

She looked up. Wilson was a bear of a man, standing well over six feet and weighing somewhere north of two-fifty, but his expression was as soft as his belly.

"Yeah."

"He'll be okay."

An insincere smile cracked her lips. "Yeah."

―――

Patterson bounced in the passenger seat as Rachette pulled through the chain-link gate entrance to Preston Rock and Supply.

It had been a couple of months since they'd put the company probe on the back-burner, and her first impression was that the place had gone downhill. Unattended equipment sat parked in the middle of the internal roads. The building looked run over by weeds, but it was now June and perhaps that's how the place looked when things were just starting to pop.

"Place looks jankier than before, right?" Rachette asked.

He parked, and they got out into warm air heated by the sun lancing through a break in sporadic low clouds overhead. Down south, the sky was darkening near Williams Pass, and Patterson remembered hearing there was a good chance of afternoon thunderstorms over the next few days.

Patterson eyed the office they'd parked next to. It had been Chris Alamy's the last time were there. The windows were dark, no movement inside.

"His truck's not here," Rachette said.

"We're looking for red flagstone, not Alamy."

"Right."

Wilson's SUV rocked to a stop behind them, and Yates and Wilson climbed out.

Wilson raised his sunglasses to his SBCSD ball cap, eyeing the interior of the rock yard.

Betsy Collworth stepped out of the front door. "Is it true?"

The question was directed at Patterson. She hesitated.

"Is it true that you found him up on Huerfano Pass? It's been all over the news since yesterday." She shot looks at all four of them. "Speak."

"Yes. We did find him. I'm afraid the news is correct."

Betsy's face became somber. A tear slid from one eye.

Rachette stood nearest the woman. He looked over both shoulders and backed away.

Patterson walked over to her and put a hand on her shoulder.

The breeze picked up, bringing with it the sound of the Chautauqua howling through the bottom of the valley a short distance away. The scent of fresh water mingled with the smell of upturned earth and Betsy's perfume.

They stood in mute respect, waiting for Betsy to process the news.

Finally, the woman looked up with wet eyes. "I have to tell you guys, I think it was Chris."

Patterson straightened. "Why do you say that, Betsy?"

She shook her head. "I've just always suspected that something bad happened, you know? He wouldn't run away. He wouldn't ditch out on his business like that. He wouldn't leave me ..." She began crying again.

Patterson rubbed her soft shoulder. "Is there something that Chris has said or done that makes you think he had something to do with this?"

"He was never going on vacation." Her voice was a whisper. "He would have told me."

Patterson lowered her hand and pulled the sheet of paper from her back pocket. "Ma'am, we have a warrant to search this property for a certain type of rock."

"Okay." She blinked, and her curiosity looked to win over the grief. "What type of rock?"

"A red flagstone. Do you have it?"

"Yes."

Rachette cleared his throat, adding a meaningful grunt.

"Why?" Betsy asked.

"Can you please show us where that is?"

Betsy wiped her eyes, slathering mascara across her cheeks, and turned. "Over there. Here, follow me."

They followed her around the building, past a dumpster, across an internal road, and down a line of concrete dividers that held piles of rock.

They passed white gravel, remnants of maroon volcanic rock, then a rectangular space that held a haphazard stack of red stone slabs. Patterson was well-acquainted with the rock—the CU Boulder campus, her alma mater, was made of the stuff. Red flagstone.

"Here we are."

Rachette bent over and picked up a slab the length of his forearm, wielding it like a club.

It took all of Patterson's willpower to refrain from yelling at him.

Rachette dropped the rock and wiped his hands on his jeans faster than Betsy could notice.

"Got your five-inch Bacon Strips," Betsy said, gesturing to a row of stones. "Named for the white stripes. Got your five-inch Red Naturals. This is called the Hood Five-Inch Natural and this is the Hood-Bacon. Five inches as well."

Most of the stones were large and flat. Few could be picked up with one arm, but as Rachette had demonstrated, some made for perfect weapons.

"Is this what you're looking for?" Betsy asked.

"Yes, thank you."

"Again. Why?"

Wilson cleared his throat. "Mrs. Collworth, I'm Undersheriff Wilson. Is this where the flagstone has always been stored?"

Betsy blinked. "Yes. We've never moved it from here."

Patterson eyed the ground, knowing there was fat chance of finding any blood residue in the soil after ninety days of Colorado mountain weather.

Rachette was studying the ground like a hawk, which caused Betsy to look down, too.

"What's so special about storing it in this spot?" she asked.

She was a perceptive one, but with Rachette around, it didn't take much.

"We're just wondering if this is where the stones were kept at the time Mr. Preston went missing," Patterson said. "The flagstone itself is a part of—"

"No. It wasn't."

"Excuse me?"

"The flagstone wasn't kept here when Mr. Preston went missing. The flagstone was kept one bay over. Right here." She gestured to the next concrete bay in line.

They all shuffled to the next place, which was full of tan gravel.

"I thought you just said you never moved it," Patterson said.

"No, we never moved it. We changed vendors from the Suskeet quarry in Lyons to the Hood quarry up in Brushing. This bay used to be the Suskeet quarry. This bay over here"—she pointed to the flagstone—"is the Hood quarry."

They eyed one another.

Patterson scratched her forehead. "Okay, so at the

time of Mr. Preston's disappearance, the flagstone was here."

"Yes."

They eyed the ground again. "But then you changed storage areas because you changed vendors."

"That's what I said." Betsy shook her head. "Wish we wouldn't have, but that was one of Chris's first changes that took hold. Oh, I guess it was about a month after Warren ..." She began sobbing again. "When Warren was killed. My God. He was killed and his body was dumped up there on that pass. Is that what happened? I've been thinking, how did he get from his house, where his vehicle was found, and brought all the way up there? He'd have to have been killed and taken up there."

Patterson hooked her thumbs in her belt and walked to the flagstone bay again. "Can you tell me more about this flagstone?"

"Yes. Sorry." Betsy wiped her eyes again. "Comes from up north outside of Brushing. It's good stone, but the problem is that the quarry owner's a jackass. Warren had never liked doing business with the Hood quarry. There's a bit of history there. Anyway, when Chris came in, he had a different history with the quarry, so he went back to them. They're cheaper, but about as unpredictable as the Colorado weather. That's why Warren dropped them in the first place."

"There's history there?" Patterson asked. "What do you mean by that?"

"The quarry used to be owned by a man named Ben Hood. Guy was dishonest as the devil, and about as reliable too, so Mr. Preston stopped using him years ago.

Then Ben died of a heart attack last year and his son, Zack, took over and has been trying to get in here ever since." She shrugged. "Chris is from Brushing and used to be friends with Zack. So, hey, what do you know? We're using the Hood quarry again."

Patterson froze, staring into the pile of stone. "Thank you for your time, ma'am. If you don't mind, we'd like some time alone to take a look at these rocks."

Betsy nodded. "Yes. Of course. Let me know if you need anything else."

"And Betsy."

"Yes?"

"Where's Chris now?"

"He went home yesterday afternoon. Right after we saw on the news that they'd found Preston's body."

"Thank you. We'll let you know if we have any more questions."

They watched her leave.

When she disappeared around the front of the office, Rachette scoffed. "You hear that shit? How much you wanna bet Zack Hood's fingerprints match that partial on Preston's car handle? And we have to look at the phone records closer now. Zack Hood. His name has to show up on Chris's call records."

"They do," Patterson said. "I remember. Hood Rock Quarry. It was among the thirty-five other numbers that looked work-related, but he spoke to them, as well as a personal cell phone owned by Zack Hood."

The wind picked up while a cloud slid in front of the sun, dropping the temperature.

"Let's get some samples of this stone," she said, breaking the silence. "One of each of the four types."

Rachette picked up his club-rock and hit the edge of another slab, breaking off a chunk.

"And then we need to get our asses to Alamy's house," Yates said. "I want to know what he's up to."

Patterson couldn't have agreed more.

CHAPTER 16

WOLF SAT IN HIS SUV, staring out the windshield at the Old Bank Building.

The clock read 10:05, but he had no intention of moving any time soon. A ghost would be roaming the halls inside the hundred-and-fifty-year-old building, and it wasn't one of the original bank tellers. Memories of one of the last times he'd visited Sarah here floated in his mind. It had been cold. Just after the discovery of Stephanie Lang's body alongside County 15.

Five minutes later, the memory of MacLean's raised eyebrows made Wolf lift his hand and pull on the handle, letting in the pine-scented breeze. He twisted in the seat, and then he was outside, shutting the door.

He made his way to the sidewalk, up onto the wooden landing, and walked inside.

The reception room was just as he remembered, down to the last detail, save Sarah's picture was now fifth-to-last in a line of headshots that hung on the wall, rather than last. His heart jumped at her beautiful smile.

My God.

"Hello. David?" A middle-aged woman with dark curly hair sat at the desk to his right.

He opened his mouth, recognizing the face but coming up blank with a name.

"I'm Cheryl. We haven't met," she said. "I just saw the badge, the gun, knew you were scheduled for ten o'clock."

He smiled. "Good detective work."

She laughed, revealing a dark window where she'd lost a tooth.

The old floor squeaked under his feet as he stepped to her desk. There'd been a time when he'd known everyone in this building, including the night janitor. Now he avoided the place like the ski resort on Christmas day.

"I'm here to see a Dr. Hawkwood."

"Hello, Detective Wolf." A male voice came from the hallway beside him. He must have been stepping down the corridor at the exact same time Wolf had been walking because he hadn't heard him. Or maybe he'd been standing on the other side of the wall the whole time. Either way, Wolf distrusted the sneakiness of the man's arrival.

Wolf took him in at a glance. Barely thirty years old, wearing a carefully ironed button-up cowboy shirt tucked into slim designer jeans. His shoes gleamed in the florescent lights, polished recently. A blond beard, groomed like something out of *GQ* magazine, framed a kind smile. His eyes were sky blue, his eyebrows as blond as the beard, giving him a perpetually surprised look.

"I'm Dr. Cyrus Hawkwood," he said in a gentle voice. He stepped forward with an outstretched hand. "Please. Call me Cy."

Wolf took it with more force than necessary, but Hawkwood matched every foot-pound without flinching.

"Dave." Wolf stepped back and hooked his thumbs in his pockets.

"Please. Let's head down to the main room at the end of the hall, and we can chat."

Great. He followed, eyeing the office on the right that had been Sarah's on the way by. He swore he caught a faint whiff of her scent. The desk was the same, but there were two framed pictures of a blonde-haired girl of about five years old standing at one corner … in the same spot where a framed picture of Jack had once stood.

He recalled Jack's smile in that photo, his green eyes squinting in the sunlight, his hair a flop. Where had that picture gone when Sarah died? It was probably in her parents' new house up in Avon.

Hawkwood eyed him, clearly noting his interest in the office as they passed. "That's my daughter."

Wolf read a bit of hurt in the man's profile as he upturned his bearded chin and walked to the back room.

The large space was just as Wolf remembered: Carpeted, multi-color painted shelves covered in worn books and pamphlets, two warped glass windows looking onto the underbrush of the forest outside, plastic seats arranged in a circle in the center of the room, drawings done by kids of all ages adorning the walls.

A shaft of light streamed through the skylight in the center of the ceiling.

There were also photographs on the wall, and he double-took one and felt a pulse of shock as he recognized himself standing with his arm around Sarah's shoulder. He was wearing a cowboy hat, dirty jeans, and a soiled flannel. Smiling like someone had just cracked a joke he thought was ridiculously funny. Sarah wore a matching cowgirl outfit, minus the grime. Sunlight spilled through the holes in her hat, illuminating her wide smile. The day of the cattle branding. He remembered it like it was yesterday—the scent, the temperature, the aching in his muscles from wrestling animals to the ground for hours on end.

She'd died that year.

"Sir?"

Wolf turned, saw the young doctor studying him.

"Please. Take a seat."

Wolf sat at Hawkwood's four o'clock, wanting neither to be next to him, nor staring straight across the circle.

The skylight dimmed overhead.

"Here." Hawkwood pulled a business card from his pocket and held it toward Wolf. "Before we start with anything, I want you to know you can call me anytime."

Wolf pocketed it with a nod.

"I've spoken with Sheriff MacLean, and also to Dr. Bancroft in Vail." He gestured at the picture of Wolf and Sarah. "I'm new in town, but I've familiarized myself with your history. At least, as much as I could. It's quite extensive."

Wolf said nothing.

"I know that what happened to you comes as a surprise, especially given your past. From what I've heard, you have an action-packed career. You've handled pressure in life-or-death situations better than most people handle burning their toast or dealing with a phone gone screwy. I know how difficult this must be for a person like you."

Wolf pulled down the corners of his mouth and nodded.

Hawkwood picked up a folder from the chair next to him and opened it. "I have a full write-up here. It says you served six tours in the army as a Ranger. You excelled and were eventually promoted to lead your own squad. Upon your return, you were immediately hired by the Sluice County SD, where you worked your way up to sheriff."

Hawkwood paused, then lowered the folder and slapped it shut. "You obviously know your own history."

"I do. And now you do, too. Great. What are we doing here, Doc?"

"We're talking."

"For how long?"

"This session is scheduled for an hour."

Wolf eyed the wall clock. "What brings you up to Rocky Points? I haven't seen you around."

Hawkwood smiled. "A change of scenery. It's pretty nice scenery up here."

"Where's your wedding ring?"

Hawkwood's smile faded.

"You're not married anymore," Wolf said. "The only daily contact you have with your daughter is that picture on your desk. What happened?"

Hawkwood swallowed and his face reddened.

A clock on the wall ticked.

"You have your folder there with my history. You know about Sarah. You're sitting at her old desk. Her pictures are still on the walls. You talked to MacLean, which means you probably know about Lauren and Ella and my botched wedding last fall. So I want to hear about Dr. Cyrus Hawkwood. What's he doing moving from Denver to Rocky Points, Colorado?"

Hawkwood looked at him. "Touché. I guess you're a detective so of course you would have checked up on me first."

"I guessed about Denver. Your outfit could have been any major city these days. And you're not wearing a wedding ring. I guessed about your daughter. Give me a medal."

Hawkwood's left thumb ran over his bare ring finger.

"Anyway, I'm not interested in talking to you about my feelings. Sorry, I know you're just trying to do your job. But I'm not into it."

Hawkwood smiled without teeth and nodded. "Let me just talk for a moment, then, about feelings. Feelings sound like a mushy word. I get it. But as far as I'm concerned, they're the strongest things on this planet. And if you want to see how strong they are, just cage them up. See how hard they can thrash against the bars. No animal can fight as hard as a feeling pent-up inside of a human psyche."

Wolf frowned. "I'm not interested in talking about the caged animal in my psyche, either."

The clock ticked a few dozen times.

Hawkwood cleared his throat. "I left Denver to get away."

"And I'm going to learn how to deal with my bad memories from a man who runs from his?" Wolf felt a stab of guilt, but that lob had been straight over the plate.

Fifty minutes left, if Hawkwood was starting from the time of his late arrival.

The silence took over, and Wolf settled in for a nice long stare.

Thunder rumbled outside.

Wolf eyed the windows. It was considerably darker now. Early for a thunderstorm. They usually hit in the afternoon. A cold front moving in.

"My daughter is ten years old now."

Wolf flicked his eyes back to Hawkwood.

"I was a drinker. I used to drink a lot in college. That's where I met my wife, Stephanie—in Boulder. All through school, she was a fellow ... enthusiast. Some couples would study at the library. We would study at The Sink."

Hawkwood smiled and shook his head.

"We were damn good students though. Both of us graduated with honors. We moved down to Denver, where I got my master's at DU. We got married. Moved into a house in Englewood, and we moved from beer to wine. You know, became more sophisticated with age. We'd finish a big bottle every night. Then it became a big bottle and a small bottle some nights. Of course, I'd hit my vodka too. I kept that from her.

"And then Steph got pregnant with Tina and that changed her in a heartbeat. She quit like it was nothing.

She had a kid growing inside of her, you know? She had a compelling reason. I didn't. I figured the baby wasn't inside of me. Maybe when the baby came I'd consider it.

"And then the baby came, and I started getting pressure from Steph to kick the bottle. So I quit drinking wine and started drinking vodka behind her back. I'd heard it was the easiest to hide, and the rumors were right. I invented a whole science around hiding my drunken ass from her. I started lying about work, saying I had to travel to various destinations, but I'd stay a few miles away in a hotel and have a bender."

Hawkwood pulled his eyes from the carpet. "I drank for years, and Tina grew up, and Steph stayed in the dark. But then, right around the same time Tina started really talking a lot, something clicked with Steph. She got wise to me. Must have been something Tina told her about Daddy's bottle or something. I don't know. But I remember the day Steph started watching me closely as I spoke. I knew she knew.

"Then one day I was working from home. It was sunny out, and Tina was playing outside. Steph came into my little home office there and stared at me for a bit, then presented me with a breathalyzer. Well, that pissed me off, and I refused. Actually, I didn't refuse. I simply got up, packed a bag, and got into my car.

"I peeled out of the garage in reverse. I remember Steph running alongside, screaming at me. I ignored her, assuming she was berating me for being an asshole liar or something like that. But she'd been screaming at me to stop. My daughter was coming down the sidewalk on her bicycle at the same time I was reversing out."

Wolf held his breath.

"Tina hit the side of my car as I backed out. Slammed right into my driver's-side door. I was so angry at Steph. I was so close to just continuing, backing out, and leaving her to deal with the screaming child. It was her fault, right? She could explain to her kid why she made Daddy do this. But, Jesus Christ, thank God, I didn't. I opened the door, and saw she'd rolled halfway under the car. I could have killed her."

Hawkwood stared at the floor.

Wolf swallowed and allowed himself to breathe again.

"So, that was the end of my drinking habit, and of my family. I got sober, and have been for five years, but that's not enough for my wife." He looked at Wolf. "And I don't expect it will ever be enough. And I don't blame her one iota for thinking so."

Lightning flickered outside, and the thunder came faster this time.

Hawkwood blinked and sucked in a breath. "You can take what you want from that story. Clearly I'm not a saint, nor could I be considered an expert in marital or family affairs. And I'm not pretending to be."

Silence fell between them again, broken by a low rumble shaking the windows.

Wolf reached into his jeans pocket and pulled out his phone.

"Listen, I have to take this." He pressed the button at the bottom to wake up the device from a dead sleep. He scrolled, pressed the number for Patterson, and left the room.

CHAPTER 17

PATTERSON LOOKED out the passenger window at the passing forest. A meadow opened up down a slope, revealing bright-green aspens shimmering in the front winds of the approaching storm.

"I've seen this guy's house a million times." Rachette slowed the SUV and leaned toward the windshield.

They were driving on the county road that led to Rachette's house. Here in the sticks, outside the north-eastern edge of Rocky Points, houses were few and far between, separated by dense woods.

"So strange how it's such a small valley, yet so big. One day you think you know everyone and everyone knows what color crap you had that morning, and the next you're meeting people you've never met who've lived here for years."

Patterson pictured herself as an open window, Rachette's words passing through her like the breeze outside.

"My point is, I've driven past here thousands of

times. I've looked at his house. He's lived here for years." Rachette slowed in front of a drive cut into the trees. "This is it, right?"

She checked her phone GPS. "Yep."

"I knew it."

Rachette had been talking incessantly for a half-hour, meaning he thought there might be some upcoming action. At times like these, she liked to sit with her breath, to shut up and think. Times like these, she knew she had the wrong partner.

"Looks like his vehicle's here."

Her phone vibrated, and she checked the screen. "Wolf's calling. Hello?"

"Hey, what's going on?" His voice sounded far away, which happened with half the calls she ever made on her cell in the mountains of Colorado.

"We're up at Alamy's."

"You're inside already?"

"No. Just got here. Just pulling up to his house now."

The SUV angled up and revved as they traveled up a steep incline.

"I'll meet you there," Wolf said. The line went dead.

"What's happening?"

"Wolf's going to meet us here."

They crested a rise and the land flattened out.

"Damn, that driveway must be hell in winter." Rachette parked next to Alamy's red Ford Explorer and looked past Patterson out the window. "But the views are worth it. Look at that."

She glanced at the valley beside her. The sun was piercing the clouds, setting the carpet of trees alight.

Behind it a curtain of white preceded the dark tunnel of a storm. A fork of lightning licked the ground.

"Weather's rolling in," Rachette said. "It's not even noon yet."

She opened the door and stepped outside.

Behind them, Wilson's SUV bounced up the incline, then scraped to a stop.

The one-story house was a no-nonsense rectangle design with a sloping tar roof and clean-looking brown paint. The trees had been cut back for an acre or so on either side of the structure, giving the property a light and airy feel.

Wilson's doors popped shut and he and Yates stepped up next to them. Together, the three men had a lot of muscle mass, and she felt safer for it. She'd rolled up to a lot of properties in her time, and she had a bad feeling about this one.

"Too quiet," Wilson said, voicing her thoughts.

Thunder rumbled in the distance.

"Spoke too soon."

"Let's go." She took the lead and walked to two wooden steps leading to a front porch framed with sturdy logs.

She pressed a glowing doorbell and stepped back. A generic ding-dong floated out from the tall door. A frosted window was cut into the center of it, revealing a dark interior.

Wilson came up and stood next to her right shoulder while Rachette and Yates held back, hands on their guns.

The house remained still and silent.

She shuffled to the edge of the porch and looked

inside the window to the right. It seemed to lead into a living room. Wood blinds were cracked, showing a darkened television and a couch against the opposite wall. A blanket sat like a peeled-open burrito.

"Nothing," she said, feeling the porch sag next to her from Wilson's weight.

They stared inside for a few moments, waiting for movement that never came.

"This is definitely his car." Rachette was down off the porch, looking inside the rear windows of Alamy's Explorer. "Has rocks inside. Imagine that. Doesn't look like flagstone."

Patterson and Wilson went back down the steps, out onto a front yard of grasses and flowers mowed to shin-height.

"Let's circle the place," Wilson said.

Wilson veered right, and she followed. Yates walked in the opposite direction toward Rachette.

"Place is kept up decently," Wilson said. "New roof. New paint."

"Wolf is on his way up."

"Oh?" He looked at his watch. "Right now?"

"Yeah."

Wilson said nothing, but he was clearly not saying something.

They walked along the front edge of the house and stopped to look inside a window, but the blinds were closed.

On the side of the house were two windows, both too high for her to see inside.

"Can you reach those?"

Wilson went to the second and got on his toes. "Bathroom," he grunted. "Nobody."

As they rounded the back corner, she kept her hand on her Glock, ready for Rachette and Yates coming from the other direction.

The rear of the house had no formal porch, just a dirt clearing leading to some sliding glass doors. A circular grill stood along the siding, smelling of charcoal.

Beyond the dirt, an expanse of grass sloped gently upward, then dense forest.

She stared into the darkened spaces between trees, spotting a single deer. Then another. "Got a few deer in those woods." She'd seen Rachette pull his weapon on a rabbit before.

"Copy." Wilson kept his eyes on the windows.

Yates and Rachette rounded the other side of the house.

Rachette raised an inquisitive eyebrow at Patterson.

She shrugged.

Wilson shuffled along the rear siding to the sliding glass doors, and Rachette and Yates pulled their guns.

She pulled hers and backed up into the yard to get an angle.

Wilson took a cautious look, then swiveled to the windows and put his face against them. He knocked on the glass, keeping his nose pressed. A few moments later, he shrugged and turned around. "Nothing."

More thunder rumbled overhead. The sun had been swallowed by the clouds now and the air grew colder.

Wilson turned and looked into the woods behind them.

"Deer," Rachette said.

"All the lights are turned off."

A repetitive knocking echoed on the wind.

They all cocked an ear.

"What is that?" Rachette asked.

The breeze shifted, and the sound with it.

"It's a nail gun," she said.

"Yeah." Wilson walked back in the direction he'd come. The sound was coming from the front of the house.

They moved to the cars in front and scanned the valley for the source of the sound. There was a clearing down and to the left, further along the road, below and across it. A man straightened, looking like he was floating on the tree tops. He was on the roof or upper floor of a house he was constructing.

"What do you think?" Yates asked.

"Maybe he went out drinking last night," Rachette said. "Maybe he took an Uber into town and left his car here. Maybe he's sleeping it off on someone else's couch in town."

A low rumble came from below. They watched a vehicle pass on the dirt road, kicking up a plume of dust.

"Let's call him."

"Alamy?" Rachette asked.

"I have his cell number." She pulled out her phone.

"You have a suspect's phone number programmed into your phone?"

She dialed. Three months ago, she'd called Chris Alamy twice, and she'd added his name to the number to keep it straight.

"That's pretty disgusting," Rachette said.

"Only if he did it." The phone trilled in her ear, but nobody answered.

"Hello, this is Chris Alamy with Preston Rock and Supply. I'm unable to—"

She hung up. "He's not answering."

Another car approached below.

"There's Wolf."

They stood and watched him slow at the driveway below. His SUV turned and revved hard as it bounced up to them.

He parked behind Rachette's car and got out.

Wolf kept his eye contact with the house behind them as he joined them at the rear bumper. "What's happening?"

"He's not here, sir." Rachette folded his arms.

Wilson eyed his watch and looked at Wolf with something resembling puzzlement.

Patterson wondered what she was missing. One thing was for sure, though, if Wolf had looked off at the station earlier, he looked worse now.

"We knocked on his front door," Rachette said. "When no one answered, we checked the rear."

"Nothing?"

Wilson shook his head. "I looked through that glass for a few minutes. There's no movement. He's not here."

"Or he's stonewalling us," Yates said. "That Betsy chick at Preston Rock said he jetted work yesterday, right after he heard about us finding Preston."

Wolf nodded, appraising Alamy's vehicle.

"Did you call him?"

"No answer," Patterson said.

The world around them flashed, and thunder followed a few seconds later. Wind howled through the trees and kicked up dirt around them.

"What's this?"

Wolf locked his gaze on the ground behind Patterson.

She saw what he was looking at—two tire marks in the soil.

"Rear-wheel drive." Wolf stepped past her. "Looks like somebody in a hurry. Or did you guys do this?"

"No," Patterson said. "We pulled up and parked where we're at."

"We think he might have gone out drinking last night," Rachette said. "Could be tracks from an Uber driver. Maybe he's sleeping it off on someone's couch in town."

"Did you call the Pony?" Wolf asked.

"No."

"Did you try the front door?"

"No," Patterson said. She looked at Wilson. "We didn't try breaking and entering."

Wilson stared at him, unimpressed.

"Okay. I want to take a look around."

More lightning flickered.

"Better make it quick," Wilson said.

Wolf walked to the front windows and cupped his hands.

The valley shook with thunder as Patterson watched Wolf stalk the front of the house.

He rounded to the right where Yates and Rachette had passed before.

Patterson followed him, and the others joined at her heels.

They passed a closed one-car garage. At the side of the house, the land sloped downward toward the forest line.

Wolf whipped around and raised his nose, nostrils flaring.

The wind swirled against the house, but Patterson smelled nothing out of the ordinary—just pine, earth, maybe some rain.

"You smell something?" Yates asked.

"Smell what?" Rachette asked, sniffing too.

They stood with their noses in the air.

"Skunk?" asked Wilson.

"Weed?"

Wolf walked to the garage side door and sniffed again.

They followed him, and Patterson caught the scent of wood siding and gasoline.

She looked down and noticed Wolf had pulled his gun. "You okay?"

He holstered his piece and walked away down the side of the house, but not before she'd noted a flash of anger behind his eyes directed right at her.

The four men continued on, leaving her to contemplate what had just happened.

"I smell it," Wilson said.

Patterson blinked out of her reverie. She'd smelled it too.

"That's not weed," Rachette said.

A window at the corner of the house was darkened by

shades, but it was cracked open, releasing an odor from inside through the bug screen. Wolf had pulled his Leatherman multi-tool from the case on his belt and had a knife open. He pried it into the jamb and popped out the screen.

"What are you doing?" Wilson asked.

"Going in."

"Why?"

Wolf dropped the screen onto the grass. "Consider yourself lucky you don't recognize that smell."

"Shit." Wilson moved closer and helped him push up the window.

Wolf dove inside and disappeared as the blinds slapped up against the window.

"Hey!" Wilson pushed a hand through and lifted the wood slats. "Go to the back door and open it for us."

They went to the rear sliding glass window.

Inside, Wolf had his face pressed into his sleeve.

Patterson swallowed and steeled herself for a face-full of nauseating air. When Wolf slid open the door, the stench billowed outside as expected.

He stuck his head out, took a greedy breath of fresh air, and turned back around.

They piled into the house behind him and found themselves standing next to a kitchen table, their choked breathing filling the silence of the room.

"Awe, man. That is terrible," Rachette said, putting his sleeve over his mouth.

On the table stood a half-eaten bowl of cereal—Froot Loops judging by the circular blobs of color surrounding the spoon. The chair was pushed out.

Wolf eyed the hallway that led down to the front door. He walked and they followed, the baseboards beneath the linoleum creaking under their footfalls.

The smell grew unbearable as they came up to the front door. To the right, the darkened room that had been invisible from outside beckoned. There was a single chair in the center of the room, and a dead body lying next to it.

Yates made a heaving noise and rushed back down the hallway, almost ramming Patterson into the wall. He went out into the back yard and vomited. That sight, coupled with the immediate smell, made her own mouth start to water.

Wolf flicked on the light switch alongside the wall, setting the room ablaze.

Chris Alamy was sprawled on the ground. Congealed blood and matter from a hole in his skull had pooled near his head.

Patterson stepped forward and pointed at a pistol still clutched in his hand. "Look at that."

"He knew the jig was up," Rachette said.

More lightning flashed outside, and raindrops started popping the roof.

Without warning, Wolf ran past them, out the back door, hooked left, and disappeared out of sight.

"The hell's he doing?" Rachette jogged down the hall.

Patterson and Wilson looked at each other and followed.

Ice-cold rain slapped their heads as they went into

the back yard and blasted them all over as they rounded the house. Lightning hit close.

"Holy crap," Patterson said, just as thunder crashed.

"What are you doing?" Rachette stopped at the front of the house, yelling at Wolf.

But Wolf was inside his SUV, cranking the wheel and revving the engine. The vehicle jerked backward, then scraped to a halt and lurched toward them.

She put up her hands. "Stop!"

He honked his horn.

She held her ground.

He's gone mad, she thought. Completely, utterly mad.

Wolf honked again.

Wolf was leaning toward the windshield, peering out at her. He waved a hand for her to move to the side.

My God, what was he going to do? Ram the place? She held her ground.

Wolf opened his door. "Move!"

"No! What are you doing?"

"Covering those vehicle tracks!"

She looked down. She was standing on one of the two tracks Wolf had pointed out earlier. What she hadn't ruined with her feet was being obliterated by the huge drops of rain.

Shit.

She moved aside, and Wolf's vehicle slid in.

CHAPTER 18

PATTERSON WALKED into the room with Chris Alamy's corpse and stood at the entryway.

Wolf and Lorber were conversing near the body and stopped with her arrival.

"There she is," Lorber said. The ME lowered Alamy's dead hand to the floor and looked up over his glasses.

She noted the continued lack of eye contact from Wolf.

"What do you have?" she asked.

"Maybe some interesting stuff. Maybe not."

She eyed Wolf, who stepped back to let them talk. The sight made her bristle. She'd been dancing around the crime scene now for hours, watching Wolf dodge her wherever she went. Growing up with three older brothers, she knew what it was like to be shunned. She also knew how to deal with it.

"Interesting how?" she asked, stepping toward Wolf.

Lorber stood up and stretched his back. "Well, let's test Ms. Patterson, shall we?"

"Technically Mrs. Reed-Patterson, but whatever."

Wolf looked at her, a glint of amusement in his eye.

She smiled at him, feeling a small spike of optimism. Maybe he wasn't shunning her after all. Maybe she'd been hallucinating at the side of the house when he'd flashed that angry glare. And maybe Wolf hadn't read that she'd basically openly accused him of being a psycho by putting her arms up and standing in front of his SUV.

She felt another spike of guilt stab her in the gut. She needed a moment alone with him, but this wasn't the time or place.

"Come with me." Lorber walked out of the room and down the hallway to the kitchen table. Patterson followed, Wolf behind.

"Tell me, Detective, what's strange about this picture?"

She gestured to the bowl of cereal. "Maybe that he was sitting here, eating his bowl of Froot Loops, then decided to get up, walk to the other room, sit down, and off himself?"

Lorber smiled back at Wolf and pointed a long finger at her. "Correct."

"Rachette and I were already discussing that," she said.

Rachette was standing out in the drizzle. "What?"

"Nothing," Lorber said.

"Seems to me he was interrupted," she said. "If this was a last meal, you'd finish your Froot Loops before you did the deed."

"So, someone came over." Rachette poked his head inside the door. "That's what I was saying."

"Or he was eating," Wolf said, "and in a flash of inspiration got the idea. Went into the front room, and ... did the deed."

Patterson had to admit that could have been the case, but her gut was telling her otherwise.

"When will you have the gunshot-residue tests done?" Wolf asked.

"As soon as I get back. The GSR will take a couple of hours."

"Good." Wolf went outside and strode along the rear of the house.

Her spirits had lifted hearing Wolf speak in front of her, almost as if everything were back to normal, but they dropped a few notches as she watched his hasty exit.

"He's still not looking good," Lorber said.

"What the hell happened to him, anyway?" Rachette asked.

Patterson and Lorber eyed each other.

"What? Why's everyone being hush-hush about his heart attack? I mean, obviously it wasn't too big a deal if he's on his feet. My uncle had a heart attack and he had to hug a pillow to cough for a month because they sawed open his chest."

"I'm going to go check on him." Patterson ducked outside. She didn't want to continue down that path, and she knew that any conversation between Lorber and Rachette would fizzle out naturally before it had begun.

Sun poked through the clouds, lighting the drizzle floating out of the rear of the storm like diamond dust.

Her stomach growled, and for once it was the good kind, indicating she was hungry and not about to hurl. She was proud of herself for keeping it together while Yates had lost his lunch.

She rounded the side yard and saw the line of flashing vehicles parked along the county road at the bottom of the driveway. Uniforms swarmed the front of the house and hiked up and down the drive.

She spotted Wolf off to the left. He was walking away quickly, through the vehicles and up into the trees, as if he were headed on a nature hike. But there was urgency to his steps. Why was he running into the woods?

"What the hell?" she mumbled, because there it was again—he'd looked at his phone.

"Hey, how's Scott doing?"

She turned and saw Deputy Nelson standing next to her.

"Oh. Hey, Nelson. He's good." She pasted on a smile. "How about Elena?"

Nelson's face dropped.

"Oh, yeah. Sorry. You guys broke up. Listen, I have to go talk to Wolf. Sorry."

She marched away, threading through the vehicles and following Wolf's trail.

Dang, he was fast. Over the past few months the man had gotten in remarkable shape.

Talking to Scott a few weeks ago, she'd mentioned Wolf's new health-kick.

"Maybe he's trying to cleanse something from his system," Scott had said.

That had shut her up, because it was spot on. That

something was months of alcohol. And something else. Something mental. And she was sure of it after seeing him on the ground yesterday, writhing in that snow bank ... and now today with that gun in his hand. She hadn't hallucinated.

For the first time in the five years she'd known Wolf, she sensed he wasn't in control. The thought scared her. A world where David Wolf was not in control was a world she feared.

She climbed up the slope into the trees. Her lungs winded quickly, and she felt the baby's tiny body inside her as she stepped faster. She'd gotten lazy this pregnancy. Last time she'd worked out until the doctor had made her stop. This time, she'd ramped down her exercise routines to brisk walks and mild hikes.

She stopped for a second and listened, then spotted Wolf up near the edge of the trees at the top of the decline leading to the road.

He was staring at his phone.

She stepped lightly between the trees and stopped a stone's throw away. His lips were moving. She stared for a few seconds, trying to figure out if he was on speaker phone, reading aloud, or talking to himself. Then she pried her eyes away, feeling guilty. She needed to make her presence known now or leave.

"What?" he asked.

She hesitated, and then he turned her way. The look in his eyes startled her—like a raccoon who'd just been caught rifling a kitchen trash can. Unpredictable. Dangerous.

"I ... saw you come up here."

He pocketed his phone and looked away down the hill.

She walked toward him. "I saw you looking at your phone again."

He said nothing.

"Sir, listen. I—"

"See that construction site?" He pointed into the distance.

She stepped next to him and looked down at the wet valley. "Yeah. We saw one of those guys on the roof before the storm." She pointed at a group of three men firing nail guns. "The guy in the blue."

"We need to talk to them. See if they saw or heard anything."

She nodded. "Yeah. Of course. We'll do that."

Patches of sunlight grew and slid along the valley below, illuminating wisps of fog clinging to the trees. The snow-covered peaks above treeline shone bright.

"Pretty beautiful," she said. She sucked in a breath to apologize for her actions earlier. Or maybe she needed to stay quiet. The silence was too much.

"I have to head home." He flashed his phone and pocketed it. "Jack came up from Boulder."

"Oh, yeah. Okay."

He turned and slipped back into the trees, leaving her on the hillside.

"Bye," she said, not expecting a response. And none came.

CHAPTER 19

"Wolf!"

He stopped short of climbing in behind the wheel and turned to MacLean. "Yeah."

"So? How did it go?" MacLean marched up close.

"It looks a little suspicious with those tire tracks over there. And he left a meal uneaten, which suggests he was interrupted. Lorber has the gunshot-residue tests in progress."

MacLean made a show of flicking his eyes back and forth. "The therapy."

"Oh. Yeah. It went well." Wolf climbed into the seat and put in his keys.

MacLean wedged himself into the door. His gray eyes narrowed as he studied Wolf. Then he nodded and looked into the distance. "That's what the doctor said. I talked to him after your session. He said it was a good start."

Wolf searched for sarcasm in MacLean's voice, but found none.

"Where are you going?"

"Jack's in town. I have to head home and talk to him."

MacLean looked at his watch. "Shit. It's almost four. You get some rest." He slapped Wolf's shoulder. "Okay, go visit your son. And we'll see you tomorrow morning. We have this." MacLean stepped back and shut the door.

Wolf fired up the engine and rolled down the window. "Thanks."

It took a minute to back out of the steep driveway while avoiding the tent erected around the tire-tread evidence, but soon he was down the hill and back onto the county road. He turned right and headed west toward town, into the blazing late-day sun. He switched on the windshield wipers, swiping away blinding droplets of water, and pressed the gas.

He drove a short distance, over a rise and around a bend, then pulled over onto a muddy shoulder turnoff.

He rolled down both windows, letting in the cool, damp air. With slow deliberate inhales, he sucked in the rain and pine scent.

The phone felt like a hot coal in his pocket. A time-bomb. A vial full of deadly virus.

He pulled it out and unlocked it. The first text message held his gaze until he realized the sun had gone behind a cloud and the air streaming in had turned cold.

He hovered a shaking finger over the screen, then tapped the second message and typed out a response to Jack.

Hey. I'll be home in a few minutes.

A few seconds later a response came.

Cool. See you in a bit.

———

Thirty minutes later, Wolf pulled through the ranch headgate and saw Jack's Tacoma sitting in the circle drive.

Wolf felt shame warm his body as he pulled the vague memory of slapping his son from the depths of his mind. A week after the incident, Wolf had called Jack for two days, leaving a single voicemail saying he was sorry. He'd followed it up with a text message, which was promptly answered.

That's okay, Dad.

But it had not been okay.

The doctors were saying anxiety had overcome him the past few days, bringing him to the ground on that snowbank up on the pass, but all he felt now was warm calm as he faced seeing his son for the first time since he'd struck him.

The front door opened, and a German shepherd puppy lunged out, escaping from Jack's clutches, and ran down the steps to the front of Wolf's car.

He jammed the brakes and watched the dog zoom past, circle around, and start barking at Wolf through the glass.

Jack came out and yelled something as he ran across Wolf's bumper.

The dog sat just as Jack gripped his collar. His tail thumped, and his mouth hung open with a lolling tongue.

Wolf smiled and pulled forward to the carport.

He stepped out and walked to Jack, who was pulling back on the German shepherd's collar.

"Drifter! Heel! Sit!"

The dog was still a puppy but compared to the last time Wolf had seen him, he was huge. His ears flopped on top of his head, one of them stuck folded inside-out.

"Let him go!" Wolf said.

Jack hesitated. "What? No, I'll put him back inside."

"Let him go."

"You were just in the hospital."

"I'm fine. It was a false alarm."

Jack looked at him skeptically.

"Come on." Wolf clapped.

Jack let go of the collar.

The dog charged him, reaching full speed, and jumped from a distance.

Wolf sidestepped like a matador and watched Drifter land in a tumble.

"Whoa!" Wolf bent down and gave him a hard scratch before he could get up. Needle-like teeth clamped onto his hands.

"Drifter! No biting!"

Jack jogged up. "Shit, sorry. He's kind of out of control."

Wolf let go and allowed his son to take over.

Jack yelled commands, and for a few seconds seemed to hypnotize the dog into obeying.

Then one look to Wolf, and he began barking.

"Damn it! Shut up!" Jack looked more than frustrated.

Wolf stepped in and grabbed the collar. "Why don't you head inside?"

"Dad, let go. You had a heart attack, for Chrissakes. You go inside."

"I'm fine. It wasn't a heart attack. Like I said, it was a false alarm."

Jack gave him another doubtful look and stood back.

"Sit," Wolf said.

Drifter sat.

Wolf looked around. "You gonna be a good boy if we leave you out here?"

"He'll just run away."

Wolf brought Drifter to the barn, opened the workshop door, and fetched a long rope attached with a clip. He tethered the dog to the steel rod next to the building.

"Oh, yeah," Jack said. "I forgot you had that for Jet. I should have done that an hour ago."

Wolf found an old bone on the floor of the workshop, swept it free of cobwebs, and tossed it to Drifter. "There're a lot of canine treasures in here."

Jack appeared next to Wolf and wrapped him in a hug.

Wolf was surprised but returned the embrace without hesitation. "I'm so sorry." The words came out of Wolf's mouth like a false-starting sprinter.

"I know."

Wolf clamped his eyes shut and continued squeezing.

"Easy," Jack said.

Wolf let go and backed away.

"Geez," Jack said. "You're huge. You've been working out."

Wolf nodded. "And I see you've been keeping up with your regimen."

Some kids gained weight when they went to college, but for the past two years, Jack had taken an interest in fitness that was beyond a passing New Year's resolution. The kid was two-hundred pounds of pure muscle. His face was chiseled, speckled with short stubble that shaded his tanned face. His brown hair was thick, a few inches long, and disheveled, which had been his going style for years. He wore a hoodie and jeans. His hands were shoved in his pockets and he looked at the ground—two signs that something was bothering him.

Wolf patted his shoulder and Jack raised his gaze.

Pain lurked behind his son's green eyes, making him look younger than his twenty years.

"Where's Cassidy?" he asked.

"She's down in Gunnison with her brother for a few days. Her mom's down there, too."

Wolf nodded, sensing there was more to be said.

Jack looked at Drifter. The dog had taken up on the grass and was gnawing on the bone.

"I knew you'd be able to calm him down," Jack said.

They stared at the animal for a few seconds.

"Your house looks as clean as the last time we left."

Wolf nodded.

"And I saw that pile of glass on the side of the house."

He nodded again.

"Looks like you're doing well," Jack said. "So, what happened yesterday? Margaret called me this morning. Well, she called me last night, but I never got the message until this morning. It freaked me out. She said you'd had some sort of heart episode and no one has any information other than that. She said you left the hospital or something."

The sky was turning orange as the sun dipped behind the mountains. To the north, the storm was just a smear.

Jack's hand squeezed Wolf's shoulder.

"I'm fine now," Wolf said.

"But ... a heart attack?"

"No. It was just stress." Wolf shrugged. "That's why I was let out so early." He started walking to the kitchen entrance. "Let's get a drink."

"Stress? What's going on that's so ..." Jack stopped talking and followed.

They stepped up into the kitchen. Wolf turned on the lights and opened the refrigerator. "What do you want? I have"—he shut the door—"I have water, I guess."

Jack stood with his arms at his side, searching his father's face. "Stress?"

Wolf rolled his eyes. "I've been low on sleep lately. The job and everything. I've been working out a ton. It's just too much for my body, apparently. You know, stress."

Jack blinked and nodded, looking like he was pretending to like a meal he secretly hated.

"Anyway," Wolf said. "What's new with you?"

"Ah, nothing. Just, you know, hanging out. Working long hours at the pizza shop. Still doing that summer internship coming up in August." Jack's mouth opened to say some more. Then he closed it and nodded.

"What are you hiding from me?" Wolf asked.

"Nothing. Just ... you know, stress."

Wolf snorted. When the smile had faded from his

lips he said, "Tell me. I can read you like a *Where's Waldo* book."

Jack frowned. "And you think I can't see you're lying to me?"

They stood in silence for a beat.

"I don't know. I guess there's some stuff happening with Cassidy."

"Did you two break up?"

"No. Nothing like that." Jack turned around and looked out the window. He sighed. "Do you think ... shit, never mind."

"Do I think what?"

"Do you think you could take Drifter?"

Wolf stood in stunned silence.

Jack turned around. "Never mind. Of course you can't. You were just in the hospital because of stress. A hyped-up dog is the last thing you need right now."

Wolf silently agreed. Wholeheartedly.

Jack's eyes were tormented. He rubbed the side of his head.

"Why are you trying to get rid of the dog?" Wolf asked.

"Yeah, I know. It's evil. But ..." Jack was borderline hyperventilating.

"If you rub your hand through your hair like that enough, you might go bald."

"It's just ... Cassidy and I are going through some stuff. And we can't keep this dog. It's impossible. The thing is untrainable. I'm at work all the time and it stays home and barks. Cassidy's at work all day, too. The neighbors are complaining about him barking. The landlord is threatening us. And going forward ..."

Wolf narrowed his eyes. "Going forward, what?"

"Cassidy's pregnant."

Wolf thought he saw a flash of lightning but realized it had been his eyelids fluttering.

"Really."

"Yeah." Jack walked past Wolf, then appeared again, turned around, and did another lap across the kitchen. "Like, confirmed pregnant. Like, I've seen the ultrasound, and it's a boy, and she's definitely going to have it, and we're going to have it, and I'm definitely going to be a dad now ... and ..." Jack stopped and looked at him. "You're smiling? Shit, I thought you were going to have another heart attack at this news. But you're smiling."

"Sorry." Wolf straightened his mouth and watched his son do another anguished lap.

"So ... Cassidy's freaking out about the kid. I'm freaking out about the kid. And, meanwhile, we have this untrainable dog that's all over the place. He chews up the furniture. He's ... he's great. Please, don't get me wrong. But he's too much. We can't handle all of this at once."

A tear streamed down Jack's cheek.

Wolf pulled him into a hug.

Jack tensed under his arms, then relaxed. When Wolf let go, Jack wiped his face. "Sorry."

"For what?"

"For all of this."

Wolf shook his head. "I don't want you ever thinking you can't come to me."

"I know."

"And I'll take the dog."

Jack's eyes lifted. "No. Don't worry about it. I'll figure it out. We'll figure it out."

"I'll take the dog."

"You will?"

Wolf remembered the fur-scented breeze whipping past him a few minutes earlier. "Yeah. I will."

"I mean, you don't have Jet anymore, right? It's perfect."

"Yeah. Perfect."

Jack's face dropped. "You don't want to. Of course you don't want to." Jack paced some more. "We can't even teach him to sit. We can't get him to shut up. And now I'm here asking you to take over. How are we going to be as parents? We're going to be shit parents, I tell you that."

Wolf grabbed Jack's face with both hands. "Don't say that. Don't ever say that again. Ever in your life."

"Okay." Jack blinked. "Yeah."

"You're going to be great parents. You and Cassidy will be great." Wolf let go and stepped back, feeling heat rise in his cheeks.

They stood in silence.

Jack cleared his throat. "The dog thing really makes us doubt, you know?"

"Taking care of a dog is different than taking care of a kid. You can't put a kid in the back yard and go to work. Things will be different. They have to be. It's apples and oranges. And you'll have help. I'll do what I can, and I'm sure Cassidy's mom will do what she can."

Jack nodded, and Wolf saw a touch of confidence straighten his posture.

"You can do this."

Jack nodded again. "Thanks, Dad."

Wolf wanted to ask about Cassidy, but hesitated. He needed to take lessons from Jack and Cassidy about relationships, not the other way around.

Jack backed toward the door and reached for the knob. "Listen, I gotta go."

"Where are you going?"

"Gunnison."

"It's getting dark."

"I have to see her. It can't wait."

Wolf nodded. "Drive safe. Watch out for wildlife."

But Jack was out the door.

Wolf walked down the steps outside.

The sky was glowing like an electric oven.

Jack walked to Drifter and spoke a few words into his ear.

The dog's tail wagged, but it otherwise ignored Jack as it chewed the bone.

Jack quick-stepped to the truck and opened the door. He stopped and looked over the roof. "Thanks, Dad."

"You said that already."

"I knew that if I just came and talked to you, I'd have the strength to get through this." He ducked in, flicked on the lights, and started the engine. Then he drove down the driveway and out the headgate. And like a passing whirlwind, Jack was gone.

Wolf stared until the dust settled back to the ground in the still air.

Drifter looked at him, head cocked, as if trying to comprehend what had just happened.

"Shit. I don't have any food for you."

He picked up his phone and called Jack, but it went straight to voicemail. The cell dead zone started yards past the headgate.

Drifter barked and stood.

He could pick up some chow in the morning, but until then, the dog would have to deal with hunger.

Wolf unclipped him from the chain. "If you run away, then have a good night in the woods with the bears. Cause I ain't coming to get you."

Drifter cocked his head again.

Wolf slapped his leg. "Let's go."

They went up the stairs into the kitchen. Drifter passed Wolf's legs and darted to the far corner near the rear door.

The dog whined and wagged his tail. Against the wall stood a bag of puppy chow. Right where Jack had left it.

CHAPTER 20

NATE WATSON's house windows glowed in the pre-dawn hours. Secluded in the hills and far from other houses, Nate had little reason to worry about curtains or blinds.

Wolf pulled into the driveway. His friend had already seen him through the glass and was walking outside.

He stepped out of the SUV and heard two dogs barking in the back yard. To the side of the house, mist clung low to a meadow. Above it, the forest rose to a silhouetted mountain. The sky brightened, dotted with Venus and strafed with lenticular clouds glowing orange at the edges.

Wolf let Drifter out of the back seat and held the leash tight as he fetched the rest of the supplies from the floorboards and closed the door.

"What's happening?" Nate said, descending the steps. He wore flannel pants, a fleece, and a Colorado Rockies hat to cover the growing bald spot on his head.

Or to show his team pride. Wolf suspected it was fifty-fifty.

Wolf shut the door and clutched the hand of his life-long friend.

"You ignored my calls yesterday. I had to call the department to get answers about you."

"Yeah. Sorry about that. I got a lot of calls. I was ... ignoring them."

Nate looked at him long, then nodded. "I get it."

Wolf and Nate had known each other since elementary school. They'd fought each other, and other kids together. And they'd grown up playing football together throughout high school.

As it had been in the army with other soldiers, Wolf and Nate fighting together on the gridiron had cemented their bond. Wolf had been quarterback. Nate had been his running back and last line of protection from a charging defense. And never once had he backed down.

Nate's eldest son, Brian, had grown up with Jack, and they were still close. Nate owned a successful geological services company and spent a lot of time out of town. Aside from the occasional day fishing, the two men saw each other little nowadays, but their bond had stayed strong.

"Here's Jack's mutt, huh?" Nate bent down and scratched Drifter hard on the neck. "What's up, Drifter? How are you, boy?"

Drifter whined and wagged his tail. His tongue licked out and his whole body shook.

"Easy," Wolf said. "You're going to give him an orgasm."

Nate let go. "Thanks for that early-morning visual."

Wolf handed over the leash. "I really appreciate this."

"Yeah. No problem." Nate shook his head. "So, you're going to be a grandfather, huh?"

Wolf frowned. "How the hell did you know that?"

"Brian told me. He heard from Jack."

Wolf watched him walk away with the dog. "I don't feel so bad dropping this guy off anymore."

"He'll love it here with the two bruisers in the back yard."

Barks echoed from the rear of the house, as if Nate's two black Labs sensed fresh meat.

"Let's get a coffee next week. I'm in town," Nate said.

"Sure."

Wolf opened his door.

"Hey, Dave."

Wolf looked up and saw Brittnie, Nate's wife, standing in a robe and sipping coffee.

"Or should I say Grandpa?"

"Hi, Britt. Thanks. Bye." He shook his head and climbed in. With friends like these, who needed murders and suicides?

Twenty minutes later, he was back on the valley floor and heading for the north side of town on the highway.

The county building parking lot was full for 7 a.m. It seemed to contain most of the SBCSD fleet. Three news vans from Denver were lined up along the sidewalk, satellite booms extended. A reporter was talking into a lens with a bright light in her face. With Wolf's arrival, she gestured in his direction.

He parked and got out, and heard the reporters

coming his way before he saw them. They funneled through the cars with microphones extended, cameramen running behind them.

"Chief Detective Wolf, can we ask you a few questions about Warren Preston?"

Wolf plucked his bag from the rear seat and shut the door. For a moment, he had the vehicle between them and him. He opted to go to the front bumper and they moved to cut him off.

"Sorry, I can't comment at this time. Sheriff MacLean will talk to you later."

"Sir, is it true you had a panic attack on top of Huerfano Pass when you discovered Warren Preston's body?"

Wolf's insides lurched. He walked faster, ducking a shoulder to get through two cameramen.

A woman's voice came fast behind him. "Our sources are saying you had a panic attack, and that you were armed at the time. Do the people of Rocky Points have reason to be concerned? Wouldn't you be concerned if a civilian was armed during a panic attack?"

"It was a cardiac event," Wolf said under his breath.

"What's that, sir?"

"No comment." He reached the rear doors ahead of the swarm and went through.

One of the reporters followed him in. "Sir."

The second set of automatic doors opened, and Tammy Granger rushed toward them like a charging bear. "Get out of here!"

The reporter stopped and backed out.

Without breaking stride, Wolf went to the stairwell door and pushed it open. The door slammed shut behind him and he climbed. He stopped on the first landing and leaned against the wall.

His breaths came fast and shallow. He was close to hyperventilation.

"What the fuck?" he asked the empty stairwell.

He closed his eyes and sucked in a deep breath through his nose, then let it out his mouth. A few seconds later he was calm and collected, but still shaken. How had she known?

Wolf resisted screaming an obscenity and sucked in another couple of calming breaths. He'd battled dozens of Taliban after being ambushed in a box canyon. He'd raised a gun and shot down a boy who'd been about to blow up a crowd of people. He'd done that and then some. Why was this happening now?

He knew the answer. It was there, in his pocket, waiting on his phone.

The door above pushed open and someone started down the stairs.

Wolf pushed off the wall and walked up the steps.

"There you are."

Wolf looked up at the top of the next landing and saw MacLean. "What's up?"

MacLean waited for Wolf to get to his level.

Wolf passed him and continued upward.

"Wait a second."

Wolf kept going. "What?"

"Would you slow down?"

Wolf pushed open the third-floor exit and headed down the hall to his office.

MacLean followed in silence, but Wolf sensed him

on his heels as he ducked into the room and pulled the door closed.

"Ow, Jesus." MacLean pushed inside and clicked the door shut.

Wolf sat down and tapped the mouse.

Without speaking, MacLean took the seat across the desk.

They sat in silence for a full minute. Then MacLean leaned forward and put his elbows on his knees. "Did they ask you about the Pass?"

Wolf said nothing.

MacLean scratched his forehead and petted his mustache. "I'm under a lot of pressure. Somehow word got out. Somebody from the Vail Health Hospital or ... I don't know."

Wolf turned toward his bookshelves and stared.

"I'm going to have to address this. Which means your name's going to be thrown around. What happened is going to be public. I'm going to have to say I'm conducting an internal investigation."

Wolf rolled his neck. Tension crackled under his skin.

"It's not like you discharged your weapon into a crowd. We'll say you're undergoing therapy, which you are, and that will be that."

Wolf closed his eyes. The world seemed to swirl on the other side of his lids. Or maybe it was him swirling. "And in the meantime? What happens? You want my badge and gun?"

MacLean's silence was answer enough.

Wolf pulled his badge from his belt.

MacLean stood up. "No. I don't. But I'm putting

Patterson on case lead. Which means you do what she says, when she says."

Wolf sat back.

"Situation meeting in twenty minutes."

The sheriff walked out and shut the door.

Wolf stood, leaving his badge and gun on the desk, and faced the window. His reflection stared back at him, blocking the brightening view of the mountains outside.

He reached into his pocket and pulled out his phone. The screen glowed to life, and he pressed the messages button.

The text from Lauren stared at him—urgent, needing.

He reached inside his pocket again and pulled out the business card. He dialed the number.

"Hello?"

"This is David Wolf."

"Hello."

"I need to speak to you."

"I'm pretty booked this morning."

"This early?"

"Oh. You mean now?"

"You told me I could call you anytime. Or was that just something you say to all your patients?"

"Clients."

Wolf said nothing.

Hawkwood exhaled. "Sure. Come on over. I'll be in the office a few minutes."

"No can do."

"No can do?"

"I have to work. I want to talk now. On the phone."

Hawkwood exhaled again. "I have to pull over—just a second."

Wolf listened to the phone rustle and heard a car door opening and closing. "Okay. My first session from the road overlooking Rocky Points. Not a bad view, I must say."

"Where are you?"

"McCall Mountain Road."

Wolf knew the spot. When he'd returned from his six tours, he and Sarah had dreamed of buying a house up there, but it had been way beyond their budget.

"You live up there?" Wolf asked.

"Yeah. A townhome a couple miles up the canyon."

Wolf stared out the window toward where he pictured the doctor standing, though it was impossible to see from the angle.

"What's bothering you, David?"

Wolf rubbed his fingers into his eyes. "Everyone knows the truth about my episode on the mountain."

Hawkwood took a loud breath. "I'm sorry to hear that."

"I don't care," Wolf said. He paced the room. "It was bound to come out."

Hawkwood said nothing.

"I killed a boy once."

Hawkwood remained silent.

"I've never told anyone that in my life, except for right now. Not even my wife, when I came home from the army."

The line hissed.

"You there?"

"Yes. Sorry. What happened?"

Wolf told the story of Sri Lanka and the boy with the backpack full of explosives, and Wolf's quick decision. When he'd finished, he stared through glassy eyes out the window, sweat beading on his forehead.

"Thanks for telling me that, David. I know that must have been hard."

"I've already dealt with that," Wolf said. "I mean ... I thought I had."

"Seems like it would be hard to completely deal with that, no matter how many years passed."

"And then there was Ella."

"Lauren's eight-year-old daughter," Hawkwood said.

Wolf nodded. "Yes."

Someone knocked on Wolf's door. He turned around, walked to the knob and twisted the lock.

They left.

"So ... how do you think Ella is triggering your memory of this boy?"

"I let her down."

"How?"

"I told her I would marry her. Marry her and her mother. And then I left her."

"It was my understanding that Lauren left you. She was unable to take the stress of being the wife of a law-enforcement officer."

Wolf said nothing.

"Am I right?"

"It didn't make it any less difficult for Ella."

Hawkwood let the silence sit for a while. "Have you ever heard of a samskara?"

"No."

"The word has several meanings in Indian philosophy. I like to think of them as trapped energy stored in our hearts."

Wolf frowned. "I'm not sure I believe in this type of thing."

"When you had your episode, where was the pain?"

Wolf rubbed a hand over his chest. "Point taken."

"A samskara starts with an event. Of course, events happen to us, around us, all the time. Most events pass through us harmlessly. We walk down the hallway, hit our foot on a chair, and we stub our toe. We hiss in pain, and we move on with our lives. We might have a slight limp for a day or two, but other than that, we move on, unaffected. But what if somebody had pushed that chair in front of us and we stubbed our toe? Did Sally mean to do that? Was she trying to hurt me?"

"Sounds like it. Sally pushed a chair in front of you."

Hawkwood sighed. "The point is, the first event passed through you. You never even thought of it again. The second event? Well, now you're wondering about Sally all day. What did you say to her? What pissed her off to the point she's acting psycho around the office, trying to trip you up with a chair? Or ... maybe she accidentally knocked it, just like she told you. But, then again, maybe she meant it. Maybe she wants your job. Maybe she's always had it in for you? Or wait a minute—maybe she's pissed about that time you went out with her boyfriend in high school. Could she still be angry about something that happened twenty-five years ago?"

Wolf said nothing.

"Are you there?"

"Yes. I'm a woman who stole Sally's boyfriend."

"Right. You stole Sally's boyfriend. Or she accidentally kicked the damn chair in front of you. That's a samskara. That swirling energy inside of you. Those emotions. Now it's stuck there, sometimes forever. Every single time you think about it, it flares with the same intensity as it did during the actual event that created it. Your body goes into that state. It releases chemicals, hormones, and puts you right back into that place. Unless you let it out of you, every time you kick a chair from now on you could trigger this thing. Hell, it could get so bad that the sight of a chair sets it off."

"Okay. I'll buy it. It exists. So how do I get rid of it?"

"By letting it go."

Wolf sat down and scratched his head. "By letting it go."

"I can't complicate it any more than that."

Wolf looked at the clock on the wall—four minutes to the sit-room meeting. The sound of Hawkwood's footsteps stopped in the background.

"Listen. Thanks for taking my call, Doc. I really do have—"

"—to go. Yeah, I know. Have a good day. And you're welcome to call me anytime."

Wolf hung up and stared at the phone. He dropped it on the desktop, then picked it up again.

Without thinking, he scrolled to Lauren's text and tapped a reply into the bubble.

That's terrible to hear. Of course I'll agree to do that. When?

He stood up fast. His chair crashed into the wall behind him.

He expected an hour or two wait for a response, but the phone chimed immediately.

Thank you. How about tomorrow?

The world stopped. Tomorrow. He turned to the window and replied.

Sure. What time?

How about 4 p.m.?

See you then.

Bye.

Wolf considered a response, but he'd already said goodbye to her once.

He pocketed his phone, feeling a rush of adrenaline spiking his veins. The fuse was lit.

He unlocked the door and walked to the sit room.

CHAPTER 21

PATTERSON WAS USED to getting up in front of the squad room and speaking in front of a bunch of male deputies and personnel by now. But it always irked her to see only men staring back at her whenever she conducted the situation-room meetings.

The department, and the county building they were in, employed plenty of females, but where were they now when the fire was getting hot? Of course, she was the one they turned to, to make sure these meetings ran with purpose and precision. She guessed that was something.

As she bent over her computer and opened her presentation, whispers of Wolf's name bounced off the ceiling and walls. It seemed to be the only topic of conversation in the building this morning. She could only imagine how Wolf felt right now. She'd left the department before it had gotten to this point. She'd been a coward and run.

The room was smothered in a blanket of silence, and she didn't have to look up to know he'd entered the room.

He walked down the center aisle.

She cringed as everyone looked, like he was a bride.

ADA Hanson said something to him that sounded cordial. Wolf nodded and took his seat quickly next to Rachette.

She pried her eyes from the spectacle. It was her duty to pull the heat off him.

"All right, looks like everyone's here. Let's get started."

MacLean cleared his throat and stood. "Uh, before we do, I'd like to say a few words."

"Yes, of course, sir."

MacLean walked to the front and center. "I want to address the situation at hand, right now, with everyone in the room, before this turns into a wildfire spread by a bunch of unsubstantiated rumors."

Wolf was like a statue.

She averted her eyes and sat on the edge of the table.

"If anyone says a word to the media about what's going on with any of our fellow deputies, either with any current situation that may or may not be happening, or any future situations that might occur, I will personally shove my fist so far up their ass I'll be combing their hair through their nostrils. Thanks, Patty." He sat down.

"Thank you, sir."

A tiny ripple of laughter washed over the room.

"I am not joking!"

The room went still.

She took a breath and began. "This meeting will consist of Dr. Lorber sharing his findings from yesterday's crime scene. Our detective team has uncovered some major details, and we're still waiting on some others. We'll go over that, too. Dr. Lorber?"

Lorber stood up and Patterson took a seat in the front row next to MacLean.

The ME clicked the laser pointer and three side-by-side graphs came up onscreen.

"This left graph is a representative average emission spectrum of a positive gunshot-residue test. You can see our spikes of barium and lead." He circled the laser. "This next graph is from a subject known to have not fired a weapon for more than ten days prior to testing and has recently washed their hands with soap and water." He circled the laser again. "You can see the spikes in calcium, sodium, and potassium, but the spikes of barium and lead are absent."

Lorber circled the third graph. His point was clear—the heading above read *Chris Alamy*, and the GSR graph looked exactly like the hand-washer next to it, but he said it anyway.

"Chris Alamy has no gunshot residue on his hands."

The room murmured.

"We also found a number of prints that didn't belong to Alamy on beer bottles found in his recycling bin, on the toilet seat, and on the living-room coffee table. These suggest that Alamy was friends with this person and had spent time with him recently."

"Him?" MacLean asked.

Lorber raised an eyebrow. "Judging by the size of the prints and number of beer bottles with the prints on them, the person was a heavy drinker. And ..." Lorber turned and scrolled through a few images, landing on a partial next to a full print. "I'll just skip to the good stuff here. We have a match for our partial print on Warren Preston's door handle."

Lorber nodded at Patterson.

She stood up and took the clicker. "Thank you, Dr. Lorber."

"You got it."

She went to the laptop and clicked open the next presentation. A picture of a blue Ford pickup truck showed up onscreen. "Yesterday afternoon, we spoke to three construction workers across the street from Chris Alamy's house. All said they'd witnessed some commotion happening up at Alamy's house two days ago—the same day we were uncovering Warren Preston's body up on Huerfano Pass.

"They said a man was parked out front of Chris Alamy's in a truck exactly like this. They reported that the truck honked repeatedly, and then drove off quickly down the hill and back toward town on County 18."

Rachette raised his hand.

Patterson nodded to him.

"One of the guys was adamant that the driver had been parked there for thirty minutes," Rachette said. "So it's not like he was there to pick him up—you know, drive up and honk, and Chris comes out and hops in. I asked that, and they said, no. He was there for a half-hour, laid on his horn a few times, then peeled off down the hill."

The room flicked their eyes back to Patterson.

"Dr. Lorber and his team took casts of the tire treads," she said. "Moving on."

She clicked the pointer and a list came up. "We

compiled Chris Alamy's call history, and a single person comes up repeatedly."

She walked to the computer and called up the web browser. A business website, Hood Rock Quarry, glowed onscreen. Pictures of rocks slid by in rhythm.

"This is a flagstone rock quarry up in Brushing." She clicked on the Employees link and circled her pointer around the first picture. "This is Zack Hood, the president of the company."

She stood and paced the front of the room. "We went to Preston Rock and Supply yesterday, and learned that a month after Warren Preston's disappearance, Chris Alamy changed suppliers of their flagstone to Zack Hood's company."

"Flagstone," MacLean said. "That was the rock found in Preston's skull."

Patterson nodded and clicked to the next slide. Two more graphs shone onscreen.

Lorber took his cue and stood up. "On the left is our spectrophotometer reading of the microscopic rock fragments found in Warren Preston's skull. On the right is the rock found at Preston Rock and Supply yesterday by Patterson, Yates, and Wilson."

"And Rachette," Rachette said.

"You can see that the two samples match," Lorber continued.

"Aren't there many rock quarries selling flagstone throughout Colorado?" Wolf asked. "Could this sample in Preston's skull match the quarry, say, down in Lyons, or somewhere else?"

"No," Lorber said. "That front range quarry is a

completely different geologic formation, with a different spectral signature."

"So you checked?" Wolf asked.

Wolf seemed so calm and collected. So ... normal, even after a public humiliation not thirty minutes in his past.

"Patterson."

She blinked and saw Lorber staring at her with wide eyes. "The next slide."

"Sorry. Yes." She clicked the button.

A matrix of eight spectral graphs lit up the screen.

"I checked," Lorber said. "And you can see here that the peaks and valleys of the mineral-composition graph do not match in intensity with the others." Lorber pointed at the screen. "This is an analysis found on the USGS website of all the flagstone deposits within the state. Back one slide, Patty."

She clicked back, and the two graphs came back up.

Lorber pointed. "The flagstone found at Preston Rock and Supply was the stone used to kill Warren Preston. Furthermore, the rock was quarried at the Hood flagstone quarry in Brushing."

Lorber sat down.

"Thank you," she said.

Wilson raised a finger. "But we know Preston Rock and Supply only started carrying this version of flagstone a month ago. Which means somebody brought that rock down three months ago and smacked Warren Preston over the head with it."

"Could Preston have been up in Brushing?" MacLean asked.

"Not likely," Patterson said. "His phone was down here the whole day, on his person. I say he was killed that night with Chris Alamy. Zack Hood. He fits the bill."

DA White leaned into MacLean's ear and whispered something.

"Here's some more," she said.

"More?" MacLean scoffed. "Looks like we have ourselves a layup of a lead."

"Well, let's make it a slam dunk, shall we?" She clicked back over to Alamy's phone information again. "This is the last five days' activity on Alamy's phone. Alamy's all over the place, speaking to different suppliers spanning the western US." She circled the laser around the final number. "But guess who that last number belongs to."

"Zack Hood," Yates said.

"Yep."

MacLean leaned forward. "So, what are we saying here? Zack Hood comes down, meets with Alamy and Preston, brings down his flagstone. Then bashes Preston over the head it. Then he and Alamy do their dance, dropping off Alamy's phone at his house, dropping Preston's vehicle at his house with all his personal pocket belongings, bury Preston, and then Hood drives back to Brushing."

She nodded. "That's what we're suggesting."

"We need Zack Hood's phone records. Financials."

"That we do," she said.

Rachette stood up and handed some papers to the DA. "Here're the warrants for financials, phone records, murder weapon in the form of rock from his quarry, and arrest."

DA White straightened in his chair and perused the papers. He eyed MacLean.

MacLean flicked a glance toward Wolf.

Wolf looked at Patterson.

MacLean walked to Patterson and turned his back on the room. "You think this is solid?"

"I'd like to see his cell records for yesterday, and for back in March. Financials, too," she said.

"But he's the guy."

She looked at Wolf. He was staring back at her without expression. "He's the guy."

"All right." MacLean turned to face the room. "First things first. Let's go get Hood. Bring him in and make him talk before he lawyers up. Patterson, Rachette, Yates, bring Wilson." MacLean looked at Wolf. "Everyone's dismissed but those I just mentioned. Wolf, I need to talk to you up here."

The room erupted as people stood and streamed out.

Wolf joined his team, Wilson, and MacLean at the front of the room.

MacLean stood with his hands on his hips, staring at the floor until the room had cleared. His eyes flicked up and landed on Wolf.

Wolf stared back, unblinking.

"I want you with them when you talk to Hood," he said. "But I want you to let Rachette, Yates, and Wilson take care of bringing him in." He pointed at Patterson. "You got that? I don't want you in there either. You're to keep yourself and that baby of yours well away from any action. You and Wolf will talk to him." He pointed at Wilson. "And I want you guys picking up some muscle from Brushing PD. I'll arrange a meet before you go."

"Go where? The quarry?" Rachette asked.

"We could call, see if he's there," MacLean said.

"He knows we found Warren Preston's body. He just killed Alamy. He sees us there, he'll be jumpy," Wolf said. "I think it's best to show up unannounced. We'll start at the quarry, then go to his house or elsewhere to find him if need be."

"We, meaning Rachette, Yates, and Wilson, and the Brushing units, who will take him into custody," said MacLean.

"Got it."

MacLean narrowed one eye. "Rachette, Yates, and Wilson take him."

"You just said that. Twice," Wolf said.

"And I meant it." MacLean looked at Patterson and then back to Wolf. "Both times."

"Got it," she said.

"Move."

CHAPTER 22

WOLF DROVE ALONE in his unmarked SUV, trailing behind two more driven by Rachette and Yates.

To his relief, nobody had protested when Wolf told them he was driving himself, and nobody offered to ride with him.

He let himself be hypnotized by the dotted line as they exited the winding road of the Cave Creek wilderness and joined the high plain valley south of Brushing.

The dash thermometer read eighty-one degrees, balmy for a June morning at eighty-five-hundred feet. Bluegrass music floated from Wolf's speakers, quiet enough to remain under the radio chatter, but not loud enough to drown out his thoughts.

He kept his mind on Jack, and on what must be going through his son's mind now that he had a baby coming into this world, and while he himself was so young.

Wolf had been around the same age, and although he'd been an adult, he remembered feeling that his childhood had been robbed with Jack's arrival. Then again, he hadn't been around for much of Jack's formative years.

And then there was Sarah. She had taken to motherhood poorly, becoming hooked on painkillers.

He sucked in a deep breath and exhaled, remembering the certainty in his son's face as he'd declared how shitty a parent he was going to be.

No. Jack was different. He was the best of both of them.

The radio scratched. "Okay, we'll be taking a left on County 41, coming up in one mile," Patterson's voice came through the speaker.

"Copy," Yates said.

Wolf picked up the handset and thumbed the button. "Copy."

They drove the mile, hooked the left, and took a dirt road lined with cattle fields. A ways later, the planted fields ran out and natural landscape took over—stunted juniper and pinyon pines warped by the relentless Colorado wind.

The soil was a deep, brick red, like that in the valley between Carbondale and Aspen over the peaks that lay ahead of him.

The road climbed toward a line where pine trees took over in the distance, but Wolf saw his destination parked alongside the road much closer than that.

Three brown Brushing PD trucks were lined on the shoulder, and five officers in uniform stood at the rear of one truck, watching the SUVs approach.

So much for sneaking up on Zack Hood, he thought. Not that it took much imagination to figure out who was inside the matching maroon unmarkeds with wobbling oversized antennas. If Hood wasn't already on edge, three light-bars would definitely put him there.

Wolf pulled up last and got out.

"Damn, look at that," Rachette said, looking at the view behind Wolf.

The valley floor below was a flat checkerboard of bright green sliced in half by a sharply meandering river. Forest and frosted peaks stood tall as a backdrop.

Wolf was last up to the powwow of handshakes with the five officers from Brushing. They were all young save the lieutenant, who did the speaking.

Lieutenant Jake Poncha was a burly man a decade Wolf's senior. His stomach was bulbous, his arms cannons, his legs stumps.

"Wolf, how are you?" Wolf shook his sandpaper-rough hand and nodded, wondering how deep the question dove.

"How's Jack?"

He smiled. "He's good."

"Good to hear."

"How about your two daughters?" Wolf had forgotten their names.

"Chelsea's out in North Dakota, married to an oil rigger. Has three kids." He flipped a hand in the air. "Rachel's out in New York, working at some coffee shop."

"Central Perk?" Rachette smiled and looked around.

"What?"

"Nothing. I'm Detective Rachette."

"You said that."

"Right."

"This is Alexander, Ryder, Underman, and Patricks."

The names passed by Wolf like the breeze coming from the west, but he shook their hands in turn. They looked poised for action, but not looking forward to it.

Wolf looked to Patterson.

She cleared her throat. "So, do we know Hood's here?"

"We did a drive-by past his house in town and he wasn't there," Poncha said. "Which gives us good odds he's up at the quarry. We haven't checked yet though. Just been waiting on you guys."

"You know him?" she asked.

Poncha smirked, and so did some of the other officers. "We know him."

"In what way?"

"His dad used to own the quarry up here. Zack's worked for him all his life. Father–son operation. His dad died last year, and ever since Zack's been ... I don't know." He looked at the tallest officer behind him. "On a streak of bad behavior? Let's just say we're not surprised you're up here."

"What kind of bad behavior?" Wolf asked.

"We've had a few complaints from his neighbors for noise," Poncha said. "Then there was a co-worker who came in, all beat to hell. Apparently, Zack had accused one of his employees of cheating on his hours or something. The employee said that he'd told Zack that his father would have never accused him of something so stupid, or anything for that matter. Well, Zack didn't like that. Punched him up real good. Guy had a black eye, fat lip."

"If you have his prints on file, we can check them against the partial we found on Warren Preston's car," Patterson said. "That would be a—"

Poncha held up a hand. "We don't have them. We never processed him. Guy never pressed charges. He came in, made a statement, then came back the next morning and recanted it. As far as we know, he still works up there." Poncha shrugged. "Whatcha gonna do? Guy doesn't want us to go after him, we're not going to."

Patterson seemed less than satisfied. "Well, how far is it to the quarry?"

"About a mile, on the other side of this hill." Poncha pointed.

The road disappeared around a low mountain covered in evenly spaced pinyons. The next layer of mountains were covered with thick pine forest; beyond that, a peak above treeline.

Wolf searched the landscape for a cut in the earth or rising dust but saw neither.

Poncha followed his gaze. "They have the cut coming in from the other side."

A low rumble floated on the wind, sounding like earth-movers in the far distance.

"I'm concerned about our cover as we drive in," Wolf said.

"Our cover?" Poncha pinched his brows.

"We roll up with six vehicles, three of which are police trucks, he might do something."

"More bad behavior," Rachette said.

Poncha shrugged. "Not sure what we're going to do about that."

Wolf looked to Patterson.

She sighed. "I'm all ears for suggestions."

"I'll go in and get him. By myself."

"No."

Wolf eyed her. "I go in like I'm a customer, asking for the boss. I put him under arrest."

"You're not going in." Her tone said she was serious about MacLean's orders.

Poncha chuckled. "MacLean said you guys wanted some muscle. We're here to give you some. Let's go in there loud and proud."

She nodded. "I don't want to expose anyone. Safety in numbers."

Wolf watched as she laid out the plan.

CHAPTER 23

"STOP HERE," Patterson said.

Wolf slowed and parked the SUV on the shoulder of the dirt road.

Patterson took off her seatbelt and got out.

He watched her walk to the front bumper and tried to ignore the small part of his brain protesting the situation. Just a few short years ago she was that wide-eyed kid sitting in his office, fresh out of the academy and looking for a job. Now she was giving him orders, cock-sure in her determination to follow her own instincts and not his.

A tinge of pride eclipsed his reluctance, and he shifted into park and shut off the engine.

He stepped out and joined her at the front bumper to observe the action from a distance. Wolf had a bad feeling, and the fact that he and Patterson were a few football fields away, helpless to contribute should something go awry, helped little.

Up the road, the other five vehicles slowed, took a right turn, and sped toward the Hood quarry.

He stepped into the ditch at the side of the road, kicking up grasshoppers from the weeds, and hiked up the incline to get a clear view. Patterson followed.

They stopped in the shade of a fragrant juniper and watched.

In the distance, Rachette and Yates pulled through the gate and parked near an outbuilding. The huge cloud of red dust kicked up by their tires announced their entrance.

Inside the perimeter fence, a handful of workers milled around while others used small tractors with caged operator seats for heavy lifting. They swarmed like ants around rectangular chunks of red rock. Giant steps cut into the rock loomed behind them.

The action slowed, and some of the workers climbed out of their machines to view the action.

Wolf and Patterson stood silent, observing. In between breezes, the sun baked Wolf's neck.

And then movement caught his eye.

"You see that?" He pointed.

One of the workers jumped out of a compact Bobcat loader and sprinted toward the building.

Patterson put the radio to her lips. "We see a single worker running from the yard toward the building."

"What?" The voice was barely audible over the sound of car doors slamming.

The worker disappeared behind the structure.

She repeated herself.

"We copy," Rachette said. "Moving in."

Wolf flicked his eyes to their cavalry, and saw Rachette, Wilson, Yates, and the others moving fast toward the outbuilding. They all had their guns drawn.

The building was made of corrugated steel with an aluminum skin. Roll doors were wide open on the near and far sides, so Wolf and Patterson could see through it. Inside, their sprinter appeared, straddled a motorcycle, and began kicking the starter.

"He's in the building," Wolf said into the radio. "He's getting on a motorcycle."

"He's on a motorcycle!" Rachette's voice boomed from their speakers. "Where?"

"Inside the building."

The sound of a revving four-stroke engine reached their ears. The guy rode out of the garage and turned away from the entrance, back toward where he'd jumped out of his tractor.

The rider shifted gears and the motorcycle roared in protest.

Wolf pulled his gun. Patterson looked at him and pulled her own.

"What's he doing?" Patterson asked.

They watched in awe as the motorcycle continued to accelerate straight toward the fence.

Then it shot through.

"There's another exit," Wolf said.

The bike's motor wound down and tires scraped, kicking up a ball of dust. Wolf wondered if it had crashed but the revs started again and the bike appeared from the cloud and shot back along the outside of the fence.

"He's headed back your way," Patterson said into the radio. "Along the exterior of the fence."

The motorcycle dove down and flicked in and out of sight between the junipers.

Wolf turned and ran down the hill.

"What are you doing?" Patterson called behind him.

He reached the driver's door, got in and fired up the engine.

"Wait!" Patterson yelled.

Wolf hesitated and looked out the windshield just in time to see Patterson slipping onto her backside. While she struggled to get up, he shifted into drive and hit the gas.

Up the road, the dirt bike appeared out of the trees, dipped down into the drainage ditch, and launched into the air.

"That's Hood!" The radio burst to life. "We have confirmation—that's Hood on the motorcycle!"

"Wolf!" Patterson's voice came through the dash radio speaker.

The ease at which Hood twisted the bike in the air and landed on the road was impressive. He ducked in his seat, then shrank as he shifted through the gears and disappeared around the next bend in a deep-leaning skid.

Wolf hit the gas, looking up the quarry driveway on the way by. The other five vehicles were trying to shuffle through the entrance.

A figure burst from the trees and ran into the road in front of him.

He jammed the brakes and twisted the wheel, narrowly avoiding killing a man.

From a cloud of dust, Rachette appeared at the

passenger window. He jumped in, breathless and wide-eyed. "Go!"

Wolf hit the gas.

CHAPTER 24

"Jesus, he's a freakin' Arenacross racer!"

Wolf agreed. The V6 305-horsepower engine was having trouble catching up. On the straight stretches, Hood zipped away with suicidal speed. Around corners, he accelerated impossibly. At the last turn he flew into a hairpin turn, launched off the road, and used the steep embankment cut into the mountain as a berm.

Wolf jammed the brakes and the tires skidded, rumbling the cab.

Then Hood was gone again, a thin wisp of dust the only proof he'd ever been there.

"What's happening?" asked Patterson through the radio.

"We're in pursuit," said Rachette. "He's headed up into this canyon here. We're just following. He's fast as shit."

"Copy. We're on your tail."

Rachette lowered the radio and eyed Wolf.

Wolf gave him a sidelong glance. "She's pregnant. I didn't want her in pursuit with me."

"I didn't say anything."

They continued along the road, following the dust around three more turns. The road climbed and they entered the pine forest.

The trees were dense on either side. The road was hard-packed and less gravelly, and Hood's aerial trail had disappeared.

Rachette pointed up the mountain to Wolf's left. "There his is! He turned off there!"

Wolf hit the brakes and stopped at a two-track dirt road leading straight up through the pines at a steep angle.

"Jesus." Rachette leaned forward and craned his neck. He put his seatbelt on. "Let me guess. You're going to—"

Wolf twisted the wheel and punched the gas.

The front end rose up and the rear dipped down.

Wolf bounced hard in his seat, but he kept a firm grip on the wheel.

"Holy cow!" Rachette grabbed the ceiling bar.

The path in front of them disappeared, obscured by the hood of the SUV. Wolf kept his foot on the gas, knowing if they lost momentum they'd likely not make it any higher.

He kept the vehicle moving through a gap in the trees, hoping the tires would miss any big rocks or pits.

The engine lurched and revved high, and when the SUV slowed almost to a halt, he lifted off the gas, twisted the four-wheel knob to low and pressed the gas again.

The engine screamed, but the tires seemed to grow claws and the SUV climbed steadily.

The front end dropped, and the jeep trail re-emerged in the windshield. They were through the tough part. The rest of the way looked benign in comparison. Wolf shifted back into four-wheel-high and pressed the gas again, gaining more speed.

"We're almost at the top!" Rachette yelled a few minutes later.

Wolf saw it, too. The trees thinned out, and now they were looking at more clouds between the pines. The slope eased and they summited the mountain.

The lodgepole pines were widely spaced amid fields of grass. Beyond lay a sea of mountains, and the end of the road.

The two-track led into a dirt turnaround. A barbed-wire fence ran across the road, and on the other side the twin ruts were grown over with grass and weeds.

Wolf slid to a stop and he and Rachette got out.

A cool breeze howled in the trees, making the barbed wire sing. Sweat dripped from under Wolf's arms, and his hands were tight from the drive up.

"Where did he go?" Rachette asked.

Wolf studied the ground. No tracks.

The dash radio came to life with Patterson's voice. "... come in!"

Rachette opened the door and plucked the radio from the receiver. "Rachette here. Come in."

"Where are you guys?"

Wolf walked away from the vehicle toward the dilapidated fence. He looked down the length of it, back where they'd come. Hood could have slipped off the trail to the right and gone in the opposite direction into the forest.

He turned around. The fence extended through widely spaced lodgepoles and down a slope that ended at the pinyon pines. Further down, Brushing glittered on the valley floor.

"I said we followed him up a jeep trail. We're sitting at the top of the mountain now."

The breeze lulled for a moment, and a rumbling noise reached Wolf's ears.

He twisted around toward the way they'd come and saw Zack Hood in the distance, edging his front tire toward the barbed-wire fence a hundred or so yards away.

"There he is!" Wolf pointed.

Hood stopped the bike, raised a hand toward them, and fired two shots from a handgun.

A bullet whistled past into the valley.

"He's shooting!" Wolf ducked behind the SUV.

Rachette ducked down in the passenger seat. "Son of a bitch!"

Hood's bike reared up as he popped a wheelie. Then he crashed into the uppermost strand of barbed wire with the underside and landed hard back on both wheels.

Wolf pulled his gun and stepped out. The fence next to him pinged and bounced.

Hood was hopelessly out of range, but Wolf took two shots anyway.

The motorcycle revved hard, and then Hood was over the fence as if it were a minor obstacle, churning through gears as he disappeared over a grassy rise.

CHAPTER 25

THE SCENT of cigarette smoke coming from the two Brushing officers made Patterson feel like hurling.

"Okay, we have a chopper on the way." Poncha pocketed his cell phone and turned to her. "Got a Summit County SD bird on the way down, and they're looking to bring in a Grand Junction news copter."

"Where's that news copter from yesterday when we need it?"

"What's that?"

"Nothing. Sounds good."

A reflection down the road caught her eye, and she turned to see a truck's silver grill climbing up the canyon, trailing a plume of dust.

She walked away from the tobacco fest, back to her home team.

"There's a chopper on the way from Summit," she told Wolf.

Wolf nodded.

She was still fuming over his leaving her on her ass in

the dirt and driving away, but she was trying to let the anger evaporate. He'd been trying to keep her safe. Or was he pissed that she was running the show?

That was the question.

"What's up?"

Wolf's words startled her. She realized she'd been staring at him. "Nothing."

"I'm sorry for leaving you back there."

She nodded. "I know you were just trying to protect me, right?"

"Who's gonna ride those puppies?" Rachette stepped between them, pointing at the truck.

The pickup parked behind their line of vehicles.

Dust washed over them, and Patterson held her breath and squinted until it blew past on a gust of wind.

The men gathered around the trailer.

Strapped onto the flatbed stood two dirt-bikes and four four-wheeler ATVs. The ATVs were blazoned with the Sluice–Byron County logo. The dirt-bikes were blue, dotted with stickers. One had a sixty-nine on the front number plate.

Within a few minutes the six vehicles were off the ramp and parked at the rear of the trailer.

After losing Zack Hood, Wolf and Rachette had descended the steep trail to the road and met Patterson and the others. Alexander had driven away quickly under Poncha's orders. Now he was back with their goodies.

That Hood had fired shots at Rachette and Wolf sent a jolt of adrenaline into Patterson's system whenever she thought about it. The stress was compacting her insides, especially with the baby inside of her. The more they waited around, the worse it got.

She'd wanted to move earlier, but the local boys were adamant that the mountains surrounding them had hundreds of miles of trails and dirt roads and any effort would be wasted, if not counterproductive. Now that they had eyes in the sky and ATVs they could move.

"Whose bikes?" Rachette asked Alexander.

"Yours truly. You ride?"

Rachette scoffed. "I can do ATVs. Not bikes though."

"I do," Wolf said.

Patterson watched in resignation as he took the helmet from Alexander's hand and slipped it over his head.

Wolf pulled it off and nodded. "Good fit."

Alexander started giving Wolf a tour of the bike. She considered protesting Wolf's involvement but decided that ship had sailed.

A couple of Brushing officers grabbed an ATV, and Yates and Rachette volunteered to take the other two. They were like teenagers at day camp.

Patterson left the motor-heads to their business and walked back to Poncha's truck. A map was spread on the hood. She hated that she had to get on her tip-toes to see what they were looking at, but she did and saw they were just re-hashing the same routes they'd been talking about for the past hour.

With every minute, Hood would be deeper into the trail web. He might have gotten off the trails, too. How long could a man stay hidden in this vast wilderness? They were going to find out.

"He's going to get cold tonight," Poncha said. "You saw what he was wearing. A T-shirt and jeans. Shit. Turn that camper around!"

Patterson turned and saw a truck towing a camper. The driver had stopped and was leaning out the window, talking to one of the officers with animated hand gestures.

It was Friday afternoon, and this was the third camper they'd turned around and sent back to the valley floor.

A thumping echoed through the canyon, and they looked up as a helicopter passed overhead. The aircraft disappeared behind the mountain in front of them—the same that Wolf and Rachette had gung-hoed up an hour ago.

Patterson's eyes lingered on the clouds sliding across the sky above. The view of the south was blocked by the mountainside, but the sun had been snuffed out by approaching clouds. The air was growing colder and a wind was kicking up fine specks of dirt that stung her arms.

"Copy that," Poncha said into a handheld radio, his finger pressed against an earpiece. "Okay, the pilot's saying there's a storm coming in within the hour, so he doesn't know how long he has."

Patterson's watch read 2:05 p.m.

She looked back and saw Wolf and Yates donning their SBCSD rain gear from the trucks.

A minute later, the canyon was a cacophony of engine revving.

She ducked into Wolf's SUV and sat behind the wheel, savoring the warm seat and relative quiet.

The passenger door opened and a face poked inside. She recognized one of the Brushing PD officers.

"Hey, mind if I ride with you?"

"Hop in."

The man lurched into the passenger seat. "I'm Ryder."

"Patterson."

She caught the scent of cigarette smoke coming off his clothes and sighed inwardly.

"You okay?" he asked.

Poncha's vehicle took off in front of her. Wolf, Yates, Rachette, and the other three men revved hard as they shot up the jeep trail and out of sight.

She rolled down the windows. The dust and exhaust might as well have been potpourri.

"Yeah, let's roll."

CHAPTER 26

WOLF SAT FORWARD and felt the rear wheel skid side to side.

The 450-cc engine was whining high in second gear as he made his way up the steep trail. Too high? He shifted into third and felt it bog down, so he clicked back into second.

He snuck a look over his shoulder and wondered if his move had caused a slowdown for the ATVs behind him, but the four-wheelers were far behind, the last one just now creeping onto the bottom of the trail from the road.

Up ahead, Alexander had already pulled away, tearing up the right track of the road and around a bend. Wolf had watched the bike bucking and lurching under the man, engine screaming and tires spitting. He wondered if Alexander and Hood rode the same racing circuit.

Wolf kept a solid grip on the throttle and, in what seemed like seconds, reached the flatter part of the road, and then the top of the mountain.

Alexander was waiting for him, one foot down and looking over his shoulder.

Wolf stopped and they idled next to one another, waiting for the four ATVs to appear over the rise.

Rachette came first, followed by the two Brushing officers, and finally Yates.

Wolf pointed forward, and Alexander tore away like he was gunning for the first turn in a race.

As they neared the fence, Alexander slowed and waved Wolf forward. Wolf rolled through crispy weeds and over a downed pine bough. He stopped by the tire marks left by Zack Hood. He put down the kickstand and got off, then walked to the barbed-wire fence and cut it with a set of heavy-duty wire cutters.

He got back on and gave the thumbs-up to the men behind him. Rachette pumped his fist, eyes wide behind his clear visor. The other two men looked comfortable enough on their machines, but Yates was staring ahead.

Wolf followed his eyes to the crested horizon. The helicopter hovered over the next peak to the south and west. Beyond it, the sky was dark. A stroke of lightning licked out of a white curtain sweeping down into a valley in the distance, and even over the six revving engines and helicopter, they heard a deep rumble shake the air.

The helicopter reacted, twisting in their direction and dropping its nose. A few seconds later it passed overhead like a dog with its tail between its legs.

Wolf watched, then lowered his eyes to Yates's ATV. While the other three ATVs had flat metal beds attached behind the seats, now packed with camping and survival gear should they need it, Yates had a radio box with a wobbling antenna jutting from the rear fender into the sky a few feet above his head.

Yates followed Wolf's gaze and twisted in his seat, and when he whipped his helmet forward, his eyes were considerably wider.

Alexander revved three quick times and took off.

Wolf gave Yates a downward gesture. *We're going down.*

Yates nodded.

Wolf went next, over the grounded barbed wire and through sparse grass. Hidden rocks bucked and kicked the bike, but the faster he went the better he kept his balance.

Up ahead, Alexander took a sharp left, and they all tacked to follow. Then he jammed the brakes, veered right, and sped across the crest of the hill in the opposite direction.

Wolf slowed, considering whether or not to stop and rein him in over the radio, but Alexander waved over his head for them to follow. They did, and found the man had found a trail. They rolled slowly down the slope and onto a jeep trail, this one much flatter than the prior one. It extended across the side of the mountain and down into the trees.

Alexander skidded to a halt.

Wolf pulled up next to him.

"Look at that!" Alexander pointed.

Wolf could barely hear Alexander's voice through his helmet and over the engines, but didn't need to. He spotted the scrape coming down the hill, and the recent peel mark of a motorcycle's tire as it had sped off.

Wolf nodded, his spirits lifting. They were on the scent, and their pursuit would take them off the top of the mountain.

"Looks like he went down!" Alexander yelled through his helmet. "Thank God!"

Wolf nodded again, eyeing the electrical storm barreling in. The world had gone dark, the wind eerily still. "Let's go!"

CHAPTER 27

"THE HELICOPTER'S grounded in Brushing until the storm passes," Ryder said, lowering the radio.

The speaker was on, but Patterson opted to not point that out. Ryder was a genuine soul, just trying to be helpful. She'd noticed that from the beginning. First, he'd asked if the side-view mirror needed adjusting, which it had. Then he'd offered to drive, but not an I'm-a-man way. He'd also apologized for the cigarette-smoke smell, explaining that he'd quit last year, but with all the action, felt like he'd needed one.

"I've never been in pursuit like this," he said as he looked out his passenger window.

"Really? Not much action up here, huh?"

"Well, there was a murder a couple of years ago in town. Domestic violence. And we had a kidnapped woman a couple of years before that, but I wasn't on either of the cases." His eyes searched the steep forested canyon on either side of the SUV. "Well, in truth, I wasn't around."

She looked at him. "Really? Why?"

"I'm new. This is my third month on the job."

She nodded, feeling perhaps a smidge more exposed if she were honest. "Well, no time like the present to get some experience, right?"

"How about you? You ever been in any sort of action like this?"

She blinked. "A few times."

"Really? Like what?"

They came around a bend and a National Forest Campground sign loomed off the side of the road. "Here's another campground. Keep your eyes peeled. He could be in here."

They'd already driven through a campground down the road, but it had been vacant—not surprising with all the traffic they'd turned around earlier on the road.

Ryder pulled his gun and set it on his leg.

Patterson eyed it. "Why don't you keep your weapon holstered for now?"

"Oh. Yeah, okay. Sorry."

The sky above them was darkening, and a flicker of lightning lit up the valley, followed by a rumble.

She slowed and turned off the main dirt road into the campground. From a slight rise, she could see it was a big circle that looped off the river, dotted with camping spaces separated by well-spaced pines. Two camping spaces were occupied.

She took a right around the track, toward the river that butted up against the spots on that side.

She crept over a deep pothole, went up over a rise,

and then over a big exposed rock jutting out of the ground.

The first spot was a flat expanse of grass next to the river. Three tents had been erected, and a family was outside gathering things and shoving them inside the shelters.

She slowed and rolled down the passenger window.

Ryder leaned back, letting her speak.

"Hi there," she said.

A man, woman, and two young children looked toward them.

The man nodded. "Hi."

"Can we ask you a few questions?"

The man set down a camping chair and walked toward the SUV, eyeing the sky on the way. "Sure. How's it going, Officers?"

"We're looking for a man on a motorcycle, a blue dirt bike. He's wearing a short-sleeved T-shirt and jeans. Have you seen him?"

The man stood and crossed his arms. "No." His brow furrowed with concern. "Why?"

Patterson considered her response. "He could be dangerous." She thought about Zack Hood firing at her fellow detectives, then looked at the kids scrambling behind the man. "He is dangerous."

The man put his hands on his hips. "Should we be concerned?"

"I would be," she said. "There's no sense in being out here right now with your kids."

"We just got here."

She shrugged and watched the man come to his senses.

"Okay. We'll pack up." He looked back into the sky and walked to his wife.

Patterson drove away.

"Sucks for them," Ryder said.

"I'd rather them have a ruined weekend than be harmed by a psycho on the run. The guy's already killed twice. The first kill is always the hardest. After that ... you're dealing with a different person altogether."

Ryder said nothing.

They bucked and bounced through the campground. The next occupied site was over a rise, out of view of the other spot but still along the river.

A few small rain drops appeared on the windshield, flecking the view of a large camper and a pickup truck. A man was inside the pickup and the reverse lights were on.

A light glowed inside the camper. Though Patterson loved living in the mountains of Colorado, she was less than enthusiastic when it came to setting up a tent and letting ants invade every nook and cranny of her gear and her body.

"That's my kind of camping." She shifted into park. "Let's go give them the news."

"Looks like he's leaving," Ryder said.

The man saw them and parked his pickup.

Patterson stepped outside.

The air was literally electric. The kind that made you duck your head.

The picnic table was strewn with two paper plates and two half-eaten meals.

The door of the pickup opened and the man came out. "Hey, how's it going?" He slammed the door behind him and stood in front of them, hands propped on his hips.

"You about to leave?" she asked.

The man looked back at his camping trailer, then back at them, and nodded. He wore a red Cincinnati Reds jacket unbuttoned all the way. He scratched his thumb over his eyebrow. His eyes darted to the camper and back to them.

He was breathing heavy—his body tense. His eyes were bloodshot.

Then she caught a whiff of weed. The problem with marijuana was that it made some people downright psycho. There was probably a fresh bag sitting in his pocket.

"Have you seen a man riding a motorcycle? He was wearing a T-shirt and—"

"Yes."

"And jeans," she said.

"Yes. T-shirt and jeans. I've seen him."

She and Ryder exchanged a glance. "Where?"

The man pointed past them. "He came in here. Went to that pump over there."

Patterson and Ryder followed his finger. A handled water pump stood near a clump of pine trees.

"What color was the motorcycle?" she asked.

"Blue."

She and Ryder looked at each other again.

"When exactly was this?"

"Recently. Like, twenty minutes ago."

Lightning flickered. Thunder followed a few seconds later.

Patterson waited for the man to expound, but he stared at them, stoned.

"Do you remember which way he went?"

"He sat there for a few minutes at the pump, then got back on his bike and rode away." He pointed down the valley, further in the direction they'd been driving before they'd stopped at the campsite.

"Thanks."

"You got it."

"Listen, the man could be dangerous. Are you here with your family?"

The man swallowed, looking guilty again. "My daughter."

"Ah," Patterson said. "Well, I'd recommend heading out. You might as well not be around if there's a dangerous individual on the loose."

A tarp flapped in the wind, weighted down by rocks. The legs of what looked like a gas grill poked out, and the wind buffeted against more things the man no doubt intended to keep covered from the approaching elements.

Two plastic cups blew around the campsite. One of the paper plates, still full of beans and a half-eaten hotdog, were about to blow over too.

"You'd better get everything shored up. This storm's coming in hard."

"Will do. Thanks, Officers." He turned and picked up the cups and made a quick lap around the picnic table, stacking paper plates and shoving them in a trash bag hanging from a branch.

Rain fell in cold, large drops. One hit the side of Patterson's neck and slid down her shirt.

"Let's go." She ducked and jogged toward the SUV.

Ryder followed.

They got back in the SUV just as the sky opened up.

Patterson fired up the engine and hit the gas, rounding the end of the loop and back out of the campground.

"Poncha, do you copy?"

They bounced harder this time as Patterson drove through the potholes with more urgency.

The seatbelt wrenched against her stomach. "Shit." She jammed the brakes and eased over the exposed rock.

"You okay?" Ryder asked, looking down at her belly.

She was shell-shocked for a few seconds, her senses drifting inward to the baby. Everything felt normal. "Yeah."

"This is Poncha. Go ahead." The voice on the radio was barely audible over the rain pinging on the roof.

"We have a confirmed sighting at the Imnaha Campground on County 832. According to a camper, Hood was here twenty minutes ago using a water pump." She pulled up, stopped perpendicular to County 832, and looked south. "Look at that," she said.

The road to the right disappeared into a wall of rain.

"Did the camper see which way he went?"

"The camper pointed south on County 832. I repeat, Hood was last seen twenty minutes ago heading south on County 832 at Imnaha campground."

"Copy. We're over on 994. We'll have to loop in from the south. Maybe we'll run straight into him. Nice work."

She turned onto 832 and faced the oncoming deluge. "I'd say odds are good he's no longer on the road and taking shelter somewhere."

"Agreed!" said Poncha over static. "Which means keep your eyes peeled on the sides of the road. Head our way, and we'll head yours. Let's not get in a head-on collision, shall we?"

"Sounds like a good idea to me. We'll keep a close eye out for you." She thumbed the radio button again. "Deputy Yates, do you copy?"

There was no answer.

The rain hit at what sounded like a thousand bullets per second.

The wipers, even on the highest setting, did nothing.

"What are you thinking?" Ryder asked.

She looked at the man. His skin was pale and wet. He looked like he was sick with fever and covered in sweat. She remembered when she'd first been thrust into action, and felt for him.

She smiled. "I think I'm glad I'm not on an ATV or a motorcycle right now."

CHAPTER 28

THUNDER CRASHED, making the 450-cc engine between Wolf's legs sound like a rattling tin can by comparison.

The trees either side of the trail blocked his view of the approaching storm, but God's electric fingers slammed into the ground unremittingly and the pines lit up like lightning rods.

The last mile of the trail had dropped in elevation—a major check in the plus column. But they'd been headed straight into the storm the whole time. He thought about Yates and his antenna, and felt for the man.

Wolf rounded another corner, and again saw no sign of Alexander ahead of him. He vowed that at the first sign of rain he'd stop and let the others catch up. Two Coleman instant-pop-up tents were strapped to the back of Rachette's ATV, and they were going to need them.

The trail ahead looked relatively straight for a stretch, so he twisted the throttle, ignoring the trees as they whipped past at body-crushing speed.

The further he rode, the more comfortable he felt. In

high school, he'd lived on his dirt bike for an entire summer, riding the trails above the ranch and up and down the valley. And the adrenaline felt good. For once, the past and future were pinched out of existence. All that mattered was the wind whipping over his helmet, his vibrating arms, and his flexing shoulders.

And the trail.

He jammed the brakes and pulled the clutch. The motor went quiet, leaving only the sound of rubber scraping over dirt and rock toward a precipitous dip where the trail seemed to vanish.

He continued forward, dangerously close at this speed now, and then the front end dropped. Instinct told him to skid sideways, jump off, anything but ride it out. The back end slid sideways, and he eased off the brakes.

The bike whined as it picked up speed.

The seat bucked up and hit him in the butt, pushing him up and over the handlebars, legs in the air. He lost hold of the clutch and the motor revved. Then by some stroke of luck or a random jolt of his wrist, the bike accelerated under him and he landed back on.

The ground flattened, and the suspension bottomed out as his full weight pressed down.

The bike shot out from under him, and he went back-first into the dirt.

He hit hard, and his vision tumbled as he rolled. He body-checked a tree and his helmet connected with something hard.

And then he was turning on the small of his back in the center of the trail. The sky and trees swirled in his face-shield, then slowed to a stop.

He lay there for a few moments, sucking in deep breaths and taking stock.

Lightning forked across the sky above him, followed by a crash.

"Holy shit! Are you okay?" Footsteps came down the trail. "Sir! Detective Wolf!"

Wolf rolled to his stomach and got onto his knees.

"Are you okay?"

It was Alexander, coming down the trail. He'd navigated the dip with ease, of course, and was backtracking on foot.

"Shit, sorry. I should have stopped before it, but it came up so fast."

Wolf sat back on his heels and stared up. The man held his helmet at his side.

Alexander ducked down and put his face close to Wolf's shield. "Are you okay?"

Wolf nodded.

"Shit. Stop! Don't come down here! Stop!"

Wolf heard skidding tires and engines being killed.

"What happened?" Rachette's voice called down. "Wolf!"

Wolf pulled off his helmet, savoring the cool moist air as it licked the sweat off his head. "I'm okay!"

The taste of blood in his mouth suggested otherwise, as did the crimson that came off his tongue and onto his glove, but given that seconds earlier he'd thought he was dead, he felt like a million dollars.

Hurried footsteps came down the trail and the other men gathered around.

"Help me up."

They did.

He stood, his legs shaking.

Rachette got in his face. "You're bleeding pretty good out of your mouth. You sure you're okay?"

Wolf nodded.

The forest hissed as rain drops fell through the trees.

Alexander was looking at Wolf's motorcycle, which had tumbled a few yards down the hill. It lay on its side, pointing straight uphill. The front fender had snapped off and was stuck in tree branches.

"Sorry about your bike."

"We have to take shelter," Yates said, eyeing the sky. "It's about to open up. That last lightning strike was right on us."

"Help me lift this!" Alexander skidded on his heels down to the bike.

They stared at him.

"Come on!"

Wolf snapped out of the shock and stepped off the trail. Other than the damaged fender and a few scrapes, the bike looked to be in one piece.

But the slope was too steep and Wolf couldn't imagine riding or pushing it anywhere but straight down.

Alexander lifted the bike, straddled the seat, and began to kick it into life.

Two attempts and the motor roared. "Push me!"

Wolf reached Alexander, stood to the side and pushed against Alexander's back up the hill. Yates, Rachette, and the other two Brushing men came up, and together they were able to get leverage, though the effort still seemed futile.

Alexander revved and put both feet onto the pegs. "Okay, move!"

They watched in awe as the man throttled hard and accelerated up towards the slope, angling back the way Wolf had tumbled down. Dirt spat from the wheels like water from a firehose, and they ducked away from the spray.

With screaming engine, Alexander moved at a constant crawling speed upward, never once looking off-balance as he did so, and then popped the front end onto the trail. The man planted a foot and with a hard rev the bike flipped around almost one hundred and eighty degrees in the direction Wolf had been going.

Alexander stared at the slope in front of him, revving the engine in short bursts like Morse code. Then he released the clutch and flew upward.

The engine howled a single note. Tires spat. He accelerated fast up the slope. Then he was airborne at the top, and out of sight.

"Ho-ly-shit," Rachette said. "Did you see that?"

A few seconds later Alexander appeared on foot. "Okay, ATVs have to go around and above these rocks! There's an easy route—just go up into the trees. It's a gradual slope. We'll meet on the other side."

"Says Spider Man on a freakin' motorcycle," Rachette said.

They climbed the short distance back to the trail.

"You sure you're all right?" Rachette squeezed Wolf's shoulder.

There was blast of static from Rachette's radio. Wolf held out his hand. "Let me see that."

Rachette passed it over.

Wolf thumbed the button. "Patterson, do you copy?"

No answer.

"Lieutenant Poncha, do you copy?"

Still no answer.

"I'm not getting anything either." Yates's voice scratched over the radio.

Wolf gave the radio back to Rachette and hiked up with him. "Let's go."

CHAPTER 29

"What did you say?"

Wolf watched Alexander's lips move but could hear nothing over the rain pounding the synthetic fiber roof of the Coleman pop-tent.

"I said, it's really coming down now!"

Wolf nodded and pulled open the tent door to look outside.

The trees whipped back and forth. He squinted as mist flew into his face. The rain came down in sheets, swirling on the fierce wind.

The lightning struck more intermittently now, but they were in no less danger. Twice, bolts had struck so close that the flash and crash of thunder were one. The tent had been erected in a flat clearing off the edge of the trail. Wolf wondered if standing with golf clubs over their heads would have been a better idea.

They'd leaned the ATVs against trees to keep them upright. Four drenched mechanical horses.

"I can't hear shit!"

Wolf turned back to the interior of the tent.

There was room enough for six men to sit cross-legged and wait out the storm.

Rachette had the radio near his face. "Patty, do you copy?" He twisted dials and shook his head. "Nothing."

"There's no way we're heading down the trail in this rain, anyway," Alexander said. "Even if it stops, it's gonna be crazy slick." He glanced at Wolf, no doubt imagining him laying down his prized dirt bike a few more times and ripping off the other fender.

Wolf sat and pulled out his phone. Still no reception.

A light hanging from the ceiling swayed, illuminating the men with a florescent glow. They looked cold and tired. Wolf's rain gear had held out while he'd helped erect the tent and park the vehicles, but he still felt like a wet dog.

Rachette pulled out a can of Copenhagen and put a pinch into his bottom lip.

Alexander double-took the silver topped hockey-puck container. "Hey, you have another one of those?"

"Yeah, full can." Rachette tossed it and Alexander caught it.

"How about me?" Yates asked.

"Whatever. Pass it around."

Wolf looked at his cell phone—3:10 p.m. They'd been stuck here for over an hour.

Rachette went to the front flap and spat out into the rain. "It's definitely letting up."

The pounding on top of the tent settled to a patter, and shortly after stopped completely, save for the occasional pop.

They stepped out of the tent and into matted-down grass amid still pines.

Sun lanced through the clouds, illuminating rising mist.

Alexander walked over to the trail and put his foot down. His boot slid with the slightest pressure. "I hate to say it, but it's still dangerous as hell. That was a big downpour, and it's going to be hard staying upright." He looked around. "Even for me."

"If this man says it's hard to ride, I believe him." Rachette spat and looked at Wolf. "Then what do we do? We're dead in the water."

Wolf held out his hand for the radio and Rachette gave it to him.

Wolf stepped over to the vehicles. A new stream with hundreds of burbling tributaries snaked down the center of the trail, pooling at the edges and running into the forest.

He could see down the hillside but the bottom of the valley disappeared underneath a belt of white fog.

He raised the radio to his lips and pressed the button. "Patterson, this is Wolf. Do you copy?"

There was a scratch and faint noise.

"Lieutenant Poncha, this is Chief Detective Wolf. Do you copy?"

He gazed along the tops of the mountains. The higher peaks were appearing from behind the mist, gleaming in sun.

"Anybody?" Rachette appeared next to him.

"Nope."

They stood in silence, listening to the sounds of water leaching through the ground and trees.

"How are you doing?"

He looked at his detective and nodded. "I'm doing okay, Tom. Thanks. Just a little bruised. Could have been worse."

Rachette gave him a lopsided grin and glanced over his shoulder at the other men. They stood laughing and telling stories. One of the Brushing men had lit a cigarette. The smoke hung like a veil in the dense air.

"Sir?"

"Yeah."

Rachette cleared his throat. "Is it true?"

Wolf looked at his detective. "Is what true?"

Rachette said nothing.

The radio scratched and a male voice came through. "—up there? Do you copy?"

Wolf thumbed the button. "This is Detective Wolf. We copy. Who's this?"

"Wolf! It's Wilson."

"Hey, happy to hear your voice. What's happening?"

"We have an official sighting, but still no Hood. Patterson talked to a man who saw him come through one of the campsites on County 832. Imnaha Camping Grounds. He was only there for a few minutes and headed south on 832 after that. We covered the entire stretch of road for twenty miles south, but there's no sign of him. Of course, with that storm, it's no wonder."

Wolf turned around. The other men had walked over to listen in.

"What's happening up there?" Wilson asked. "You

guys okay? That was a soaker of a storm. Lots of lightning."

"Yeah. We're okay, but I'm afraid we're stuck. It's too dangerous to descend this trail right now."

"Roger that. MacLean's arrived with another six units at the rock quarry. They're on their way to meet us. We'll get that bird back up in the air soon. It's grounded in Brushing until this clears up."

"Where's Patterson?" he asked.

"Hey," she said. "Right here with Wilson."

"How you holding up?"

"I'm fine. Thanks."

Wilson's voice came back on. "Radio contact's intermittent through these valleys."

"Roger that," Wolf said. "Don't worry about us. We'll get down as soon as we can. You go find Zack Hood."

"Roger that. Keep your radio on."

They said their goodbyes and Wolf handed the radio back to Rachette.

Yates and the other men went back to the tent, leaving Wolf and Rachette by the ATVs.

A patch of blue sky grew in the south. Wolf noticed Rachette still looking at him. "What?"

"You don't have to answer."

"Answer what?" Wolf exhaled long and eyed the others loitering by the tent. "Oh, yeah. Is it true that I cracked up on top of that mountain yesterday? That I had a panic attack?"

Rachette's face was stone.

"Yeah. It's true."

Rachette shrugged. "I wouldn't worry about it too much."

Wolf nodded. "Yeah. Thanks."

"I mean, you've been through a lot. Shit, you had your pinkie blown off. That's a major, painful, life-changing, gut-wrenching, I don't know, badass thing to happen to somebody." Rachette eyed his own left hand and stretched his fingers. The stump where his pinkie had been severed two years ago wriggled.

Wolf looked at him.

"But, seriously. You've been through a lot lately. With what happened with Lauren ... and Ella? I ... don't know how that must feel inside, you know, ditching out on that little girl. Or, you know, feeling like you ditched out on her. But it's gotta be pretty bad."

"You have a way of speaking bluntly about the most awkward of subjects."

Rachette patted his shoulder and walked away.

Wolf reached for him and snatched his arm with an iron grip.

Rachette froze.

"Thanks."

"Yeah." Rachette pulled free and slapped Wolf's back again. "And, damn, your birthday next week? Forty-six?"

"Forty-seven."

"That's gotta be eating at you, too. Cause you're really old."

"Thanks."

"You're welcome." Rachette walked away.

CHAPTER 30

"All right. I'll lead the way." Wilson stood outside Patterson's window and slapped the roof.

"Listen." She looked up at the mountains rising on either side of the road. The sunlight reflecting off the dripping forest. "I'd rather stick here with Ryder, if that's okay with you. We have radio contact with Wolf and the other team. What if Hood came down only for a few minutes, then climbed back up into the trails? What if they run into him, and we're none the wiser?"

Wilson nodded. "It's probably a good idea. Radio's shit in these tight valleys." He looked up and down the road. "Okay. Fine. You two stay here. I'll head back and rendezvous with MacLean and Poncha, and we'll be back within the hour with reinforcements. Then I say we backtrack. Hood would have been hiding out during that storm. No way he rode through that in his clothing. He's still close."

She nodded. "Agreed."

A pickup truck towing a camper rounded the corner and slowed to pass them.

"Here's the guy who saw Hood earlier," she said.

Wilson turned. The trailer bounced heavily on the wet road, kicking up mud as it passed.

The man waved on the way by.

"I told him the man we saw was dangerous," she said. "Why the hell's he going in the same direction he pointed us in?"

"Probably lives down in Points," Wilson said. "You can take this all the way down to Rainbow Creek Canyon."

"Or he's high."

"What's that?"

"Nothing."

Wilson slapped the roof again and walked away. "We'll be back soon."

Patterson nodded and watched in her side-view mirror until the trailer edged around a bend and out of sight. The last thing she saw was a gas grill strapped to the back.

"What are we going to do?" Ryder asked, snapping her from her thoughts.

She shrugged, watching Wilson drive away at speed. "Sit here and wait for reinforcements. Hope we catch a break."

"I gotta take a leak."

"Enjoy yourself."

Ryder hopped out and walked to a bush, leaving Patterson looking through the windshield at a wispy patch of fog swirling up the side of the mountain.

Ryder returned and sat down heavily. "Man, I tell you what, it's nice out there now. Calm. Almost warm."

The sun shone brighter now. Steam gathered in a light blanket along the road. Patterson turned the key and rolled down the windows, letting in the scent of wet forest and the sound of birds.

She stared at the beaded water on the hood, then the side windows. Mud streaked everywhere, some of it running down with the water as it shed off the vehicle.

"Why would they cover up the gas grill with a tarp when they're just going to carry it on the back of the camper, completely exposed to the elements?" The question came out of her mouth without thinking.

"What?"

"There was mud flipping up all over it," she said.

"The gas grill? What are you talking about?"

She flicked her eyes to the side-view mirror. "Remember that tarp at that guy's campground? It was covering a gas grill and some other stuff. I'm asking, why? Why go through the trouble sheltering it from the coming storm? It seems to be built to weather the elements. It was strapped to the back of the camping trailer. Like, holstered in."

"So ... you're saying the tarp was covering something else?"

They sat in silence for a beat.

She picked up the radio and pressed the button. "Wilson, do you copy?"

There was no answer.

"Wilson, do you copy?"

Still no answer.

"Anybody. Do you copy?"

"Yeah, we copy." Rachette's voice came over the speaker.

"Shit."

Ryder turned in the seat toward her. "What are you thinking?"

"What if the guy wasn't stoned? What if he was scared?"

Ryder's face dropped.

"What's up?" Rachette asked.

She put the radio to his lips. "I ... think we may have ..." She lowered the radio and sucked in a breath.

"What? You broke up. Think we may have what?"

"Shit. I'm probably just freaking out." She raised the radio again. "We'll be in touch. Over."

Rachette waited a few seconds and said, "Sure. Whatever."

Patterson hung the radio, cranked the wheel, and turned the SUV around.

Ryder pulled his gun again, setting it on his lap. Patterson looked at it but said nothing.

The engine revved as they accelerated up the road and around the corner. Mud flipped up and slapped the underside of the vehicle.

The dirt road was vacant, so she pressed the gas harder. The mist split a few yards in front of the bumper as the SUV reached fifty miles per hour.

She pumped the brakes for the next turn. The road was rocky, but there were still large swaths of mud that could send them sliding into the drainage ditch.

"There he is," she said, rounding the next corner.

The trailer lumbered forward in the distance, like a large, slow-moving animal. They were a cheetah, catching up fast.

She flicked on the lightbar.

The trailer's brake lights blossomed and the truck towing it pulled over and came to a stop.

She parked in the middle of the road, a short distance from the left rear of the camper.

"What do we do?" Ryder asked. His voice sounded strained, his breathing rapid.

Patterson looked over at him. "We stay ready for anything, but we just go talk to our guy and assess the situation."

Ryder nodded.

She eyed his heaving chest. "Hey."

"What?"

"You take point at the right rear of the camper. I'll go talk to him at the driver's side."

"Got it."

"Deep, slow breaths from now on. Got it?"

He looked at her and nodded again, sucking a deep breath through his nose. "Yeah."

She picked up the radio again. "Wilson, do you copy?"

The speakers remained quiet. She waited for a snarky comment from Rachette, which she would have welcomed, but none came.

"Let's go." She popped the handle and stepped out.

The sun beat down, and the rising mist seemed to envelope her. It was no more than sixty degrees, but it felt like walking in a sauna.

She pulled her weapon and held it in both hands.

Ryder stopped walking, taking a spot between the SUV and the rear of the trailer.

Patterson nodded her reassurance and continued onward until Ryder slid from view. She flicked her eyes between the windows of the trailer and the rear of the pickup. It looked like the man driving was alone.

Alarm bells started ringing in her head. There had been two half-eaten plates on the picnic table, so where was the second person?

She sucked in a breath. Maybe somebody was lying down in the truck cab, or was too short to be seen over the headrest. Maybe a child was sitting in the passenger seat. She dismissed that idea—the seatbelt wasn't stretched from its pulley near the door and since the driver wore his, she had to assume the guy would have made a child wear theirs.

He was alone.

She edged nearer the truck bed.

The blue tarp was stretched over the back. Her stomach lurched at the shape poking up beneath it.

She reached over, lifted the edge of the fabric, and saw a motorcycle tire.

CHAPTER 31

Wolf watched as Rachette lifted the radio to his mouth. "Patty, do you copy?"

Wolf didn't remember having approached Rachette, but he was standing right next to him. They'd all heard the strain in Patterson's voice.

"What's going on?" Yates came up behind them, the other men in tow.

Wolf held out his hand and Rachette handed over the radio.

"What's happening, Patterson?" Wolf asked.

The radio remained silent.

Wolf flinched as two bangs echoed up the mountain.

"The fuck was that?" Rachette asked.

Another shot rang out.

"Patterson, come in!"

"Shots fired, officer down!" Patterson's voice vibrated the radio. "It's him! It's Hood! He's shot Officer Ryder! Wolf, do you copy? Rachette!"

"Yes! Patterson we hear you. Do you copy?"

"—Wolf! Do you hear me!"

"Shit."

"She can't hear you," Rachette said.

Alexander ran to the trail and looked down at the bottom of the valley. "Down there. Those shots were right at the bottom."

"We have to get down there," Wolf said. "I don't care if we have to slide down backward."

Alexander nodded. "Not on the motorcycles."

Alexander looked hard into Wolf's eyes. "I'm also good with four-wheelers. I'll go."

"I'm going, too."

Alexander looked down at the mud, then back at Wolf with a shake of his head. "You're gonna have to get on back with me."

"I'm a hundred and ninety pounds."

"Even better." Alexander leaped onto the back of the nearest ATV, twisted the key, and pressed the starter.

The engine fired and he thumbed the throttle. "We're gonna need all the weight we can get! More traction that way!"

Wolf jumped on and wrapped his arms around the man's torso.

"Hang on!"

Wolf doubled the strength of his bear hug as Alexander took off.

The engine whined loudly, but the vehicle accelerated slowly. The rear wheels slipped down toward the edge of the trail, where a steep drop-off promised a quick and violent end to their descent. But Alexander seemed only to grow bolder, revving the engine higher and spitting mud over the edge.

The ATV straightened out, and before long the trees were again whipping past at bone-crushing speed.

The wind buffeted Wolf's eyes. In their haste, they hadn't put on their helmets.

He thought about Patterson, and the baby in her belly, and her husband and son waiting at home.

"Go faster!"

Alexander said nothing, but the engine howled louder in response.

The trail was relatively straight, bending to the right along the mountain's contour. The ATV slid from side to side in the mud like a boat.

"Hang on!"

Then the world flipped around almost one hundred and eighty degrees. The revs died and for a split-second Wolf considered jumping off, wondering if they were at the start of a bad fall.

Then the engine screamed to life again and the tires spat huge swaths of mud.

They slowed almost to a stop, and then the wind was whipping through Wolf's hair again as they accelerated in the opposite direction. Alexander had just navigated a hairpin turn as if it were nothing.

"That was close!" Alexander yelled. "Hang on!"

Wolf clenched with all his might and shut his eyes.

Under the noise of the engine, Wolf heard a heated conversation through the radio clipped to his belt, but he dared not let go of Alexander to listen in. More gunshots rang out.

The descent continued, and twice more Alexander navigated turns with hair-raising aggression. Wolf's arms and his inner thighs ached from holding on. But they were lower, into the fog, and now below it.

And then Alexander yelled, "Lean left!"

Wolf obeyed, and the world twisted again around them. They spun a half-circle and came to a stop. They were in the middle of a dirt road.

"We made it!" Alexander said.

Wolf relaxed his grip and looked up and down the road.

"Which way?" Alexander asked.

Wolf plucked the radio from his belt. "Patterson, this is Wolf. Do you copy?"

"This is Patterson. I copy."

"Where are you?"

"I'm on County 832. I don't know ..." She sounded more panicked than before.

One direction lifted into mountains and tight canyons. The other seemed more open.

The fresh tire tracks gouged into the road told him nothing. They were too numerous, overlapping, and traveling in both directions.

"Are you surrounded by steep mountains or meadows?" he asked.

"A mountain on one side," she said. "A meadow on the other."

Wolf pointed away from the tight canyons. "Go!"

Alexander punched it.

They rounded the first bend. An RV was parked on the right side, though taking up most of the road. Behind it stood Wolf's SBCSD unmarked. Patterson was crouched at the bumper, waving at them.

Between the two vehicles lay a man in a tan Brushing PD uniform.

The side door of the trailer opened. A man came out, towing a child behind him. He raised a gun and fired.

A bullet zipped past the ATV.

"Shit!"

Alexander swerved, then overcorrected.

Wolf held on hard as they flipped up on two wheels.

They slowed and got back on four, and Alexander drove to the left side of the road, putting Patterson and her vehicle in between them and the shooter.

More shots rang out and Patterson ducked as a side window shattered.

"Stop!"

As the ATV slowed, Wolf jumped off and continued in an all-out sprint to Patterson. Alexander's footsteps were close behind.

The shots stopped, and they got to Patterson a few seconds later.

She stared at them with a resigned, cold glare. "He has a little girl."

Wolf ducked down next to her.

Alexander crouched next to Wolf. "What happened to Ryder?"

"He shot him."

"Is he okay?" Alexander peeked through the windows. "Ryder!"

There was no answer, but Ryder moved slightly.

"We have to get him," Alexander said.

"Calm down," Wolf said, putting a hand on Alexander's arm.

Alexander looked down like Wolf's hand was a spider.

"Relax."

The man blinked and nodded.

"What's happened so far?" Wolf asked.

Patterson stared at him.

"Patterson."

"I walked up to the truck's driver's side. Officer Ryder took position at the rear. I went up, saw there was a motorcycle covered with a tarp in the truck bed. So I knew it was Hood. I was on the other side of the trailer. He came out of the trailer and opened fire. I didn't see what happened. When I got to the other side, Ryder was down. I couldn't get to him. Hood took a shot at me, and I saw the little girl so I didn't return fire. I've just been here. I tried to talk to him. He keeps yelling and shooting."

Wolf nodded. "Okay."

He raised himself and put his hands on the back of the SUV, then shuffled to the side and poked his head out.

Zack Hood stood next to the RV. He held a girl in front of him, a handgun leveled at her head.

Hood saw him. "Don't you dare, pig!"

Wolf ducked back. "Give me your gun."

Patterson blinked. "What?"

"Give me your gun."

She hesitated.

"Patterson, give it to me."

She handed over the Glock.

Wolf shoved it down the front of his pants.

"What are you doing?"

The sound of a helicopter rose in the distance.

They turned and saw it coming full speed from the north. It reared back and slowed above them.

"Hey, down there." A voice came over Wolf's and Patterson's radio. "This is MacLean. What's happening?"

Two gunshots rang out and a spark showered off the bottom of the helicopter.

"Turn around and get out of here," Wolf said into the radio. "We have Hood. He has a little girl and a gun. Officer down. Get the cavalry up here, but keep your distance."

The helicopter was already over the nearest mountain and out of sight.

"Roger that," MacLean said. "Shit."

Wolf nodded and turned off the radio. He took off his jacket, dropped it on the ground, and hooked the radio onto his belt.

"Zack!" Wolf put his head out, ready to pull it back in at the first sign of a gun.

Hood still stood with the girl in front of him.

Wolf raised his left hand and took his gun from its paddle holster, held it barrel-down between thumb and forefinger, and dangled it out the side of the SUV. "I'm not armed!"

He took a big step out into the open.

He studied Zack Hood in the flesh for the first time. The man had a closely cropped oval scalp that shone in the late-afternoon light. His teeth were bared, almost glowing from the shadow that covered his face. His chin was down, and he looked at Wolf with menacing eyes.

"What do you want, Superman?"

"I'm going to throw my gun away."

Hood didn't blink.

Wolf tossed his Glock into the drainage ditch.

"Probably have another weapon in your belt. You think I ain't seen the movies?"

Slowly, Wolf lifted his jacket, exposing his stomach. He turned a full circle. "I'm not armed."

"Probably one strapped to the bottom of your leg."

Wolf lifted his pant legs, exposing his shins.

"What the hell do you want?"

Wolf looked at the girl.

She was six or seven years old, her face covered in snot and tears. Past the point of horrified, now a few stages into shock. Her eyes were calm pools of resignation, locked on Wolf's.

Wolf felt his chest constrict. It was sudden, like the shockwave after an explosion. His vision swam for an instant.

A deep breath and a shake of the head, and the sunlit valley righted itself.

Hood tilted his head.

"Please," Wolf said. "We don't have to involve the little girl in this anymore."

Hood smiled, then laughed. "Yeah, we do." Hood flicked his eyes to the sky, then back at Wolf.

The helicopter sounded like it was hovering a valley or two over.

"What do you want?" Wolf asked.

Hood stared at him for a beat. "I don't know. Far as I see it, this is the end, here. It's just a matter of who comes with me, I guess."

Wolf shook his head. "No." He took slow steps forward.

Hood raised his weapon. "What are you doing?"

"I'm coming to talk to you. I'm not armed. I'm just coming to talk."

Hood put the barrel back to the girl's head.

Wolf stopped.

"Thought you were coming to talk to me."

Wolf looked down at Ryder. Eyes stared back at him. Blood seeped out of the man's mouth, and a hole had opened up on his shoulder, covering his torso in blood, but his eyes were calm and alert. He'd fallen onto the muddy road so that his back faced Hood. He clutched his service piece in his right hand.

Wolf lifted his eyes to Hood again. "Please. Can I approach you and talk for a few minutes?"

"What good is that going to do?"

"We're going to bargain, okay? We're going to strike a deal. You give me the girl, and I'll get you a ride out."

"A ride out? You think I'm stupid?"

Wolf turned his chin to the air. "We have a chopper right over there. We can give you a ride out of here."

Hood pulled the girl closer to him.

"And you can take me," Wolf said. "You need someone as a hostage. I get that. You can take me, and you can leave the girl."

Hood narrowed his eyes. "Not as good a hostage."

"Why?"

Hood lowered the gun.

Wolf took a few steps forward and stopped in line with the rear of the trailer. His arms were out, and he flipped his palms to the sky. "What do you say?"

Hood was thinking, calculating. His eyes blinked rapidly. He gripped and re-gripped the gun.

Wolf saw the white tension in Hood's trigger finger and realized his own breathing had ceased. Despite the adrenaline coursing through his veins, he felt suddenly, completely exhausted. Like he was teetering on stilts.

The girl watched him. She closed her eyes, and her face twisted as she began to cry.

"Shut up!" Hood shook her.

The sight cooled Wolf's blood. "Come on, let's do this. I'll get the helicopter to land right over there, okay? We'll make everyone but the pilot get off. Me and you will walk over there, hop on the chopper, and take a ride."

"Then what?" Hood shook his head. "You ever heard of anyone getting away like that?"

The girl whimpered.

"Shut up!"

"It's okay, honey," Wolf said. "Just calm down, okay? Just close your eyes and take deep breaths, and this will all be over soon."

The girl did as she was told.

"This is screwed up," said Hood.

Wolf nodded. "Let me be your guy. I'll call the chopper now. We'll have him hop us down to Mexico. Once you get there, extradition's a bitch. With everything that's been going on politically, you think Mexico's ready to cooperate with a few hillbillies up in Colorado? Hell no."

Hood looked him in the eye.

Wolf nodded. "I'm taking the radio off my belt."

Hood remained almost still. His grip on the gun had steadied, and he looked at the ground, as if considering Wolf's proposal.

Wolf had to keep the situation moving. Stagnancy was death.

He brought the handheld to his mouth. "MacLean, do you copy?"

Come on.

"Copy. What the hell's going on down there with that psycho?"

Wolf cringed. "Change of plan. I need you to come pick me and Hood up in the chopper. I'm here right now, talking with Hood and the girl."

Silence.

"Do you copy?"

"I copy ... and what are we doing?"

Wolf nodded again, looking Hood in the eye. "We're going to leap it down to Juarez, Mexico. We'll have to refuel in Santa Fe, and probably somewhere just this side of the border. I want you to get that going. But in the meantime, I want you to come in from the west, directly over us from the west, and land in the meadow to the east of the trailer. Do you copy?"

Another few seconds of silence, and then MacLean said, "Copy that. It's going to take some doing on the refuels, but ... I'll work on it."

The volume of the rotors increased, and the helicopter appeared behind Wolf, far in the distance over the SUV. He saw Patterson's face poking out, and Alexander's above hers.

The bird skimmed the sky from right to left. As it disappeared again behind the mountain next to the road, the sound was snuffed out.

He turned back to Hood. "Okay. Here they come."

The girl's eyes were wide with hope. She shuffled her feet, and Wolf noticed she'd wet herself. The sight sent a spear through his heart.

"Hood. Come on. Let her go now. Let her go to my deputy back there by the SUV. I'll stay right here with you. Okay?"

Hood lifted his arm so the girl was no longer in a headlock, but he clamped a hand on her shoulder.

"Come on." Wolf narrowed his eyes with the most earnest look he could muster. He fought the tension in his chest, willing his lungs to relax as he spoke. "Point the gun at me now."

Hood raised the barrel towards Wolf.

"That's it." Wolf nodded. "I'm your guy."

Wolf ignored the black hole of the barrel, and looked straight into Hood's eyes. "Thank you."

The girl stepped forward and ducked, and Hood's hand came free from her shoulder.

"Go on, honey," Wolf said. "You can go now. Go to the car back there."

The girl walked fast toward Wolf. Tears flowed down her cheeks as she passed.

"Run, baby."

She ran past him.

Hood blinked, and his face twisted, as if realizing he'd been duped.

"No!" Wolf yelled. He pointed up into the sky with wide eyes. "There! Here it is!"

Hood looked up.

There was nothing there. The ruse had clearly pissed him off—his lips downturned and he raised his weapon, aiming carefully at Wolf's chest.

The helicopter came over the top of the mountain, and hovered overhead. The noise came out of nowhere, like a bomb.

"See?" Wolf sidestepped to stay in front of the muzzle.

Hood looked up again. This time he had to twist his head almost backward to see it.

Wolf dove his hand into his pants and pulled out the Glock.

He raised the gun and aimed, but just before he pulled the trigger, gunshots rang out from behind and blood spurted from Hood's chest.

Hood dropped like his legs had disappeared.

Wolf turned around. The shots had come from Ryder.

"Hold your fire!"

The officer lowered his weapon and rolled onto his back.

Wolf ran forward and kicked the weapon from Hood's hand.

Hood's lips were moving.

"You piece of shit," Wolf said with a voice shaking with rage.

Behind him by the SUV, the girl was trying to escape Patterson's clutches, screaming at the top of her lungs, though he couldn't make out what she was saying above the noise of the helicopter and the pounding in his ears.

Wolf knelt next to Hood, making sure he was close in case there was more fight in the man. "You piece of shit."

Hood coughed, and warm blood spattered Wolf's face.

"I ... done it again."

Wolf ignored him.

A man came tumbling out of the passenger door of the truck. "Is she okay? Is my daughter okay?"

"She's okay." Wolf pointed back, realizing the girl had been yelling for her father.

The man sprinted to his daughter. The girl broke from Patterson and dove into her dad's embrace.

"That asshole ..."

Wolf looked down at Hood. His chin was covered in blood. The hole in the center of his chest spat like a geyser, but still his lips were moving like a fish out of water. He was determined to speak.

"That ass ... hole ... called my daddy a liar and a cheat." Hood's throat gurgled. "If I could bash his head in all over again ... I would." He smiled, showing red teeth. "He ... dead now."

"Yeah," Wolf said. "And how about your best friend? What did he do to you?"

Hood's smile vanished.

"Yeah. I don't think it's that funny killing people either."

"What ... happened ..." Hood said.

Wolf shook his head and stood up. He took deep breaths to stave off the light-headedness. When was the last time he'd inhaled?

"... Chris ... dead ..."

Wolf looked down. "Now it's time for you to join him."

Hood closed his eyes and did as he was told.

CHAPTER 32

WOLF'S BED shook as Drifter whimpered in his sleep. The dog's legs kicked, perhaps chasing a rabbit in dreamland.

He'd never seen a dog with so much balled-up energy in a dead sleep. Then again, he couldn't remember the last time he'd had a puppy.

Maddie had been the name of his golden retriever growing up. He'd been too young to remember when his family had gotten her. She'd simply always been there in Wolf's childhood.

He stared at the fan twirling on the ceiling and allowed his mind to wander for the next half-hour ... his mother screaming at him for feeding Maddie a bag of Twizzlers and the trip to the vet .... the vet who'd come over to the ranch and look after the cattle ... Wolf and his father riding horses along the fence line, the calf stuck in the barbed wire, and how he and his father had wrestled with it, untangling the hoof.

Before he knew it, the sun was back up.

And so was Drifter.

"You gotta pee?"

Drifter jumped off the bed and wagged his tail.

Wolf stared at him. Straight out of a night's sleep, he was a mellow dog. Last night, when he'd picked him up from Nate's, Britt had all but thrown Drifter into his arms. Drifter had peed three times inside the Watson house and had demonstrated a taste for wooden furniture legs.

Drifter barked.

"Come on."

Wolf slipped on his jeans and a flannel and went to the front door. He considered letting the dog out unattended but remembered Jack's warning—*He'll just run away.*

They went out into the cool morning air and stood in the front yard, both relieving their bladders.

Wolf watched the dog run circles, blocked him as he raked Wolf's legs with his claws, and ended up tethering him near the barn with bowls of kibble and water.

The morning went faster than the night had as he busied himself inside with chores. He wanted it to look like he kept a spotless house, just in case they came in. He spent the afternoon outside, preparing.

By two, Wolf had completed his digging and removed the leash from Drifter's neck. The dog went far and fast, but always stayed within sight.

As four o'clock neared, he shoveled the last of the broken bottles from the side of the house into the barrow and wheeled it back to the barn. He'd finish that chore later.

It was time.

He felt as if he were suspended over a ravine, with somebody set to drop him at any moment, but he didn't know when.

3:55 p.m.

"Drifter!"

The dog was sniffing something in the field.

He took the dog by the collar and walked towards the house.

Drifter followed without protest and Wolf put him inside the doorway and pointed at him. "Take a nap."

Drifter looked past him and tilted his head.

A vehicle came into view and Wolf shut the door.

Lauren had been driving an Audi the last he'd known. Now, a big pickup truck barreled down the drive, kicking up a plume of dust.

The sun reflected off the windshield, obscuring the occupants.

He checked his watch. 4:02—suspiciously punctual.

Still, his breathing calmed. The moment he'd been dreading seemed to have been postponed for the time being.

The truck turned, and his heart leaped. Ella looked out at him from the rear window.

He walked forward on numb legs, watching as they parked.

Lauren and Ella climbed out of the tall truck.

Ella landed on sure feet, slammed the door, and turned to him.

She smiled, and his own mouth stretched wide.

Her red hair was darker now. And longer, pulled out

of her face and clipped against her head. Her eyes were just as big, squinting as she showed her smile was just as bright.

She jogged to him, and he moved toward her.

Then he stopped. He was not supposed to do this. He was supposed to be distant, to keep it to clipped, short sentences. To—

Her feet thumped up and she latched onto him, hugging tight around his waist.

"Hi." He returned the hug and looked up to see Lauren rounding the rear of the truck.

He expected concern to etch her face, but she stood and looked out on the landscape, pointedly ignoring Ella's interaction with him as if it were none of her business.

Ella let go and walked back to her mother, as if she'd just finished something pre-planned.

Wolf followed her.

Lauren's hair was shorter, cut in a bob, also colored darker. Her eyes were as green as ever, but there was no smile stretching her pretty, freckled face as she turned toward him.

"Hi, David."

"Hi."

She pulled her bangs behind her ear and gestured to the truck bed. "Thanks for agreeing to do this."

"Of course." He popped open the tailgate, noting the rental plates.

"He was too big to fit in my car," she said.

Wolf lowered the gate and believed it when he saw

the dog casket. It was at least five feet long, half that wide and tall.

"It's big, I know. That's all they had at the place I went to. Had to get the two neighbor guys to help me load it."

"No sweat. One second." Wolf walked to the edge of the barn and upturned the wheelbarrow. The glass crashed into the dirt. He brushed the remaining slivers out of the bed and returned, noting how Ella took special interest in the pile of glass behind him. She was still the most inquisitive person he'd ever met.

Drifter barked inside, and her head whipped around. "Is that a dog?"

Wolf smiled. "Yeah."

Lauren had turned and wrestled Jet's casket into position.

Wolf pictured the dog inside, old and thin. According to Lauren's text messages, Jet had fought the cancer long and hard, but the German shepherd had lost the battle two days earlier.

With strained muscles, still aching from the motor-cycle adventure, Wolf tipped Jet's coffin onto the wheel-barrow bed, then slowly lowered it with Lauren's help. They worked in unison without speaking. They'd always worked well as a team.

Lauren backed away and looked around. "Where do you ..."

He nodded into the distance. "I've prepared a hole over there." He pointed at the lone pine at the edge of the meadow.

"That's where he always used to sit," Ella said. "He'd watch me practice my cartwheels."

Wolf nodded. "That's what I was thinking when I chose that spot."

Ella looked toward the door again as Drifter barked inside.

Wolf lifted the wheelbarrow and pushed it through the bumpy field. Their separation was palpable. Lauren and Ella followed a good distance behind.

They reached the tree and Wolf set down the handles.

They shuffled and grunted, and finally Jet's casket was lowered into the hole.

While digging that afternoon, Wolf had wondered if he'd been overzealous. Now he wished he'd added an extra six inches on all sides.

But the old boy fit.

Wolf grabbed the shovel leaning against the tree.

"Wait," Ella said. "I wanted to say some things I wrote down." She pulled a folded piece of paper out of pocket and waved it at Wolf.

He nodded. "Yes, of course. That's a good idea."

She stood at the hole's edge. "Jet. You were a good dog. You always followed me wherever I went. You always played when I wanted to. Or you watched while I did if you didn't want to. You tooted a lot." She smiled and looked up at Wolf and Lauren.

They smiled in turn, though Lauren kept her eyes glued to the earth.

"And you always went crazy at raccoons. And ..." Ella

sniffed, and tears rolled down her cheeks. "I'm going to miss you. A lot."

Wolf felt an electric jolt as Ella looked up at him.

"But it's okay," she said. "Because, as my mommy says, all good things must come to an end. But that doesn't mean they weren't good." She looked back down at the paper and found her place. "So we say goodbye, and remember the fun times we had. And we leave you here ... forever ... but we'll see you again up in heaven."

She folded the paper and shoved it back in her pocket.

Wolf's eyes slid to Lauren. She was looking at him.

Drifter barked again, louder than before.

They all turned as the bug screen on Wolf's bedroom window hit the ground. Drifter's head jammed outside and disappeared.

"Oh, he's a German shepherd! He's a puppy!" Ella walked toward the house like she was hooked in a tractor beam.

"Do you want to see him?" Wolf asked.

She turned. "Yes. Can I?"

He nodded. "Go let him out before he breaks down a wall."

She ran.

"His name is Drifter!"

"Drifter!" she said in mid-stride.

Wolf pushed the dirt onto the casket.

Lauren stood by his side, watching in silence as he finished the job.

"You look good," she said.

He stood tall, leaning on the shovel.

"Tired. But good."

He nodded. "Thanks. You do too. You both look great."

Lauren looked at the fresh earth mound. "Thanks so much. I wasn't sure if you were going to answer me."

"Yeah. Sorry about that. But ... I didn't feel like ..."

"Like what?"

He looked toward the house. "Like letting Ella down again."

She shook her head. "You never let her down. I never let her down. It's nobody's fault we didn't work out. It's just ... life."

He nodded. "I think she just said it best."

Ella was on her hands and feet, butt in the air. Drifter jumped up onto her back, sending her head first to the ground.

"My God," Lauren said, shaking her head. "I forgot how crazy puppies are."

"Yeah."

She sucked in a breath and let it out. "I'm not sure I can handle one of those things rampaging around the house. But there's no way I can say no to her."

"You're getting a puppy?"

She smiled. "Yeah."

"You're going to get one. You haven't gotten one yet."

"Yes." She narrowed her eyes. "What? Why?"

"Please." He stood in front of her. "I beg of you. If you're serious, please consider taking this dog."

She blinked. A smile cracked through her confusion.

"I would pay you. A large sum of money."

She laughed. "What's going on with this dog? You have to explain."

He explained the Jack and Cassidy story.

"They're having a baby?"

He nodded.

"Oh, David, that's so wonderful."

"It is."

"So ..." She looked at Ella and Drifter. "You really are serious."

"I can take care of him if need be. Please don't feel pressured. But, yes, I am."

They walked slowly toward the house, watching Ella as she let Drifter tackle her to the ground.

Lauren looked at Wolf with suspicion. "Are you telling the truth about Jack and Cassidy?"

He rolled his eyes.

"Sorry, of course you wouldn't lie about something like that."

He said nothing, watching the gears turn behind her eyes.

"Perfect timing," she said. "You have to listen when God gives you perfect timing. My dad said that to me once." She stopped and scrunched her face. "Okay, fine. We'll take him."

He smiled. "You won't regret this."

Now she rolled her eyes. "Why is it when somebody says that, you immediately regret your decision?"

"I guess I should warn you—he likes to chew furniture."

"Oh, good. Anything else?"

He smiled.

They stood in silence, watching Ella and Drifter's antics some more.

Wolf felt like his chest had been connected to an air hose set on high.

"You gonna tell her?" he asked.

"I probably should. Hey, Ella!"

"What?"

Lauren gave Wolf a knowing smirk. "It's time to go."

"Awwwwwww. I'm playing with Drifter."

Wolf watched as Lauren walked over and quietly gave her the news.

Ella squealed, then looked at her mother, and then to Wolf.

Wolf nodded.

She squealed again, and wrapped her arms around Drifter.

Drifter peed on her shoe.

"I have a kennel you guys can take."

Lauren smiled. "That would be great."

"I'll throw in a blanket or two as well."

Ella ran over and hugged Wolf's legs. This time, instead of turning away, she looked up at him. "Thank you."

"Thank you, Ella."

They hugged again, and Ella walked to her mother.

Wolf gathered some canine paraphernalia, and Lauren packed it in the truck.

Ella strapped herself in next to the kennel in the back seat.

Lauren stood staring at the ground for a moment,

then looked up at him with her kaleidoscope eyes. "Goodbye, David."

"Bye, Lauren."

Ella rolled down her window. "Bye!"

Wolf smiled. "Bye! You take care of that dog, now!"

"I will!" The window went up.

Lauren climbed into the truck and drove away.

Wolf stood and watched until the truck disappeared through the headgate.

The sun perched on the tip of the western peaks, blazing in the cloudless sky.

He shut his eyes, letting the warmth fill his body. When he opened them, the sun had begun to dip behind the mountain.

He started at the sight of an elk staring at him from the trees. It raised its snout into the air and took a sniff, then lowered his head and ate some grass.

Wolf went up the steps, through the door, and stood in the living room.

His ears rang faintly over the dead silence.

As if in a trance, he walked to his bedroom.

He climbed onto the bed, lay down, and went to sleep.

CHAPTER 33

WOLF'S EYES snapped open to a sound.

He sucked in a deep breath, then stretched and yawned. When the fabric of his flannel pulled on his skin, he realized he still had his clothes on.

His body felt heavy, a sensation he recalled from his teenage years when he'd slept in until noon.

There was that sound again, like a buzz saw.

Outside his bedroom windows the sky was aglow with subdued sunlight.

He sat up quickly and twisted. He put his feet down on the floor, noting his boots were still laced to his feet.

The noise again. The phone vibrating on his nightstand.

"Hello?" His voice croaked like he hadn't used it for six months.

"Hey, sorry. Wake you up?" It was MacLean.

"Nah."

"You slept?"

Wolf stood and stretched again, and had to cycle

through a long yawn before he could speak. Out the window, the eastern sky was lit, not the west. "I guess. What's up?"

"Rise and shine. Happy Sunday morning. We're having a debrief at oh-nine-hundred."

"Okay."

"How are you holding up? You get any rest yesterday?"

Cool air leaked into his window. He saw the screen lying on the grass outside, and the scar in the earth where he'd scraped up the pile of broken Scotch bottles. Two deer were eating at the treeline. Beyond that was the mound of earth—Jet's final resting place.

"Hey, you there?"

"Yeah, sorry. It was good," he said. "Much needed R and R."

"Yeah? Glad you enjoyed it. I spent my Saturday trying to explain how we didn't get this guy three months ago to a bunch of media jackals and self-righteous council members. Blood-sucking bastards can't give us a pat on the back for solving the case. They want it done faster. I love election years."

Wolf made his way to the kitchen.

"Anyway," MacLean said, "time to join reality again. And Wolf?"

"Yeah."

"Me, you, and White need to have a private debriefing."

"Okay."

"I wouldn't worry about it," MacLean said. "You showed your true colors Friday. Anyway, we'll do that at oh-eight-hundred, an hour earlier than the official debrief. My office."

"Got it." Wolf ended the call and started the coffee.

He grabbed a quick shower, shaved, and got dressed. The refrigerator had enough greens for him to make only a small smoothie, so he added a few eggs and toast to his breakfast and got out the door with an hour and a half to spare before the meeting.

He stopped at his rear bumper and slowly scanned the world around him. He sucked in a breath through his nose, taking in the scent of the barn's weathered wood and the wet forest.

His vision seemed wider. It was as if he'd been wearing a baseball cap pulled down low, and somebody had pulled it off.

As he climbed into the SUV and backed out of the carport, Lauren's words echoed in his mind.

You have to listen when God gives you perfect timing.

A sprained ankle had brought him and Lauren together. He'd been waking up every day, ruminating over that perfect timing for the better part of a year. Now he could only think of the permanent smile plastered on Ella's face as she drove away next to that puppy, and he couldn't stop smiling himself.

He shifted into drive and hit the gas. Patterson had been driving his SUV during the Zack Hood incident, so his own vehicle sat in Lorber's bomb shelter as evidence. The acceleration of this temporary cruiser was sluggish in comparison. That and the cupholder was too narrow for his preferred to-go coffee mug.

He jammed the brakes and came to a stop before the headgate, spilling some of the hot liquid on his hand.

Lauren's words echoed again.

Perfect timing.

He shifted into park, and shut off the engine, letting the silence envelop him. Like the raging Chautauqua below, ideas flowed into his mind.

He got out of the car, pulled his phone from his pocket, and dialed Margaret Hitchens.

"Yeah?"

"Hey."

"What's up?" She spoke loud over a hissing background noise.

"I need to ask you a few questions."

"I'm driving. Can I call you back?"

"No. Pull over."

"Are you serious?"

"Yes. It's important."

She sighed heavily into the phone and the noise dissipated. "Okay. I'm not driving anymore. What's up?"

"What's going to happen to Warren Preston's land?"

She scoffed. "Funny you should ask. I was on my way to speak to some prospective developers right now."

"Today?"

"Yes."

"Who?"

"A firm from Denver."

He frowned. "How? I mean it's Sunday. Has Preston Rock and Supply even shut their doors yet? We've only just pulled Warren Preston out of that snow. Chris Alamy just died."

"Preston was leasing the land. The owner will sell it. And I said prospective developers. There's nothing going on yet, but when it goes for sale people will have to move fast. You snooze, you lose on that piece of land. They want to discuss feasibility with me. Pricing for units, cost of construction, permits, etcetera."

Wolf paced in the grass next to the headgate. "Who's the owner?"

"A man named Rod Bloom. Lives up on Cold Lake."

"This guy Bloom will develop it?"

"No. Whoever decides to buy it will."

"So now that he has his land back, he's selling it to developers."

"Well, actually, no. The deal is more complicated than that."

"More complicated how?"

"I don't know all the details. Like I said, I'm just helping this one firm. But from what I gather, Bloom sold an option for purchasing the land to another firm. The firm I'm talking to has an inside track to put in an offer."

"Do you know which firm owns this option?"

"No. I'll know more after this meeting. Why? What's going on?"

"Do you have Rod what's-his-name's number?"

"Rod Bloom." She sighed. "I don't know how to do that with my phone while I'm on it."

He said nothing.

"Okay, let me look." After some fumbling and cursing, she read the number aloud.

"Thanks."

"You're welcome. So why are you asking all these questions?"

"I have to go."

"Oh, of course you aren't going to tell me. Fine. Goodbye. I'm driving." She hung up.

He typed in the number and hit the call button.

THURSDAY, 8:34 a.m

Five days later ...

Wolf parked his SUV and got out into cool dense air scented with lake water and pine.

Forest hid any houses that might have lurked in the woods, although Wolf guessed that if there were neighbors, they were a good distance away. The trees had been cleared for a few acres, and in the middle of a gently sloping lawn stood a hulking home built from sturdy logs and plenty of glass.

The lawn ran down to the shore of Cold Lake. A dock jutted out into Sluice–Byron County's largest body of fresh water. A piercing reflection lanced off the wood finish of a Chris Craft Riviera-style boat as it bobbed on a passing wake.

"Mr. Wolf!"

Wolf peeled his eyes away from the waves. A man in jeans and a salmon sweater stood waving on the front porch.

"Mr. Bloom?"

"That's me."

A man in a suit and tie came out of the front door and stood next to Bloom.

Wolf shut his vehicle door and walked past a Mercedes SUV that was ticking and radiating heat from the hood.

"Thanks for agreeing to speak to me," Wolf said.

"Please, come on up. We'll sit on the porch."

Wolf's boots crunched along a gravel path to the front entrance. Flower boxes burst with color all over the exterior of the house, like a swiss-style chalet.

Wolf stepped up the stairs and took the man's hand. "Chief Detective Dave Wolf."

"Nice to meet you. I'm Rod Bloom. You can call me Rod."

"You can call me Dave."

Bloom smiled and looked like he meant it. Wolf supposed it was tough to frown living here. And since Wolf had called Rod Bloom for the first time five days ago, he'd learned that Bloom had plenty of other reasons to smile. The man owned vast tracts of land across the country, from ranches near Telluride, to farms in Tennessee, to an island in the Caribbean, to this estate on the southern shores of Cold Lake.

"Nice place."

"Thank you. This is my lawyer, Henry Tiller." Bloom steered Wolf away from the man and led him along the deck. The lawyer, a tall, skinny man, followed them mutely.

They walked along the exterior of the house on a

wrap-around porch until they reached a deck overlooking the lake below.

"I'm sorry we couldn't meet earlier this week," Bloom said. "But as I said, I've been on business in New York for too long. Please, take a seat."

Wolf wondered what kind of deals a man like Rod Bloom had been working in New York.

Two coffee cups sat upside-down on a black metal table. Bloom gestured to a cushioned chair and Wolf sat.

The waves below sparkled like diamonds. A fishing boat sped past and disappeared around a bend.

"I always love coming back here after a trip to a big city. Give me forest, lake, and mountains over skyscrapers any day."

Wolf silently agreed.

A sliding glass door opened, and a pretty woman in her sixties stepped out with a carafe. She stood and smiled warmly at Wolf. "Hello."

"Pia, this is Dave Wolf. Dave, this is my wife, Pia."

"Dave," Wolf said. "Nice to meet you, ma'am."

Pia upturned the coffee cups and poured. "Room for cream?" She had a thick accent that Wolf failed to pinpoint.

"No, thank you."

She finished and went back inside. The glass door hissed shut.

"Please." Bloom gestured to the steaming liquid.

"Thank you." Wolf took a sip and was pleased to find it strong and hot.

"I'm sure you can understand the presence of my lawyer."

"Of course."

The lawyer stood with hands clasped behind his back.

Bloom slipped on some sunglasses from his pocket. "I must say, your insistence to come meet me was a little annoying at first. But, as I read about the details of this case, I have to say I'm intrigued. What is it I can do for you?"

Wolf pulled out his notebook and flipped to the pages of notes he'd accumulated over the past few days. "Just to be clear," he said, "you owned the Preston Rock and Supply land yourself, correct? There were no partnerships with other people or companies?"

The lawyer said his first words. "He never owned that land."

Bloom waved him off. "I own a corporation that owned that land. Henry's trying to throw you off with technicalities. But, yes, I owned the land myself. Without other partners."

"Could you please describe the lease agreement you had with Warren Preston that enabled him to run his rock business on that property?"

"He signed a forty-year lease to operate."

"Forty years?"

"Forty years is relatively short for a ground lease," the lawyer said.

Bloom nodded. "It's true."

"Okay. But there's so much development happening these days along that section of the river."

"Yes. So?"

"Wouldn't you want to develop that land? It's my

understanding that you could make a lot more money with a single project, say, a condo complex, than a forty-year lease on a business. Millions instead of thousands."

Bloom shrugged and gazed over the water. "Warren Preston signed that forty-year lease in the heart of the economic downturn, when there wasn't anything along that portion of river, and no prospect of any development in the Chautauqua Valley. I was grateful for the income back then. And now ... well, I was grateful that Warren could run his business at a relatively small cost in return."

"Relatively small cost?"

"I gave him competitive terms."

Wolf nodded. He knew all these technicalities from interviews with Betsy Collworth and with help from Margaret, but he wanted to hear the answers from this man's mouth. So far, Rod Bloom seemed to be shooting straight.

Bloom narrowed his eyes. "Why?"

"I guess I'm wondering if you ever regretted your decision to lease the land. On competitive terms."

"No. A deal's a deal. I don't play woulda-shoulda-coulda. I've learned to never regret the past, Detective."

The lawyer walked to the table and took up position behind Bloom's shoulder.

"Can you please tell me about your sale of the rock yard land?" Wolf asked.

"I sold an option to a firm in Rocky Points a few years ago. They're doing what they want with it. It's not my problem anymore."

"What were the terms of that option?"

Bloom raised a hand to keep his suit-man at bay. "Ten-year option for a percentage of market value."

"And, so, now that Preston and Alamy are gone, and the rock business is gone, the option has been exercised, and you will earn market value for the land."

"A percentage of the market value."

"You'll earn millions."

The lawyer bent down and whispered in his ear.

Bloom smiled. "I don't have anything to hide, Henry. Yes, Mr. Wolf, I'll make a percentage of the market value of that land."

Wolf narrowed his eyes and nodded. "Why would you do that? Why not just sell it yourself to get the full market value rather than a percentage?"

Bloom shrugged. "I took a calculated risk. Preston was a workhorse. If that asshole Zack Hood hadn't killed him, he'd have kept paying the lease for another twenty-five years and I would have made money on the option and the lease. Then you'd be calling me smart in this meeting, rather than questioning my sanity." Bloom smiled and gestured to his house. "It doesn't matter to me. I'll come out okay in the end with a percentage."

Wolf looked at his notes.

"Mr. Wolf, as you would expect, I've been keeping up with this case the best I can, seeing as it took place on my land. I read all the newspapers. Your investigation found that Warren Preston was murdered by that man up in Brushing, Zack Hood. Chris Alamy, the manager at Preston Rock and Supply, was also present at the murder. Hood killed him to keep him quiet. And then there was

Hood's demise, when your heroic actions saved that little girl's life." Bloom looked at him hard.

Wolf held his gaze and saw through the man's eyes to the thoughts lurking behind them. This past week, local news stories had never strayed far from mentioning Wolf's panic attack on the mountain.

"Are you here to tell me you think I have something to do with all of this?"

Wolf said nothing.

"Please, Mr. Wolf, get to what you want to know. Or you're going to wear out your welcome fast."

Wolf nodded. "You say it's a company that purchased the option to buy your land. But really, like you and your corporation holding the property, it's a single person, correct?"

Bloom raised his sunglasses, revealing a hawk's glare.

"S & S Development," Wolf said. "That's the company who purchased the option."

"Yes. And I don't know if it's a one-man operation."

"But you met the one man, correct? Only dealt with the one individual."

Bloom's eyes glazed over. His face dropped. "My God. You think he's involved?"

Wolf studied Bloom hard. "I do. But more importantly, Mr. Bloom, I don't think you were involved."

Wolf flipped his notebook shut. "I hope I can count on your continued cooperation in our investigation should we need it in the near future."

Bloom stood frozen.

"Mr. Bloom?"

"I don't get it."

Wolf took a final sip from his coffee and stood from his chair. "I'm sure you'll have plenty of chances to read about it in the papers."

CHAPTER 35

WOLF CROSSED one leg over the other and checked his watch.

"What's he doing?" MacLean looked toward his office windows.

Wolf followed the sheriff's eyes but saw nothing past the shut blinds. His watch read 1:12 p.m.—twelve minutes past meeting time.

"I guess I'll call again." MacLean huffed and picked up his desk phone.

The door opened, and White strode in. He stopped at the chair next to Wolf, unbuttoned his suit jacket, and smoothed his canary-yellow tie before sitting down.

"Hello, gentlemen." White nodded at the sheriff. "Listen, sorry I'm late, but I have a lot on my plate this afternoon." He slid a look to Wolf. "If we could please make this as brief as possible."

"Sure," Wolf said.

White settled in, checked his watch, and crossed a leg. "So?"

"We have a new angle on the Preston case," Wolf said.

"What kind of new angle? I thought we were pretty clear on all the angles in this case, and they're all dead."

"What do you think the odds are that Dr. Sheffield was hiking up on that pass the day Warren Preston's body emerged from the snow?"

White blinked rapidly. "What?"

"It had rained almost an inch on top of Huerfano Pass the night before. The rain lowered the snowpack, washing a good portion of it down into the valley. That storm was responsible for uncovering Warren Preston's body."

White looked like his brain was rebooting.

Wolf opened a folder on his lap, pulled a sheet of paper from the stack, and handed it over. "I found Sheffield's perfect timing rather odd that he was on top of that pass in the right place, at the right time, to see the body as it emerged from that snowbank. If he'd been a week or two later, maybe even only a few days later, who knows what could have happened to that body? The wildlife might have scattered it across the Rockies. And why hike there? The body was a good hundred yards off the trail, and then in a snowbank."

"He said he saw the crows," White said.

"Look at that."

White looked down at the paper. "What is this? Cell records for Sheffield? I never signed off on this warrant."

"You can see," Wolf said, "that the odds are good that Sheffield would be there at that exact moment because it was the thirty-third time in the last three months he'd been up on that pass."

White set the paper on MacLean's desk. "You may as well have just spoken Cantonese to me, Wolf. Got a full schedule, gentlemen. So far, I'm not liking the pace or content of what I'm hearing."

"Sheffield killed Chris Alamy," Wolf said.

White turned slowly to Wolf.

"And I have proof."

"You have proof. Well, I would hope so. Otherwise that accusation would look downright crazy." He flashed a condescending smile and looked at his phone.

"I know Sheffield's all but in the county council at this stage of his campaign, and I know he's recently been publicly endorsing you. I thought you'd want to hear this sooner rather than later, so that you don't inadvertently look bad. But if you want to get back to your full plate, by all means go ahead."

White pocketed his phone. "Consider my schedule cleared."

"Let's, uh, go ahead and tell your story, Wolf," MacLean said.

"Before Zack Hood died, he told me that Preston had called his father a cheat and a liar. That's why he bashed his head in—his words, not mine. He said he'd do it all over again if he could. I mentioned Chris Alamy, asked him why he'd killed his friend. And, yes, I was in an excited state of mind, a little bit crazy"—he glanced at White—"but I could have sworn he looked like he didn't know what I was talking about. Then he died."

"Okay," White said. "Let me get this correct, then.

You're saying Hood didn't kill Alamy? That Sheffield did it? What about those construction workers across the street from Alamy's? They saw Zack Hood's blue truck honking at the scene, taking off down the hill—speeding away from the crime. Hood's prints are all over the house, on beer bottles, on the toilet."

Wolf opened the folder and pulled another sheet. "From the first time I heard the story, I wondered why Hood would sit there and blast his horn, right after he'd shot and killed his friend and staged it to look like a suicide. Why would he do that?"

White shrugged. "Because your detective misinter- preted what the construction worker said?"

"Or Hood wanted to make himself seen by the construction workers across the street. So why would Hood want to make himself seen?"

White blinked.

"Because it wasn't Hood," Wolf said. "It was Sheffield making sure those construction workers looked over and saw that blue truck as it peeled away ... so we would all think it was Hood."

White looked nonplussed.

"Here's one of Sheffield's credit-card statements." Wolf handed over the piece of paper.

"Again, I never signed off on a warrant to check Sheffield's cell records, or his financials."

"We went straight to the judge."

White looked at MacLean.

The sheriff shrugged.

"We didn't want to hit any resistance," Wolf said. "Look at the circled transaction, please."

White looked down. "A car rental."

"Sheffield used his personal credit card to rent a pickup truck from a rental agency over in Grand Junction last week." Wolf reached over and tapped the page. "You can see the date. It's the day he came into our office with the pictures of Preston's body."

White squinted.

"Here's a photograph of the actual truck he rented."

White looked at it and lowered it to his lap. "A blue Ford F-250."

"The exact same model owned by Zack Hood. We went to Grand Junction two days ago and got casts of the tires on that rental truck. Last night in his lab, Lorber definitively matched the treads to the ones found at Alamy's house." Wolf tapped a finger on the edge of MacLean's desk. "It was Sheffield. He came to us with the photos. Then he drove to Grand Junction, got the truck, came back, went to Alamy's. He shot him, left the clean, untraceable gun in Chris's hand, then left with his horn blaring."

White stared into nothing.

MacLean pushed a piece of paper toward the DA. "Sawyer, we'll need you to sign off on this warrant to search Sheffield's house for clothing with GSR traces. We'll also be bringing him in, taking us a good look at his hands for residue there, too."

White stared into nothing.

"Sawyer." MacLean held a pen in his face.

"Yes. Of course." White took the pen and signed. When he was done he sat back, deflated. "What is this? What does this mean? I mean ... why? He brought the pictures to us. But ... Alamy and Hood had to have killed Preston." He looked at Wolf. "Right?"

"It all comes down to what would happen to the land under Preston Rock and Supply should the business fail," Wolf said. "You know those condominium complexes that line the river on the way to the rock yard?"

White nodded. "Yes."

"Through Margaret Hitchens, I've been speaking to some developers this week. It turns out that multiple groups have been in contact with Warren Preston over the years. Anybody with a pulse and a construction business is interested in turning his scarred piece of riverfront property into a couple of condo buildings, and millions in profits. They've been running into a brick wall, however, in the form of Warren Preston."

White's phone rang in his pocket. He pulled it out and silenced it. "So Preston was sticking it out. Thumbing it in the faces of the developers," White said.

"Preston never even owned the land," MacLean said. "But he was entitled to stay."

"You've gotten to know Sheffield recently," Wolf said. "He doesn't live in that big house up on Sunnyside just from the profits of his clinic in town, does he?"

White shook his head. "No. He doesn't."

"It turns out he dabbles quite a bit in Rocky Points real estate. In fact, his own company partnered with another firm to build one of the condo complexes at the base of Rocky Points Resort."

"Yeah." White's voice was low.

"I've spoken to the owner of the land under Preston

Rock and Supply," Wolf said. "A man named Rod Bloom. Ever heard of him?"

White shook his head.

"I hadn't either," Wolf said. "He likes to keep quiet. Apparently, these developers have been calling him for years, too. He tells them all the same thing—he's not interested in kicking Preston off his land. He tells them he pays his bill every month as per the terms of the lease, and that's fine by him.

"But, Mr. Bloom takes opportunities when they're given. So when a firm offered him hundreds of thousands of dollars to purchase a ten-year option on the land, should Preston Rock and Supply default on their lease within that period, he took the deal."

"And what company purchased that option?" White asked.

"S & S Development Corporation," Wolf said. "The first S stands for Sheffield. And apparently so does the second one. The articles of incorporation only list the doctor."

White stood and walked to the window behind MacLean. He stayed silent and looked down on the street below. "I don't get it. Was he involved in Preston's killing or not?"

"No," Wolf said. "Ever since he bought the option, his mission has been to kill Preston's business, not the man. I think his plan was to sabotage the equipment at the rock yard—death by a thousand paper cuts. I think he was the one cutting brake lines and hydraulic lines. And according to Betsy Collworth, he was doing a pretty good job of bleeding them over the past year. The business was struggling to keep up with repairs and fulfilling orders, which was leading to a lot of lost orders."

"You say *you think*," White said.

Wolf nodded.

"That's going to be tough to prove."

Wolf continued. "Through Zack Hood's records found in his quarry office, and after talking to his business colleagues, we've put together a pretty good picture of what happened the night of Preston's death. Remember, Zack Hood took over his flagstone quarry business from his father last year. His father had pissed off Warren Preston years ago, so the Hood quarry never supplied Preston after that. But after his father's death, Zack was giving it another try. He bragged to his colleagues about how he was going to meet with Preston. Told them he'd get the account back.

"Hood used his best contact at Preston Rock and Supply, his high-school buddy Chris Alamy, to get a meeting with the boss. That Saturday night, Hood came down with rock samples and a sales pitch. According to Hood's last words, Warren Preston told him what he thought of his father, and that meeting ended with Hood killing Preston with one of those rock samples. And we know what Chris and Zack did next—they drove around town, dropping off Alamy's phone at his house, bringing up Preston's car to Preston's house and leaving his personal contents to make it seem like he'd been there. Then they dumped Preston's body up on Huerfano Pass."

"But Sheffield." White turned around and shook his head.

Wolf picked another sheet out of the stack. "Sheffield's phone records tell quite a tale. He wasn't as careful as Chris Alamy had been with his phone that night. We may as well have had a tracking collar on the doctor. On the Saturday night in question, Sheffield's phone spent just under two hours hooked into Preston Rock and Supply's wireless network IP address."

White raised his eyebrows and took the paper from Wolf's hand.

"Look at the exact time," Wolf said.

"6:38 p.m. to 8:23 p.m.," White said.

"He was there when the murder happened," Wolf said. "Right during that window when Alamy drove home to drop off his phone and vehicle."

"And Sheffield was there," MacLean said. "At the rock yard. Bleeding steering fluid on one of those front-end loaders, or whatever his next booby-trap was. My theory is he got stuck inside the lot. Probably thought the place would be deserted on a Saturday night. But then everyone started showing up. He got stuck and witnessed the whole thing."

White handed back the paper. "Okay. So he sees the murder. Then what?"

"While Alamy and Hood drove back to Alamy's to drop off Alamy's vehicle and phone, Sheffield must have still been at the rock yard. Probably wondering how he was going to take advantage of this situation. He had options. He could come to us, tell us what he saw, and put away Alamy for murder. Preston was dead. The company would have gone under. He would have been sitting in a good position for his land option."

"But then Alamy and Hood came back," MacLean said. "They took the body, and they drove away in Hood's truck and Preston's vehicle. At that point, we think Sheffield got in his own vehicle and followed them. Because them leaving changed things. There was no more body, no more murder. If Sheffield came to us, he'd have to explain what he'd seen, and that would lead to why he'd been on the property in the first place. He would have looked suspicious. So he must have followed them on their escapades, going up to Preston's house to drop off the vehicle, and then up to Huerfano Pass to dump the body."

Wolf nodded. "He would have kept at a distance. Alamy and Hood must have parked at the gate on the top of the pass, given where we found the body. Think of Sheffield—he drives up behind them, knowing they're disposing of the body. He sees their truck parked at the top of the pass, but he can't get any closer. Maybe he even comes back later that night to see what happened. But it snowed. Hard. He would have been driven from his search."

White shook his head emphatically. "Jesus. And if he came back the next day, any and all tracks would have been erased under feet of snow."

"And then we got the case when Alamy came in saying his boss was missing," Wolf said. "Only we were stumped, because ... no body, no murder."

MacLean picked the sheet of paper showing Sheffield's phone GPS locations and waved it. "So Sheffield began frequenting Huerfano Pass, hoping one day he'd find the body. Thirty-three times in three months. The thirty-third time's a charm."

"He scoured that pass for clues," Wolf said. "And then, the day after that rain storm, he hit the jackpot. He saw the crows and knew he'd found the body.

"So now we had a body, and Sheffield knew we'd be right back on Chris Alamy. Sheffield knew about Zack Hood, but we didn't yet. He saw a sure-fire way to get rid of Alamy—to kill him and make it look like Zack Hood had done it. So he goes over there in the rented truck. He stages a suspicious-looking suicide, which points to an actual murder by Zack Hood. He honks the horn, makes sure the construction workers see. He even picks up Alamy's cell phone and makes one final call to Zack Hood, knowing we'll see that on the records. One final pointer to the man we need to go after."

"So now we're onto Hood," MacLean said. "We go after him, and he goes ape-shit and gets himself killed. But even if he'd come in quietly, we would have made everything stick on him. It all fit too well."

"Meanwhile," Wolf said, "Sheffield would have already relayed the land to the highest bidder, quickly ducking back into the shadows, away from any suspicion. The odds of us digging that deep into that land deal would have been low."

"Nil," MacLean said.

White shook his head, looking like he'd just woken up from a daydream. "This is too ... sensational. Unbelievable."

"Try on two other words for size," MacLean said. "High profile."

White pretended not to hear. Or maybe visions of press conferences, interviews, and news reports—attention and votes—were taking up too much cognition.

"We need to proceed very cautiously with this one," the DA finally said.

Wolf shut the folder and held it out. "I don't know how to tie a bow."

White grabbed the folder with both hands. He turned and left the room without another word.

MacLean stared at the swinging door. "Damn. That's a lot of publicity in that folder he just left with. Ready for four more years with that asshole?"

"Nope."

"Me neither."

CHAPTER 36

Wolf walked into the Old Bank Building and smiled at the woman sitting behind the desk. "Hello ... Cheryl, isn't it?"

"Yes. Mr. Wolf. Good to see you again. Dr. Hawkwood is in back waiting for you."

"Thanks."

Wolf turned the corner and walked down the hallway, this time not bothering to look inside Sarah's old office on the way past.

"Hey, there he is." Hawkwood shelved a book and walked over.

Wolf shook his hand. "Here I am."

"Good to see you."

Wolf nodded, unsure how to respond, and settled for "Good to see you, too."

"Please. Take a seat."

Wolf did as he was told, taking four o'clock on the dial again to Hawkwood's twelve.

The skylight beamed a shaft of sunshine onto the

carpet in the middle of the circle of chairs. The windows on the far wall were open, letting in the afternoon breeze.

Hawkwood wore a tight flannel, buttoned halfway, revealing a Gibson guitars T-shirt underneath.

"You play?" Wolf asked.

"Huh?"

"Your shirt."

"Oh. Yeah. I have an ES-335 and a Les Paul. You?"

Wolf shook his head. "I have an old Martin D-18 my dad left when he died. I don't play it much anymore."

"Oh, wow." Hawkwood's eyes lit up. "You'll have to show me that guitar sometime."

They let silence take over for a beat.

"So. I've been reading the newspapers," Hawkwood said. "You've been a busy man since the last time I talked to you."

Wolf nodded.

Hawkwood's expression became serious. "How do you feel about what happened to you?"

"Which part?"

"I hear there was a shootout. The guy had a gun to that girl's head. You talked him into letting her go. He was shot down right in front of you. Died right in front of you."

"Oh, yeah. That."

Hawkwood chuckled. "Yeah. That."

Wolf shrugged. "It's over. She's okay. Her father's okay."

Hawkwood stared at him. "Right." He shifted position and crossed his legs. "So I'm glad you made it to your session."

Wolf nodded.

After a moment of silence, Hawkwood said, "Listen, I know you're not enthused about the visits. You're following orders."

"Thanks for taking my call last week."

Hawkwood nodded. "You're welcome. Did our conversation help?"

"The bit about the Sriracha?"

"That's a hot sauce."

"Oh. Yeah." Wolf let out a breath. "Yeah. It helped. It helped a lot."

"Good. Care to tell me about it?"

Wolf said nothing.

Hawkwood pointed to the clock. "Forty-one more minutes. You can spend that time offloading your stuff onto me, or you can spend it thinking. Since I don't have any truth serum on me, I'll leave it up to you. Of course, we both know how each of those choices play out, don't we?"

Hawkwood sat back and preened a nail.

He was good.

"Okay, fine," Wolf said.

He hesitated for another minute, wondering where to begin, and then he told Hawkwood about Ella and Lauren contacting him and coming to bury Jet on his property. He told about Jack's visit, and Cassidy's pregnancy, and the pride of becoming a grandfather, and the shame as he'd remembered the countless times he'd been an imperfect dad.

Hawkwood listened attentively and pressed when Wolf stalled, and Wolf responded to the prodding by letting thoughts tumble out of his mouth. It was an utterly foreign feeling. Selfish. Unnecessary. And yet, liberating.

And then the forty-one minutes were up.

As they stood, Wolf swallowed, feeling guilty about rambling on about his son.

"Thanks again, Doc."

"You're welcome." All the facial hair preening in the world couldn't hide the solemn expression on Hawkwood's face as they shook hands.

Wolf nodded and weaved through the chairs. Before he got to the hallway, he stopped and turned around. "When was the last time you saw your daughter?"

Hawkwood was still standing in the circle like a statue. His eyes flicked to Wolf as he smiled without mirth.

"Is there anything I can do to help with that?" Wolf asked.

"It's that kind of thinking that gets you in trouble, Dave."

Wolf was less than satisfied with the answer on more than one level. "Right."

Hawkwood turned his back and made his way to the bookshelves.

"Well, we'll just save that topic for next time," Wolf said.

Hawkwood turned around with a furrowed brow.

"Later." Wolf gave the wall a slap as he walked out of the room.

CHAPTER 37

THE SUN SAT in a saddle between the mountains, its last rays sparkling off the fresh rain that had fallen on the valley only minutes earlier. A two-tiered rainbow arched across the sky. Behind it, a wall of rain receded up the valley.

Water trickled from a hanging flower pot onto Wolf's head as he strolled down the sidewalk.

Patterson was on her phone outside, having a heated conversation with somebody. She looked up and saw him, then ended the call in what looked to be mid-sentence.

"Hey, there you are." She walked down the sidewalk toward him, a strained smile stretching her face. "Good to see you. Happy birthday."

Wolf embraced her and stepped back. "Thanks."

"Who was that?"

She frowned. "Who?"

"The phone call."

"Oh. Yeah. Just ... my mom."

"How's she doing?"

"Good." She popped her eyebrows and looked around. "Pretty nice night, huh?"

Wolf smiled. "Yeah. Nice." It was the type of evening that usually had Patterson snapping photos with her phone. But, clearly, she was preoccupied.

"You ready for some pizza?" she asked, thumbing over her shoulder to the entrance of Black Diamond Pizza.

It was six o'clock on a Saturday night, but nobody streamed in or out of the place.

"We got a table. Rachette and Charlotte should be here pretty soon with TJ."

"Oh." He looked past her. "Cool. How about Margaret?"

Patterson's eyes narrowed. "Margaret? She was ... I never invited her to the dinner." Her face softened. "Oh, I'm sorry. Did you want her to come, too?"

"It's okay. I think she's here anyway. Maybe she'll join us."

Patterson whipped her head around. "Where?"

The sidewalk was empty.

"She's a block up. Sitting in her car. See the Hitchens for Mayor sign on her back window? She's parked right in front of Rachette's jeep. Didn't you say he was on his way? I guess he must have already arrived."

She turned around, keeping her eyes on the ground.

"And isn't this Burton's Chevy truck?" He gestured to the truck parked a few feet away. "Has that dent where he backed into the flower pot last year."

She looked up with narrowed eyes. "Yeah, sure. I

316 / JEFF CARSON

guess he's here, too. It's a bar on a Saturday night. Guy's a fish."

"And Jack's truck is parked two vehicles from mine in the parking lot back there. I thought that was a bit odd, since he's supposedly down in Boulder with Cassidy."

"Are you done?"

He smiled.

She closed her eyes and exhaled mightily. "Are you going to at least pretend like you're surprised?"

Wolf watched as Margaret ducked behind a vehicle up the road. The Wilson family minivan was parked one block in front of her campaign-machine. MacLean's wife's Audi was in front of that. Yates didn't yet have privileges to drive his unmarked while off duty, and his beat-up yellow Chevy truck sat across the street.

Margaret appeared on the sidewalk and approached with her arms out. "Hey, guys! What are you doing here? Nice night for—"

"Go inside, Margaret. He knows. Pretend like you don't know he knows."

"Okay." Margaret veered into the restaurant.

"Damn it. It's like herding monkeys."

"I am surprised."

"No, you're not."

"Well, no. I figured it out weeks ago."

Her eyes went to the sidewalk. "I wondered if I should keep it a surprise or not. I've been deliberating for days."

"You decided to risk putting me back in the hospital."

She looked up and her eyes were wide with concern.

"Hey." He smiled and put a hand on her shoulder.

"Thank you. People were suspiciously lax with the secret. I overheard mention of the party numerous times over the last week when I was in earshot. I even had somebody push the invitation under my office door."

"They did?"

"But you never told me."

She lifted her chin. "I wasn't going to chicken out. I knew you could handle it. I know you're back."

He stared at his detective. Her eyes matched every bit of intensity he felt inside.

"I never doubted you," she said. "You know that, right?"

He nodded. "I know."

"I knew you could get through whatever it was you were going through. And if you're still not through it, I just want you to know that I'm here, and everyone's here to help you. All of these people crammed into this tiny little restaurant—that with hindsight probably should have been Beer Goggles—will help you through it."

He gripped her face and kissed her on the forehead. "Thank you."

She wiped an eye and sniffed. "Dang it. We have to go inside soon. They're probably wondering what's going on."

He looked down Main Street again. "Is that shiny black Interceptor with government plates whose I think it is?"

She smiled. "Yep. And she looks really good."

His chest quickened, and the feeling brought a smile to his lips.

"Then let's go." He walked toward the door.

"And I want that invitation. I'll dust it for prints and kill whoever did that."

"Watch this. Did I tell you I took an acting class in high school?" He grabbed the handle.

"No. You didn't."

"Yeah, got a D-plus. Teacher hated me."

"Surprise!"

THE END

Thank you for reading Drifted. I hope you enjoyed the story, and if you did, thank you for taking a few moments to leave a review. As an independent author, exposure is everything. If you'd consider leaving a review and helping me with that exposure, I'd be very grateful.

CLICK HERE TO LEAVE A REVIEW

I love interacting with readers so please feel free to email me at jeff@jeffcarson.co so I can thank you personally. Otherwise, thanks for your support via other means, such as sharing the books with your friends/family/book clubs/the weird guy who wears tight women's yoga pants at the gas station, or anyone else you think might be interested in reading the David Wolf series. Thanks again for spending time in Wolf's world.

Would you like to know about future David Wolf books the moment they are published? You can visit my blog and sign up for the New Release Newsletter at this link – http://www.jeffcarson.co/p/newsletter.html.

As a gift for signing up you'll receive a complimentary copy of Gut Decision—A David Wolf Short Story, which is a harrowing tale that takes place years ago during David Wolf's first days in the Sluice County Sheriff's Department.

Made in United States
Troutdale, OR
01/14/2024

16943561R00198